"Everyone to the garage . . ."

The space, meant to house three cars, was empty except for a large tarpaulin-covered object in the middle of the floor. A bright red bow perched on the top suggested it was a gift; by its shape and location, it had to be a car.

"Happy birthday, hon," Jed stood back proudly as the ribbon fell to the floor and with it the tarpaulin.

It was a gray 740 turbocharged Volvo, fully equipped with air-conditioning, electric door locks, a burglar alarm, a tinted sunroof, a stereo AM/FM radio, a tape deck, and a built-in compact disk player.

Sitting in the driver's seat was Dawn Elliot. And she was dead.

Also by Valerie Wolzien
Published by Fawcett Gold Medal Books:

MURDER AT THE PTA LUNCHEON

THE FORTIETH BIRTHDAY BODY

A SUBURBAN MYSTERY

VALERIE WOLZIEN

FAWCETT GOLD MEDAL • NEW YORK

To Trevor

FORTY YEARS MINUS
THREE DAYS

I

" . . . AND WITH WINDS OF THIRTY MILES AN HOUR, THIS snow won't stay off the roads for long, so we can look forward to a difficult rush hour tonight. And that's the forecast for today: more blustery winter weather. Sleet changing to snow during the morning with an eight- to ten-inch accumulation expected before tapering off around midnight. Alternate side of the street parking . . ."

Susan forced her eyes open and sat up in bed. It wasn't a dream: There was snow coming down outside her bedroom window. She squinted over her husband's shoulder at the clock-radio on the nightstand by his side of the bed. Six A.M. Too early for him to get up. Why had she set the alarm half an hour ahead last night?

A gust of wind hit the north side of the house, its chill piercing the well-insulated walls. She shivered. The automatic thermostat wouldn't turn on until six-thirty. Grabbing a robe from the back of the mirrored closet door, she hurried downstairs to turn up the heat.

Minutes later, a creamy cashmere robe tightly wrapped around her, shoulder-length brown hair pulled from her freshly scrubbed face into a skimpy ponytail, glasses perched on her nose where they would remain until she was awake enough to face her contact lenses, she was in her kitchen on a stool near the vent directly over the furnace, a mug of instant coffee cradled in her cold hands. So why was she up so early? A glance at the family's calendar didn't enlighten her. As far as it was concerned, nothing important enough to write down was happening early this morning.

She peered out the window into the light beginning to illuminate her backyard. This was going to be some storm. Already the ground was covered and small drifts were forming at the corners of the bluestone patio. The flakes were falling so fast she could barely see through them to the half-dozen tall willows lining the brook that marked the end of their property.

As she watched, the wind shifted and the willows' long, leafless stems lashed about the bending limbs. She hoped the trees survived the storm. True, she and Jed were always saying that they should have them taken down before they fell down. But every year in the spring, when their leaves first turned green and dipped into the water, she knew the trees would be left to die naturally.

She had spent her first afternoon in this house under those trees, picnicking with Chrissy, trying to show the then four-year-old child that moving from the city would be lots of fun. And probably trying to convince herself that it didn't mean giving up everything that she had grown to love in the six years she and Jed had occupied a tiny one-bedroom walk-up on the West Side of New York City. A year later, she had sat in the privacy of the willows and nursed her baby son. That child, Chad, had fallen from the top of one of the trees only four years later—his first trip to the hospital emergency room. She sighed, then smiled at herself: It was amazing how sentimental she was becoming as her children grew up. Oh well, she thought, reaching into the freezer for breakfast. Maybe frozen waffles . . . She paused and read the calorie count printed on the back of the box. Could they possibly be that fattening without syrup? She put them back and decided on toast. She'd just remembered why the alarm was set. She had been planning to get up early and ''Exercise with Irma'' on the local cable channel. Just because she had missed that was no reason to pig out.

"Mom! Did anyone call? Is school canceled?"

"Not that I know of, Chad. There isn't even an inch of snow on the ground yet," she hollered up the stairs. "Wear your heavy Mets sweatshirt. It's going to be cold."

"I ripped it playing field hockey in gym. Remember? I told you and you said you'd fix it. I'll wear the Ferrari shirt. It's warm."

"Okay." She hated that shirt as much as her son loved it. She had agreed to buy it, hoping its fluorescent colors would fade after repeated washings. Thanks to the wonders of modern science, that hadn't happened, but it wasn't something to start the day arguing over. She should have remembered to mend the other. She looked out the window again and wished for the survival of the willows before returning to reality and the confusion that was her weekday morning.

"I don't have time for breakfast. Just some coffee if it's ready," her husband announced from the doorway to the kitchen. "This storm's going to mess up the trains. I think I'll drive your car in, if you don't mind."

"My car?"

"The Mercedes is due at the garage this morning. I told you about it last week, remember? I think it's just the fuel injector, but it may be something more complicated. Make sure they have my number at the office in case they want to reach me." He crossed the room and absently kissed his wife good-bye, caressing her shoulder with one hand and accepting the coffee she had poured for him with the other. "Thanks. I'll call, but you can plan on me being late with this weather," he commented, peering out the window before leaving for his job as vice president of financial affairs at a large ad agency in New York City. "I didn't need this. I shouldn't have scheduled that meeting with the graphics department for nine."

Their ten-year-old son ran into the room, nearly colliding with his father. "Watch out, Chad. I almost spilled hot coffee on you." He raised his cup in the air. "I've really got to go.

You help your mother with the snow on the walks and the drive until the plow comes," he ordered, and then added, "I'll pay you. Just keep track of how long it takes. 'Bye," he finished and was gone.

"Oh, good, frozen waffles," the child said, not answering his father but watching his mother open the microwave door. "I'll get the syrup."

"Mom, you know I can't eat waffles. Kathy and I just started our new diet. I told you last night." The protest announced her daughter's arrival.

"I remember," her mother replied, handing the thirteen-year-old girl a glass of juice and a plate of Ry-Krisps. "But this won't hurt your waistline and I hate sending you off to school without something in your stomach. Do you have your boo—Oh damn." Still holding her mug of coffee she ran into the hall after her husband. "Jed! Jed!" Flinging open the front door, she watched her little green Datsun sedan scoot down the street. "Damn," she repeated and returned to her children. "My boots are in the trunk."

"Mine are in my locker at school," her son informed her complacently, pouring an excess of syrup over two waffles.

"Good move, Slick," his sister commented and then turned her attention to other matters. "Mom, Kathy's mother's going to drive me to school. And don't forget that you have an appointment with my art teacher this afternoon. She said it was important."

"If this snow keeps up she'll probably want to make it another day and get home to her family. But don't worry. I wouldn't forget an appointment with a teacher," Susan lied. "And I'll call the school in a few hours to see if she wants to change the time."

"This is very important to me, Mom," her daughter reminded her. "I think she may want to tell you about the trip to European art museums that she runs each summer. And you know how I want to major in art in college."

"I know, but I'm not promising anything, Chrissy," Susan said. She did know what it meant to the child, so she worked to keep the irritation from her voice. This wasn't promising to be a great day. "What good are your boots going to do you if you leave them in your locker, Chad?" she asked rhetorically.

"They don't do me much good anyway," was the reply. "There are holes in both of 'em. There's your ride, Chrissy," he added as a horn sounded in the driveway.

A loud knock on the back door preceded the arrival of a girl in a shocking pink parka with a turquoise sweater and bright orange tights hanging below and bleached blond friz above. "Hi, Mrs. Henshaw. Hi, Chrissy . . . oh, Ry-Krisps. I wish my mom had thought of them. I'm starving."

"Hi, Kathy. You girls better hurry," Susan interrupted, knowing that once they started talking about their diets they would hang around the kitchen forever.

"Oh, my mom says not to rush, Mrs. Henshaw. She knows it's early and she says she'll just sit in the car and warm the engine until Chrissy's ready."

"Well, take her this mug of coffee and tell her I asked if she'd drive Chad over to the elementary school on her way to Hancock Junior," Susan requested.

"Sure, Mrs. Henshaw, I'll ask her. She won't mind." Snow blew in the open door as she left.

"I can't imagine what Stephanie is thinking of to let her daughter dress like that," Susan commented.

"Mother, she looks wonderful," loyally protested her daughter.

Susan reminded herself that it was too early in the day to deal with conflict. "Is your homework in your backpack, Chad?"

"Yeah. I don't have time for two more waffles, do I?"

"No. I appreciate you going with Mrs. King," said his mother, who knew that her boisterous son was surprisingly shy around strange adults. "I have to get the Mercedes to the dealer this morning and . . ."

"It's okay, Mom. I like going to school with Mrs. King. You should see the way she takes the corners in that new Jaguar of hers. Outta sight!" He waved his arms in the air to demonstrate how the car careened around turns.

"A new Jaguar?" Susan asked, peering out the window through the snow.

"Yeah. It's fantastic! Two-twenty horsepower . . ."

"A burgundy sedan," Susan mumbled to herself, the car's expensive newness undiminished by the snow. "Nice. Now don't keep Mrs. King waiting. Get your backpack and hurry. And don't forget to wear your boots home; even with holes, they're better than nothing," she added. "And look at your spelling words before the test. Remember gymnasium is spelled g . . . y . . . m . . ." She gave up the lesson and watched as her son sank his Reeboks in the largest drift he could find between the house and the car.

She braved the now heavy snowfall long enough to wave to the last of her family before returning to the kitchen.

The willows creaked from a particularly torturous blast of cold air and then, sighing, righted themselves.

II

"You know how it is: We have two cars and the one that doesn't work is mine," Susan said into the phone while emptying the dishwasher of last night's china before adding the morning's accumulation. "Sure. I'd appreciate it, but do you have the time? Well, starting a new business always takes a lot of . . . I know, but don't get discouraged. Did the Smalls get in touch with you? I know they were very unhappy with their system after their most recent burglary . . . Yes, their most recent. They've been broken into three times in the last three years. Well, maybe you ought to give them a call. It couldn't hurt." She stopped cleaning to concentrate on the voice at the other end of the line. "Look, I know how you feel. But at least you're doing something. You're not just taking care of other people." She listened again, a slight smile on her face. "Okay. Maybe it's just the weather or maybe it's my birthday coming up. All I know is that I feel more and more like I don't have a life of my own, and taking a car that I only get to drive on weekends in for service isn't helping any . . . Okay, you're right. I'd better get going. I'll drop off the Mercedes and meet you at the Inn at noon. Okay? . . . No, I don't think we'll need reservations in this weather, but get them if it would make you feel better. Great. See you then.''

She hung up and, flipping the switch that would start her dishwasher humming, left the kitchen and headed up the stairs, a cacophony of sounds greeting her arrival on the second floor. She went first into her daughter's room and then into her son's, turning off their respective radios, each set for a different rock station. In her own bedroom, an all news radio station was reporting on the myriad of traffic and train delays in and around the city. In the corner of the room, Bryant Gumbel and Jane Pauley were chatting happily. She reached to turn off the radio as the phone rang again.

''Susan.'' The voice on the other end of the line sounded excited. Susan didn't anticipate the same response, and reached out with her free hand for the remote control that had spent the night tucked down in the sheets between her husband and herself. ''Have you heard who's coming back to town?''

''No.'' She'd succeeded in turning off an interview with the rock star who had just written a book, and she flung the line of the phone across the mattress so she could reach her dresser drawer while talking. She found her underwear, but where was that moss green turtleneck?

''Dawn Elliot.''

Susan froze, but her caller continued.

''It'll be interesting to see her after so long, won't it? I wonder if she's still as gorgeous as ever. Or as skinny. Maybe she's stopped smoking and gotten fat . . .'' And on and on.

Susan couldn't think of anything to say. Oddly enough, she found she was thinking only of the frill of ivory lace hanging from the cup of the bra she was wearing. Should she mend it? Was it worth the time? Did she even like this bra? Maybe the style made her look fat . . . or flat?

''So what do you think?''

''I . . . I have to go. I have to drop off Jed's car at the dealer, and I'm meeting Kathleen for lunch and . . . I really do have to go,'' she insisted.

"Oh. I didn't know you were in a hurry. But think about when we can get together with Dawn. I want to give her a party. Or maybe it would be more fun if we just get a bunch of women together for a lunch. I like that idea. Let's do it. I'll call around and check to see what dates are free and get back to you tonight. Okay? Drive carefully. The snow sure is coming down."

"I will. 'Bye." Susan hung up and stood studying the telephone, feeling like she'd taken a bad fall and had the breath knocked out of her, a gray gloom wrapping her in its envelope. "No way." She pulled herself together. "That bitch isn't going to get to me now." She flung her cashmere sweater over her head, tugged on tweedy wool pants and tall leather boots, and stamped down the stairs to the hall closet. So what if the weather was too rotten for her to wear her new nutria coat. Today her morale needed it.

III

"Don't worry, Mrs. Henshaw. If we have a problem, we'll just call your husband. I have his number in the city right here. Now, do you need a ride home? The courtesy van is due back in a few minutes and we'd be glad to give you a lift."

"Thanks. But I have a date for lunch and I'm going to shop until then. I appreciate the offer, though," Susan replied, handing an extra set of car keys to the man on the other side of the service desk.

"Why don't you leave through the showroom then? We keep the front of the place shoveled, and you're less likely to slip in the snow. Sure is coming down, isn't it?"

"Sure is," she agreed, not particularly anxious to chat. "Maybe I'll look at the new cars on the way out."

"Good idea. Check out that signal-red 560SL. Perfect car for a nice lady like you," he urged.

Susan smiled. Why not? If wrapping herself in an expensive fur was good for the morale, just how would she feel if she and her fur stepped into an expensive new car? She was moving across the deep rug of the lush showroom when, out of the corner of her eye, she saw a well-dressed salesman starting in her direction. He was probably surprised to see a customer in this weather. She decided to view the car another time. That man had a lot of time to spare and, in her present mood, she just might find herself ordering a dozen 560s—each in a different color, please. She changed direction and hurried toward the door.

IV

"I thought you probably knew all about it."

"How many people are allowed to go through their fortieth birthday without a surprise party?"

"I'm sure Jed's giving it for you because he wants to make you happy. I mean . . ."

"Oh, I know that, Kathleen." She smiled across the table at the stunning blonde. "I'm not being very nice about this, am I? I guess I'm just in a bad mood today."

"Anything I can do? Or is it just turning forty? You know, it really isn't the end of the world."

"You're not going to tell me 'life begins at forty,' are you?"

"Not me. And I always thought that it was 'life begins at fifty.' "

"Oh, good. You mean I have ten more years to wait?"

"Yup. Have another hot buttered rum while you're waiting."

"Good idea. Where'd that waitress go to?" Susan swallowed the last of the creamy, warm liquid from her tall white mug and looked around. She might be depressed, but she'd picked a great place to be depressed in. The Hancock Inn, a very successful restaurant in a Connecticut town of very successful people, had added this room last fall. Now the Colonial stone front of the building was balanced by a sun room in the rear. At first, resisting change, Susan had disliked the addition, but, during the winter, she'd come to love it. The large copper and glass room was filled with spring flowers in wooden window boxes and hanging baskets, their green lushness dripping down to the tile floor or growing up toward

the moisture-covered glass ceiling. As she spied their waitress and nodded, Susan thought that she would be happy to
sit here forever, the warm artificial spring protecting her from
the snow and cold outside.

"Two more hot buttered rums and an appetizer tray,
please," Kathleen ordered. When the waitress hurried off,
she respected the other woman's silence and joined her in
staring out into the swirling snow.

"Do you ever think about that summer?" Susan asked,
interrupting the silence.

"Of course."

"But it wasn't as dramatic for you, was it? To you it was
just another murder investigation—just another job."

"And to you . . ."

"It was the loss of two friends. And then learning to accept
that a person we all knew was the murderer. Sometimes I
still can't believe it."

Kathleen had spent many years as a policewoman, and
knew well the upset and confusion that a violent death nearly
always brought with it.

"Do you think that anyone could become a killer like that?
If pushed far enough, do you think we're all capable of striking back like that? Of killing someone?" Susan continued
her questions.

"I used to know cops that thought that was true—that
thought everyone was capable of killing. And, heaven knows,
I've met some unusual murderers, but I think that most people, no matter what happened in their lives, wouldn't kill
someone they knew. They might kill a stranger in a war, or
they might want to hurt someone so badly that they think
they would kill him. But I believe most people stop short of
murder."

Susan sipped the hot drink that the waitress brought and
wondered if Kathleen was right. Just how much did she hate
Dawn? She asked herself if Kathleen wondered why she was
asking these questions. They were good friends, but their
relationship had begun only a year and a half ago. There
were lots of things each didn't know about the other's past.

They hadn't even seen each other for the months following the murder investigation that had brought Kathleen to Hancock in the first place. Then, after running into each other on a weekend trip into the city, Susan had introduced Kathleen to a friend of her husband's, a widower who worked in the same ad agency. He was now Kathleen's husband. "How is Jerry?" she asked, suddenly remembering her manners.

"Good question," was the rueful response. "He's working so hard, I don't see him much. If you want to know about him, ask your husband. Jed talks to him more than I do. At least they go in and out of the city together most days."

"But you're not . . . ?" Susan asked, instantly concerned.

"We're happy together," Kathleen assured her. "Really we are. And I'm told that everything is going to clear up once the fall campaigns are in the can. I have nothing to complain about." She looked at her friend and beamed. "Have I told you how happy I am to have a perfect husband and a perfect friend?"

"And a perfect life in the suburbs?" Susan teased, picking up a raw mushroom.

"Well, let's just say it's not as bad as I thought it would be."

"Were you really dreading it?" Susan asked. "I thought that Jerry offered to move into the city when you and he got married. I wondered then just why you were staying here. It's not as though he had any children in the schools to worry about. I always thought that he might want to get away from where it all happened."

"You mean the accident."

"Yes." She paused. "You know, you've made him very happy, Kathleen. I'll never forget the way he looked that night when he came to the door and told Jed and me about the crash. I don't think I've ever seen such anguish on a person's face."

"It's not often that a man is told that his entire family, his wife and both of his children, have been wiped out in one horrible tangle of cars. He still has nightmares that it's happening all over again, you know."

"God."

"Yes." Kathleen sipped her drink and studied the plate of vegetables the waitress had brought.

"You're not . . . you're not jealous, are you?" Susan asked, hesitantly.

"Of course not. He loved them and now he loves me. I'm not twenty years old. I understand that life changes and that the past, no matter how important, doesn't negate the present. Jerry loves me and I love him. We don't begrudge each other the years before we met." She seemed to make up her mind and she speared a carrot with her fork.

"Of course not," Susan agreed. But what if it had happened after they had met? Stop it, she ordered herself. You're confusing your life and Kathleen's. "The dip looks good. What is it?"

"Something green. Maybe spinach. Definitely sour cream. Try some. Maybe it's not as fattening as it tastes. Hey . . ." She remembered something. "Did you go to the caterer's this morning like you were threatening to?"

"No. I went by, but they were closed. I'm still tempted to call them up, though. You don't happen to know if . . ."

"If I know the answer to your question, I still won't tell you," Kathleen insisted, remembering the spiced shrimp balls, the stone crab claws, the lobster, and the clams that Jed had discussed repeatedly with her. Determined to have all his wife's favorites, he chose to ignore the possibility of a shellfish allergy among his guests. But she wasn't going to talk about it. Nor would she mention the hours that she and Jed had talked about the proper guest list (although they had finally decided to invite almost everyone that could possibly be considered an appropriate guest, both of them being unwilling to offend anyone through an accidental omission as well as a simple acceptance of the axiom "the more the merrier"). Nor would she even offer a hint about the gift Jed was planning to present publicly. She hadn't been consulted about that, merely informed. In fact, Kathleen just wasn't going to talk about the party—that way she knew she wouldn't let anything slip. There was a bit of guilt in this decision: A comment of hers had confirmed Susan's suspicion that there was to be a party at all. "I still feel badly that you know about the whole thing," she said.

"Don't be silly. I'd rather know. Otherwise I wouldn't get the chance to shop for the perfect dress."

"We're still going out? In this weather?" Kathleen was incredulous.

"You'd prefer to sit home and worry about the drive our husbands will be making home from the city?"

"Okay. You're right. I never feel really comfortable on these snowy days until Jerry's home in the evening. We'd better order lunch and we could, of course, have one more drink."

"Excellent idea."

The waitress was waiting for their signal.

V

"Do you mind if we stop at Growls and Grins first? I have to buy a gift," Susan asked, as she and Kathleen walked out into the storm. "It's on the way."

"Of course not. Chrissy or Chad going to a birthday party?"

"No, I still haven't gotten a present for the Bower's new little girl. I went over to see the baby—I guess we should start calling her Missy now—right after they got her, but I still haven't sent a gift."

"Isn't she the cutest thing? But I don't know what you're going to buy. I stopped in yesterday and that child has everything a baby could possibly use or need—including enough silver mugs and porringers to seat a dozen other babies at a formal brunch."

"I think everyone is just so thrilled that they finally got her. You haven't been in town long enough to understand all they've been through: They got married knowing that, if they wanted children, they would have to adopt one, but they never thought that it was going to be so very difficult to get a baby. They had almost given up when they heard about this lawyer in San Francisco who arranges private adoptions."

"They were lucky to get her," Kathleen commented. "There just aren't that many babies needing to be adopted."

"True," Susan agreed. "And they've been working at this for years. They practically changed their entire lives to get a baby."

"You're kidding," Kathleen said, peering at a display in one of the shop windows.

"No, they started going to church regularly and Gloria volunteered for all sorts of community service. Why, she practically runs the hospital thrift shop single-handedly . . . Here we are. Don't slip on the steps. It's getting icy." She pulled open the door of the tiny shop, revealing a riot of stuffed animals, mechanical toys, games, and children's clothes.

"Well, you have a lot to choose from," Kathleen commented, stamping the snow from her boots on the provided floor mat.

"I don't think that's going to make it easier." Susan sighed, heading over to an exhibit of stuffed forest animals. "Do you think she'd like a life-size raccoon?"

"Not particularly. I don't think there's anything cute about an animal that dumps your garbage cans and then eats the garbage."

"I guess not," Susan agreed. "You know, I wanted to buy Chrissy the stuffed Steiff giraffe before she was born. I used to go into F.A.O. Schwartz—the big store on Fifth in the city—and drool over it."

"But you didn't buy it?"

"Jed had just started at the agency. He wasn't making very much money and we had to pay off the loans that had gotten him his M.B.A. If I'd spent two thousand dollars on a stuffed animal, he'd have had me committed. Besides the fact that we were living in a small apartment. We didn't have room for the baby, so where were we going to put a seven-foot toy?"

"What about when Chad was born?"

"We were doing better then, of course. But we still didn't have that kind of money. That's probably one reason Missy's getting so many great gifts. We all had our children before we had any spare cash. It's great to finally be able to buy just what we want even if our own kids are too old now to appreciate it.''

''Would they ever have?''

''Probably not. They'd have been happier with something plastic and trashy. I guess the stuffed animals are for the parents.''

''These must be,'' Kathleen agreed, reading the tag attached to a particularly cuddly jaguar. ''It says not for children under three years of age.''

''That's because the eyes can fall out and a young child might swallow one,'' said the elderly saleslady coming up to them. ''Toys for children under three have to meet certain safety requirements set by the federal government. Can I help either of you?''

''We're looking for a gift for the baby who has everything,'' Susan stated, putting down the panda bear she was stroking.

''And you're interested in a stuffed animal?''

''Not really . . . Look at those. They're wonderful,'' Susan interrupted herself. ''Chad would love them for his bedroom.''

''I don't know. . . .'' The saleswoman began, looking around to see what interested her customer.

''Oh, you're right,'' Kathleen agreed, reaching across the piles of animals and grabbing a satin pillow embossed with the arrogant lion that was the Porsche emblem.

''Oh, look. The Ferrari and Mercedes symbols, too,'' Susan enthused. ''These really would look great on his bed. And his birthday's coming up in a few months. I could get them now, and be ready ahead of time for once.''

''You're not talking about a baby present,'' the saleslady said, catching on. ''We also have pillows with the BMW shield, the Jaguar shield or, I think, a Corvette and a Lamborghini logo. Let's see.'' She knelt down and started sorting through the colorful pile.

''Fantastic.'' Susan joined her search. In a few minutes,

they had found seven different pillows and had them laid out on a low shelf. Susan sat back on her heels and examined the different designs. "Well, I like the Porsche, Jaguar, and the Ferrari—that design is great."

"Are those the cars that he likes best?" Kathleen asked.

"Good question. He'll probably care more about that than about the designs."

"Well, you should know what he likes—he talks about expensive sports cars enough, doesn't he?"

"Yes. But I don't really listen," Susan admitted with a frown.

"I suppose one of each is a bit much," the saleswoman suggested, fluffing up the round satin Mercedes emblem.

"Definitely," agreed Susan, who had had a chance to examine the price tags. "But it is his eleventh birthday and he'll love them. Let's pick out five," she decided. "The Ferrari, the Lamborghini, the Jaguar, the Corvette, the Porsche. The BMW and the Mercedes are too yuppie—a little boring or something. What do you think?" she asked her friend.

"Fine," Kathleen agreed, thinking that they were getting near something she didn't want to talk about.

"Wonderful choice," enthused the saleswoman, gathering up the pillows. "Shall I wrap them, or do you want me to put them in bags?" She glanced out the window at the still falling snow. "They're going to be very bulky."

"Could you wrap them? And I'll come in for them in a few days when this weather clears up a bit," Susan said, handing over her gold card.

"Of course, Mrs. . . . ." she glanced down at the name embossed on the plastic ". . . Henshaw. I'll gift wrap them and put them in the back with your name on them. So even if another salesperson is here, you just tell her your name and she'll be able to get them for you. I'll wrap each pillow separately, shall I? Little boys love opening presents, don't they?"

"That would be great. I'll be in soon," Susan agreed, drifting away from the sales desk and back to her friend, now examining hand-painted mobiles of lions, clowns, ducks, and other assorted baby-appropriate themes.

"That doesn't solve the problem we came in with," Kathleen said. "We still need a baby gift for Missy, remember?"

"I know. But I've had an idea. Pickwick Papers—the bookstore around the corner—has a great selection of children's books. What would you think about something like that? Or is a baby too young to appreciate books?"

"Missy's too young to appreciate silver porringers, but that didn't stop people from giving her a dozen. I think books are a great idea. I love reading to my nieces and nephews, and I remember doing it when they were still too young to sit by themselves. Let's go look. I want to check out their selection of books about Greece. Jerry and I are thinking of going there in the fall, you know."

"If you'll just sign here, Mrs. Henshaw," the saleswoman suggested.

Susan rushed back to the desk. "Of course."

"And could you put your address and phone number underneath?"

Susan did as requested and slipped the card back into her wallet.

"You can come in for these anytime," she was reminded.

"Does the snow seem to be letting up?" Kathleen asked, pulling up the hood of her coat and heading over to the door.

"Not appreciably. Thank you for all your help," Susan said to the woman now trying to hold the five pillows all at once. "I'll be back soon."

The wind blew snow in the door as they left the warmth of the shop. "The bookstore isn't very far, is it?" Kathleen asked.

"Just follow me," was the reply, almost lost in the now-howling wind.

"No one else is crazy enough to go out shopping in this stuff," Kathleen insisted when, a few minutes later, they were once again inside where it was warm.

"Looks like you're right," Susan agreed, looking around the brightly lit room full of books and almost devoid of people. "We'd better shake off our clothes or we'll drip on the books."

"I'm sorry, ma'am, but we're closing the store early to-day—because of the snow." A young man with long hair falling across his smudged horn-rimmed glasses approached them. "The police have declared a state of emergency and asked us to close. We haven't had any customers all morning really, so it will be a relief to get home," he added.

Susan, who had always thought that the reason to have a job in a bookstore was that on slow days you would have all that time for reading, smiled uncertainly. Then the meaning of what he had said sunk in. "What about the schools?" she asked anxiously.

"They were called off a while ago. At least, that's what the radio's been reporting."

"Chad and Chrissy. Where could they be?" Susan grabbed her friend's arm anxiously. "I know you want to leave, but could I use your phone for just a few minutes?" she asked the salesman.

"Of course. There's no rush. My wife is coming to pick me up and she won't be here for a while. Help yourself. It's behind the computer on the desk by the door."

Susan rushed over to the desk and Kathleen, realizing for the first time just how much snow she had brought into the room with her, stood still, dripping on the linoleum by the door. She smiled uncertainly at the man beside her as a trickle from her coat slid across the floor in the direction of a shelf of best-sellers. He smiled back before reaching for a sponge, hidden from view by an unopened box of books, and bent down to mop up the liquid.

"I'm very sorry . . ." Kathleen began.

"They're fine," Susan interrupted. "Both Chrissy and Chad are at the Kings' house. Stephanie drove them both to school, but by the time she had made it to the junior high school with Chrissy and Kathy, the decision had been made to close up for the day. So she turned around and collected Chad from his school and took them both home with her. The Calhouns live next door and their son is in Chad's class so the two of them are out in the backyard making a snow fort.'' The question of whether her son's boots had ever made it out of his locker flashed through her mind. Damn.

''And Chrissy?''

''She and Kathy are going through fashion magazines and trying to think of a snack that will fill them up but has no calories. They'll be fine. And I called over to the dress shop. They're going to stay open and we can still look for that dress, if you don't mind.''

''Great. Let's get going.''

VI

But there are some days when, no matter how hard you look, no matter how much you try on, everything makes you look old, fat, or just plain horrible. For Susan, it was that type of day.

''At least I have a new dress to wear to your party,'' Kathleen stated, leaning forward to peer through the windshield of her Subaru sports coupe.

''Three of them,'' Susan corrected. ''And new slacks, a new skirt and two new sweaters. I, on the other hand, have three pairs of beige stockings and a headache.''

''I think I'll get a lot of use out of that black skirt,'' Kathleen stated, beginning to justify spending so much money.

''Yes. And I love the length.''

''Not too short? Damn.'' She pulled hard on the steering wheel. ''Did you see that? That car almost plowed right into us. I wish people who can't drive in snow would stay off . . . Oh no. Hang on.''

Susan felt the car swerve, heard the wrenching jangle of metal meeting metal, and closed her eyes. When she opened them, she could see through the snow enough to realize that Kathleen's car had just become one with a Jeep. ''I thought they were supposed to be able to maneuver so well on slick roads,'' she commented, referring to the Jeep.

''Not unless someone is steering them. That Jeep is parked.''

"It's going to be hard to say it was the other driver's fault."

"I'll tell you whose fault it was. It was the maniac driving that beige Cadillac that swerved out in front of me. If I hadn't had to dodge that car, I wouldn't have lost control and skidded into this one. If I ever meet that driver, I'll kill him." Kathleen slammed her hand into her steering wheel in frustration.

"I think you're going to get your chance right now. Look." Susan pointed. The Cadillac was backing slowly, carefully toward them. Skidding slightly, it came to a stop and, flashers blinking, the door opened.

"Are you all right? I saw what happened and I just had to stop. Why did you serve like that? Shall I find a phone and call an ambulance?" An elderly lady, wearing a down coat that resembled a large sleeping bag with an unlikely flowered hat perched crookedly over slightly blue hair, stepped out of the car and walked toward them.

"No. We're fine," Kathleen said. "Thank you for stopping, though."

"Now you're sure about that? I can just hop over to one of those houses there and have the owner call the police if you would like me to."

"We really are okay," Susan insisted, craning her neck to peer out Kathleen's window at their good Samaritan.

"How did you ever get into a skid like that?"

"We were dodging you," Kathleen stated.

"Now, now, dearie, blaming someone else won't help." And with that thought, she returned to her car and drove off.

"Did you get her license plate?" Susan asked.

"No need. I'll just file a report that I skidded to my insurance company. They'll be getting a whole slew of minor fender bender reports on a day like this. My worry is the owner of the Jeep. I guess I'll have to leave a note on his windshield and give him my name and address and phone number and he'll get in touch with me."

"So what's the matter with that?"

"How would you feel if you came back to your car assuming it was fine and discovered its side was smashed in?"

"Yeah. I know what you mean, but I don't think it's going to be a problem."

"Do you know some way to find the owner?"

"I think he's found you."

VII

"But he didn't make a big stink, did he?"

"Well, he was pretty unhappy at first," Susan replied, pushing a small bubble up the faucet with her big toe. "Poor guy. You see, the Jeep was brand-new. And he had borrowed it from a friend or something. So while everyone else was going 'not another storm,' he was thrilled to death at the chance to try out its four-wheel drive traction. So here he comes ready to leap into this macho new black Jeep and head for the hills, or his home, or something, and the whole side is smashed in."

"How badly?"

"Well, Kathleen's right fender hit the left side of the Jeep: The whole driver's side was dented in pretty badly. In fact, he couldn't open the door. He had to crawl in over the passenger's seat."

"Well, I can see how that would make him mad."

"I think he was madder when he thought I'd been driving than when he saw Kathleen. Once he got a look at her he calmed down a lot—a whole lot. I wonder what it would be like to be so attractive that all men fall in love with you a little?"

"I think what you're talking about is all men falling in lust with you, and I'm not sure it's a situation that a man wants his wife to be in," Jed said, reaching down into the bubble bath that surrounded her.

"I told the kids you would make them some of your famous sloppy joes," Susan told him.

"That's a hint."

"I guess so. It's been a long day and I have some thinking to do." She smiled up at him from her tubful of bubble bath.

"Okay." He stood up and, grabbing a bright green towel, dried off his hand. "How about you?"

"About me?"

"Dinner. I thought the kids and I were the only ones who savored my gourmet sloppy joes."

"Don't worry about me. I'm not getting out of here until I turn into a prune, and then I'll stick a Lean Cuisine into the microwave."

"Okay. Don't fall asleep and drown. You look a little tired."

Her smile became a frown as the door closed behind him. Not only weren't strange men falling in love with her, but her own husband's only comment on her looks was that she'd been getting too little sleep. She sighed and reached for the faucet: The water was getting a little cold.

Returning to her previous position under the scented bubbles, Susan relaxed. Getting Kathleen's car separated from the Jeep hadn't been all that easy. With the owner of the Jeep and herself pushing, it had taken a few minutes of working muscles ignored in her aerobics classes to accomplish the task. Then Susan had fallen on the ice and, for one horrible moment, had thought that one of the cars was going to roll across her. She picked up a thick terry washcloth, wet it, and placed it across her face. Maybe it would have been better if it had, she thought, remembering what she had been trying to forget all day. Of all the things she needed with her fortieth birthday coming, a visit from Dawn Elliot wasn't one.

When her husband came back into the room a few minutes later, a glass of chablis for her in his hand, he found that she was still in the tub. Crying.

FORTY

I

"YOU STAY RIGHT THERE AND GET SOME EXTRA SLEEP. The kids'll bring up your breakfast." Jed crossed the bedroom to the door. "Now don't get up. Chrissy and Chad have been planning this all week," he ordered, leaving the room and slamming the door behind him. "Oh, by the way," he called back into the room. "Happy birthday."

Oh shit: her party tonight. She'd been trying to forget. Susan rolled on her back, pulling the sheet and quilt up over her naked shoulders. But that wasn't enough; if the kids were coming up she'd better put on her nightgown. She felt around under the covers with her toes. It must be here somewhere. . . .

After searching through the sheets and pillows and even getting up to look under the bed, she gave up and pulled a different nightgown from the dresser. She had just yanked it over her head and gotten back into bed when the door opened and Chrissy entered, a very full tray shaking in her hands.

"Happy birthday. You don't look forty, you know," the child stated, placing the tray, tilted, down on the bed.

"Thank you," Susan replied, knowing that her daughter was doing her best to console her. "That looks wonderful," she continued, surveying the food. And it did: fresh strawberries in a bowl set next to a cup of sugar and a tiny pitcher of cream, crisp slices of bacon on a plate accompanying a mushroom omelet, coffee, and a tall red rose. A big breakfast eater when she wasn't dieting, Susan enjoyed the prospect of this meal. But not on her, she thought, grabbing the tray before it dumped everything across her thighs.

"Mommy, Mommy. Look at this. I found the RC car Daddy is making me right here in this magazine and they painted it blue and yellow. Do you think we can paint mine like it?"

"Chad, be careful," Susan ordered, taking the magazine thrust at her with a sigh.

"You didn't even wish Mommy a happy birthday, Chad. Think how she must feel today—she's forty, you know."

"I know. But I want to know about . . ." He would have gone on but his sister interrupted.

"Chad!" she cried.

"I wasn't going to say anything about Mommy's birthday, Chrissy. I just came in to show her this magazine. You're the only one saying anything about her birthday!" he protested indignantly.

"And I'm looking at it, Chad. Now show me again which car your father's building you," Susan suggested, scanning a page containing photographs of more than two dozen small spiderlike vehicles with oversized spiked wheels.

"Can't you remember anything? I keep telling you . . ."

"I know, Chad, but they do all look alike to me."

"Why don't you let your mom drink her coffee and eat breakfast, Chad? Then she'll be able to concentrate on what you want to show her," Jed suggested, coming back into the room.

"Oh, okay. Hey, did I show you this?" he asked his father, leaping off the bed, magazine in hand.

Susan smiled at her son and husband bent over the page of cars together.

"How they can spend so much time on those things is beyond me," Chrissy commented in a very grown-up voice.

"Any plans for today?" her mother asked, ignoring the

last remark. She knew Chrissy would have been prepped by her father about how they were going to fill the time before the party. The kids had been granted an extra holiday at school, by parental permission, but Susan didn't know what plans they had made for the day. Kathleen had refused to reveal all and Susan didn't even know how her family had planned to carry off the surprise party.

"Well, first you have to finish your breakfast," was the reply, as Chrissy reached out and took a strawberry off her mother's tray. "Do you know how many calories there are in a strawberry?"

"Not many, I'm sure," Susan replied, her mouth full of omelet.

"Well," Chrissy returned to the question, "we've really got a great day planned. After you finish your breakfast, we're all going to put on lots of warm clothes and then we're going to . . ."

"The beach!" Susan guessed.

"How did you know?"

Susan exchanged smiles with her husband over the heads of their children. Jed knew that, in all her life, his wife had never turned down an offer of a walk on the beach. Susan glanced out the window at the blue sky.

"It's going to be cold," Jed reminded her.

"So what? Let me hurry and finish this so we can leave. Any particular beach in mind?"

"Wherever you want to go," he answered magnanimously.

"As long as we can get back in time for . . ."

"In time for the special dinner I've planned," Jed interrupted his son.

"Oh. Yes." Chad looked knowingly at his father.

"Well, why doesn't everyone get into their clothes and I'll get up and we can get going?"

"It's impossible to keep her away from the shore," Jed reminded his children. "You two hurry. We'll leave in half an hour."

II

"This is going to be great in the fireplace," Susan enthused, pulling dozens of sandy branches of driftwood from the trunk of the Mercedes. "We should do this in the fall instead of March."

"We bought a cord of hardwood in the fall and we haven't burned even half of that yet," Jed reminded her, taking an armful of wood from her and handing it over to Chrissy. "Help your mother with that load," he told his son.

"Wow! It looks like we brought most of the beach back with us," the child said, looking into the carpeted trunk.

Susan grimaced at her husband. He really didn't like a messy car. "Why don't we drive into the garage and I'll bring the shop vac up from the basement, just as soon as we pile this wood out on the patio?"

"No need for that now. I'll have plenty of time tomorrow. But does this have to go on the patio, Sue? Someone will be tripping over it every few minutes."

"Let's just stick it out back with the rest of the firewood, if you think that's a better idea," Susan agreed.

"The best idea is to worry about it tomorrow. Just pile it all up neatly by the stone wall there, kids. Then we can all go inside, take showers, and dress for dinner."

"We're going out?" Susan was surprised, wondering just when her party was scheduled to begin.

"Yes. And I'm not going to tell you where, so don't ask. Just get ready and be sure to put on your best dress."

"Are the kids coming?"

"They are not. They've already celebrated with you. Now it's our turn."

"You mean falling into a freezing ocean is Chad's way of celebrating?" his wife teased, reaching into the back of the trunk to clean out the last few small chinks of wood.

"It's better than talking about cars, isn't it?"

"Anything is better than that!"

"Anything is better than what?" asked Chad, coming around the corner, brushing the sand from his still wet jeans.

"Than dying of pneumonia. I've been having such a good time that I haven't been paying any attention to you. Now go upstairs and get right into a hot—and I mean hot—bathtub."

"I'll come inside with you, Chad," his father offered.

"I liked it better when you were having such a good time," he muttered, following his father.

III

"So where are you taking me?" Susan asked, stretching her legs out before her and resting her head on the backrest.

"It's a surprise." He reached out and put his hand over hers. "You smell good."

"It's new. Mom sent a monster bottle of White Linen bubble bath, powder, and cologne for my birthday. I think maybe I overdid it, though. Is it too strong?"

"Would I have told you how good you smell if you'd used too much? Besides, if you can't be extravagant on your fortieth birthday, when can you?"

"I think I'm supposed to start cutting down—less White Linen and more violet toilet water—as I get older."

"Don't even consider it. You're going to become a fascinating forty. I'm thinking about developing a passion for older women."

"Good thing," his wife responded, trying to keep her voice as casual and bantering as his.

"Sure. You'll probably become sultry and sleek and seductive in your old age."

"Not with my thighs." Keeping her response casual was getting to be an effort.

"Damn!"

"Did you forget something?" she asked.

Jed was tugging at his suit jacket and running his free hand through the various pockets in his pants.

"I sure did. Directions to this place. Did you see my

leather appointment book around the house? I know I had it this morning.''

"Yes. It was by the sink in the bathroom. I noticed it while I was putting on my makeup. I wondered what it was doing there.''

"I must have taken it out of the other shirt when I was changing. Damn it.''

"Do you need it right now?''

"Yes. The directions to the inn we're going to are in it. And I can't get there without them. We'll have to turn around and go back. Luckily, I left plenty of time to get there. We won't be very late.''

"Can't we just call them on the phone—there must be a pay phone around here—and ask the way? Surely we don't have to go all the way back home?'' she asked, a feeling of dread beginning.

"No. I had my new American Express card in there too. We really do have to go back. I'm sorry, honey.'' He patted her hand.

"No problem. It's a nice night for a drive,'' Susan replied, thinking furiously. She had assumed that her party was going to be at this inn Jed had been taking her to, but he certainly wouldn't plan a party in a place he couldn't find. It looked like the party was going to be at her home. Oh no! Just how much of a mess had she left the house in? She was fairly sure that the living room, den, and dining room hadn't been vacuumed in a week. And the kitchen—just what did her kitchen look like when she hadn't entered it since her family had cooked breakfast for her this morning? To make matters worse, the family's quick change after their day at the beach had left each of the three bathrooms a disaster area: shampoo dripping off counters, bathtubs unwashed, and, certainly, towels on the floors and draped across shower curtain rails. Great. For her fortieth birthday, she was going to be revealed to friends and neighbors as a slob. This decade was really starting out swell.

IV

"You knew, didn't you?"

"Just because I knew, doesn't mean I don't love it. Oh, Jed, it's the best party I've ever gone to."

"Not a bad compliment. It's only the second one I've given. The first was in my college dorm the day that I found out that I wasn't going to be drafted. All I did for that was order a keg of beer and a few pepperoni pizzas."

"You did more than that this time," Susan answered, looking around at vases of spring flowers, glowing candles, bright balloons hung in corners of all the rooms, and helium Mylar balloons climbing the stairway to the second floor. And the food! All her favorites laid out on the dining room table: piles of seafood and other goodies.

"I just called in the caterers and paid the bill: same principle as the first time. Only this time Joe's Bar and Grill isn't doing the catering."

"More champagne, madam?" A waiter appeared at her elbow.

"Yes," Jed answered for her, "she would love more champagne."

"He's right, I would," she assured the young man.

He smiled and fulfilled her request.

"How do they find such good-looking kids to wait at these things?" she whispered to her husband.

"I think they hire out-of-work actors." A voice behind the Henshaws answered her question.

"Kathleen! I've been looking all over for you!"

"Well, I've been here all along. I had a great vantage point at the top of the stairs when you and Jed made your entrance. I'll give you credit: Those guys aren't the only actors in the room. You really looked surprised!"

"I was! I opened that door expecting one of the worst messes of all time and everything was so beautiful! You had something to do with this, I expect," she continued, looking at Kathleen who, wrapped in gold lamé and white silk, was startlingly beautiful. "You didn't come over and dust in that outfit, did you?"

"You're not giving your husband enough credit. He really thought of everything; he knew that the house would need a certain amount of work before guests arrived and he hired both Mrs. Annie and Mrs. Knapp—you know her, she cleans for a lot of people on the other side of town—to come in while he was driving you around. They did a great job, too."

"Then you were here."

"Yes. Actually, Jerry and I were with the two cleaning women in the Hallards' kitchen waiting for Chrissy's call that you'd left. Then we all dashed over. And you must have passed the caterer's truck on the road. They arrived about three minutes after you left . . . I'll take some of that," she interrupted herself to accost a waiter walking by carrying a tray of snow crab claws: "The food's delicious."

"Fantastic!" A woman wearing a deep purple dress with a tight bodice and full circle skirt and a necklace of large pearls around her neck joined them. "Happy birthday, dear." She leaned over and kissed Susan. "It's a beautiful party."

"Thank you, Maureen," Susan returned her greeting. "Are those real?"

"Yes." She fingered them nervously. "I wear so little jewelry that I feel a little self-conscious wearing them. Colin bought them for me on his last trip to Hong Kong—to make up for forgetting my birthday two months ago. How do you get your husband to remember your birthdays so lavishly?"

"Well, this is only because it's my fortieth. He usually needs a few hints. I shouldn't say that," she corrected herself. "Jed's very good about giving presents. Although I don't have any pearls like that! They're gorgeous!"

"Have you seen Dawn? I hear she's running around town wearing a diamond so big she almost needs a crane to lift her left arm. I wonder how she talked Richard Elliot into buying her that?"

"I don't know who . . ." Kathleen began.

"Of course, you never met Dawn. Dawn Elliot was the

town bombshell for years. At least, she already held that position when we moved in and we've been here ten years.''

''Bombshell?''

''Are you talking about Dawn?'' Another woman leaned into their group. ''I ran into her at the Inn and I couldn't believe it—she looks better than ever. And you know she can't possibly be a day less than forty . . . Happy birthday, Susan. You don't look forty yourself, speaking of looks.''

''What I'm surprised about is that she's still with Richard. He's really put up with a lot,'' Maureen Small stated, taking a sip from the glass she held.

''No one really knows that,'' the other woman, Martha Hallard, corrected her.

''The town bombshell or the town tramp?'' Kathleen asked.

''Same thing,'' Maureen said firmly.

''Not really,'' the other woman protested. ''No one really knew whom she was sleeping with. There were just always rumors. She gives off kind of an air, you know. She has a way of dressing and moving and talking that says 'I'm available,' if you know what I mean.''

''You could say that about a lot of people,'' Kathleen said, thinking that it could have been said of her at one time in her life—and still might be if anyone was feeling bitchy.

''Yes, but with Dawn it isn't just her looks. She makes innuendos about other women's husbands and being the other woman.''

''Sounds like a bitch.''

''Oh, she is, but an interesting bitch. Oh, there's Betsy. She'll know more about Dawn, I heard she ran into her a few days ago.''

Martha and Maureen waved to a friend and headed over to her, leaving Kathleen and Susan together by the food.

''Is she a bitch?'' Kathleen asked, casually.

''It's my birthday and I'm not going to talk about it!'' Susan spun on her heel and walked away.

''You two have a fight?''

Kathleen turned to find her husband beside her.

"No, but I don't know what's going on. Maureen and Martha were talking about some woman who used to live in Hancock and has come back for a visit, and Susan just clammed up and refused to say anything."

"So maybe she doesn't like her and she has the good manners not to mention it. I wouldn't worry about it. She looks fine now." He nodded toward the hallway, where Susan and her husband were greeting some late arrivals. "When is Jed going to present his gift?"

"Right before the cake's brought out. We thought that two hours was enough to allow for dinner and then we'll all go to the garage. While everyone is there, the caterers will clear the table in the dining room and bring out coffee and cake. So, when we come back in, everything will be waiting."

"He really has this organized, doesn't he?"

"Yes. It's been great helping him because he's cared so much. He really loves her. I think it's wonderful."

"Well, I really love you." He pulled his wife to him. "Isn't that just as wonderful?"

"More. But we haven't been married seventeen years. Let's see if you love me then."

"Absolutely. But, to return to the subject, how's Jed going to get everyone to the garage?"

"I'm going to do that."

Kathleen and her husband turned around and found that Chad was sitting in a window seat behind them.

"Well, I didn't know you were still at the party. I thought I saw you and your sister heading upstairs a few minutes after your parents arrived," Jerry said.

"We wanted to catch the beginning of the 'Friday Fright Night Movie' on channel twelve, but it's one we've seen before. Chrissy is still up there watching something else. I wanted to see the speedboat races but it's her turn to choose, so I thought I'd come down and see what was going on. There are some great cars out there. Did you see the Smalls' Jag sedan? It almost collided with the Bowers' Buick just now!"

"Oh, really?" Jerry was amused, but remembered how it

was to be a boy well enough to encourage Chad. "Are they both okay?"

"Yeah." He sounded disappointed. "But it would have been terrible if something had happened to that Jag—it's brand-new. I wish the Bowers had brought their Porsche instead of the Buick. It's the best Porsche in Hancock: a 930S, bright red with red wheels and a slope nose front, the best-looking turbo on the road. I wonder why they're driving that old Buick?"

Kathleen was less interested in cars than her husband. "Aren't you hungry?" she asked.

"Yeah. I came down here to find some food."

"So why aren't you eating?" Kathleen asked. Out of the corner of her eye, she could see Susan and Jed by the front door with the Bowers. They seemed to have brought their baby with them. Kathleen wondered if this was part of their effort to appear good parents. She didn't know the answer to that, but she guessed it was the reason that the Porsche had been left at home. She might not know as much about cars as Chad, but she knew that a Porsche wouldn't carry the large amount of paraphernalia a baby required even for a short visit.

"Ugh. It's all fish," Chad was saying. "I don't eat fish. I went into the kitchen to find something, but there are all these people in there. Hey, did you see the cake? It's huge! I asked one of the waiters if it's chocolate, but he didn't know and he wouldn't let me pick away any of the icing to take a peek."

"Good for him. Listen, I saw the list of food, and somewhere around here there's Brie and crackers and some dips. There may even be a basket of something as prosaic as potato chips, if you're lucky. I'll help you find them, if you like."

"Great!"

"Hey, wait. Don't you two run off yet. I still don't know how Jed—or Chad, rather—is going to get Susan into the garage." He whispered the last word, knowing not to give away the secret.

"You'll see with everyone else," his wife replied with a

smile. "Come on, Chad. I could do with a slice of Brie myself."

A loud cry of laughter from the den led Jerry there. A couple of men were wiping their eyes and chuckling when he arrived. "Something funny?" Jerry asked a neighbor.

"Jake Bradley was just telling us about the ski weekend he and Marge spent with the Elliots up at Skull Mountain. Seems the snow was perfect and Richard and Jake and Marge skied all day while Dawn stayed at the lodge, but, in the evening, Dawn was the one so tired she had to go to bed right after supper."

Unlike his wife, Jerry knew Dawn Elliot and the stories that surrounded her. Unlike his friends, he didn't find the subject funny or interesting. "Skull Mountain, heh? That must have been before Marge shattered her femur. She'll never ski hard trails like that again."

"Probably not," was the agreement, but the conversation was set on the Elliots and nothing was going to change it. Jerry wandered away.

As he passed the front door, the bell rang. Assuming it was another tardy neighbor, he opened it.

A good-looking man in his mid-thirties was there. Dressed in a leather jacket, jeans, and handmade cowboy boots, he was expensively, if not suitably dressed for a party. He peered in the door as though the celebration surprised him.

"This is the Henshaw's house," Jerry informed him when he didn't speak.

"I must have the wrong address," was the reply.

"If you tell me who you're looking for, maybe I can help you find them. I've lived in Hancock for a long time and I know most everyone in town."

"Yeah." The man hesitated. "The Jones house. They live on Decker Drive, I think."

"I don't know any Joneses . . ."

"Oh, well . . . thanks anyway."

Jerry watched, startled, as the other man turned abruptly and hurried down the walk toward the street. "Hey . . . !"

"Thanks," came the reply, called back over his shoulder.

Jerry turned away and closed the door behind him, so he didn't see the man get into a black Jeep with a badly damaged left side and drive off down the road.

"Feeling unsocial?" A statuesque blonde appeared at his elbow.

"No, there was this man at the door . . ."

"Another guest? I thought the whole town was here already."

Jerry glanced into the rooms around the center hall in which he stood. "I know what you mean, but this was a stranger . . . at least I didn't know him."

"What did he want?"

"He was looking for the Jones house. I told him I didn't know anybody named Jones in Hancock . . . Where are you going?"

"To call the police."

"What for? Wait a minute, Brigit." Jerry grabbed her arm. "You can't just call the police because someone you don't know came to the door."

Brigit Frye brushed her short blond bangs off her forehead and looked at Jerry, a serious expression on her face. "Don't you read your mail? The police department has been sending around pamphlets almost weekly asking that anything—anything—unusual be reported to them at once. And that definitely includes strange men wandering around in the middle of the night asking for fictitious families!"

"Brigit, you leave the phone alone. I've never heard such jumping to conclusions. In the first place, it is not the middle of the night, the man was very well dressed and not really strange at all, and how can you tell that he made up the name of the family? The guy was lost and he saw a party going on and knew someone was home so he stopped here for directions. The police will think you're crazy."

"Jerry, my house has been broken into and my mother's antique silver stolen; my garage has been broken into and four expensive all-terrain bikes were stolen; Guy's car window was smashed and the radio was stolen; and the filter system for the pool was ripped off . . ."

"The pool's filter system?"

"Okay. That was probably some kids. But the point is that I've been burgled twice in the past year and I report everything! And don't tell me to have an alarm system put in. I did. Everything I own is wired: the house, the garage, both cars. I keep expecting the damn dog to beep when I pet him. But I still report strangers—it isn't just the police who say to, your own wife says to. And she's in the security business, isn't she?"

"Yes." Jerry smiled, a little embarrassed.

"Well then?"

"Okay, point made. Are you going to call or shall I?"

"No, skip it. You're right. The man probably just saw that people were home and came by for directions. Oh, I see Nathan over by the window. I've been looking for him. He has the name of the fantastic art dealer in the city who sells antique Chinese rugs at a discount. Nathan!" She ran off into the crowded living room.

"What's she in such a rush about?"

Jerry turned and found Gloria Bower behind him, a plastic bag in her hand. "Something about oriental rugs," he answered. "Did I see you with an infant?"

"Yes. We decided to bring Missy. Actually, we couldn't bring ourselves to leave her at home with a strange sitter. Harvey is upstairs with her now."

"Hey, maybe I'll take a break and go see them," Jerry said, heading toward the stairs.

"I wouldn't. They're together in the bathroom. We changed the formula that the hospital was using and she's got a slight problem. She's getting a quick wash. I was just going to the garage to get rid of her dirty diapers—we didn't want to deposit them in the wastebasket. She's a beautiful baby, but, right now, she smells."

"They all smell. Well, tell me when she's presentable, and I'll go take a look. In the meantime, I think I'll find Kathleen."

She was in the dining room, munching on shrimp and talking about another spate of burglaries in Hancock.

". . . well planned. I really don't understand it because evidence suggests that someone who knows the homes is involved . . ."

"Cleaning women! It must be the cleaning women we hire. I'm going to call Flora in the morning and tell her not to come back . . ."

"No, I think it's the lawn men. They're always around our houses and they know when we're home and what's available. Or, you know, it could be the pool companies. They dash into the backyard once a week and clean out filters and add chemicals. They could be using those times to case things out!" Another woman offered her opinion as she reached across the table for a napkin in which to wrap the shells.

"Oh, that's a problem," said the woman who was going to fire Flora. "I could clean the house myself if I had to, but Brad's too busy at his office to deal with two acres of lawn, and neither of us know anything about the garden or the pool."

"Face it, Nadine, we're at the mercy of these people. How do we even know that the man who comes in to wire our burglar alarm system isn't a thief?" said the woman who was depositing her shells in a convenient ashtray behind the group.

"You're panicking. What you're saying just isn't true. In the first place, most of the pool services and lawn services are checked out pretty carefully by the Hancock police. And if there's a problem, they're the first to be suspected. And as for the security people that come into your home, most of them are bonded. If there's ever any problem, the company takes care of it," Kathleen insisted, knowing that she was exaggerating. The truth was that this suburban town depended on outside help and that if the members of the community ever sat down and counted how many people they let into their homes during the year they would be amazed: from delivery people to chimney sweeps to floor refinishers to wallpaper hangers. The list went on indefinitely.

"So how can we stop these constant burglaries?" Nadine

asked. "You're running your own security company, you must know what can be done."

"No work. It's party time!" Kathleen was relieved that her husband had interrupted at this moment and spared her an answer. Because she knew there wasn't any. He handed her a fresh glass of champagne and passed on to another group.

"I keep hearing about this woman, Dawn . . . Enright was it?"

"Elliot. Yeah. She's back in town. You'll keep hearing about her forever. Not that some of the women in this room aren't trying to forget her."

"What do you mean?" Kathleen asked, more to keep the conversation going than because she was interested.

"Well, Dawn loved to imply that she was sleeping with other women's husbands. I don't think that anybody knew just who, though. It made some women nervous."

"Some women?"

"Well, not me," Nadine replied with a rueful laugh. "I love my Arthur, but I don't think that anyone else would be interested in him."

Kathleen privately agreed, but still didn't know what to say. Chad's arrival spared her more embarrassment.

"Mrs. Ward, how do you like your new 944?"

"My new what?" Nadine Ward looked down at the boy as though he had asked a question about her sex life.

"Your Porsche 944," he answered, looking equally amazed.

"You'll have to ask my husband that question, Chad. It's his car," she continued to Kathleen as Chad ran off, presumably in search of the owner of the Porsche. "If I had told him the truth, I'd have had to say that I hate it."

"Oh?"

"Yes. In the first place, it cost more than a college education and how Arthur thinks that we're going to pay Janie's tuition at Brown and keep Heather in Darby Day if he continues to buy expensive sports cars is beyond me. In the second place, he loves that damn automobile more than he loves me and his daughters combined.''

"Now, I'm sure that's not true," Kathleen protested.

"So you say, but believe me it is. Oh well, I suppose everyone has their faults: If Arthur's buying forty-thousand-dollar cars that's not the worst thing he could do.''

"Yes," Kathleen agreed.

"Everyone to the garage," Chrissy said as she swept by. They saw that Chad was giving the same message to everyone else, and followed the crowd out through the den and into the small mudroom that led to the door connecting the house and the garage. Susan and Jed were the last to arrive.

The space, meant to house three cars, was empty except for a large tarpaulin-covered object in the middle of the floor. A bright red bow perched on the top suggested it was a gift; by its shape and location, it had to be a car. "Happy birthday, hon." Jed, his arm around her shoulders, beamed.

Susan, truly surprised, smiled back.

"Aren't you going to look under the tarp?" someone suggested from the other side of the room.

Feeling foolish, Susan walked hesitantly toward her gift.

"Come on, hon," her husband urged.

She pulled the side of the plastic up over the back of the car. As the bumper was revealed, her smile became a bit fixed. Pulling the tarp up across the bumper, her first impression was verified: It was a Volvo and it was gray. The big expensive sedan, and a shiny metallic gray, but a gray Volvo nonetheless.

"I wanted Dad to buy her a Maserati, even the 425i sedan if he didn't like the Spyder, but he said, 'No, Chad, your mother has a Volvo type of personality,' " she heard her son explaining.

"Beautiful, discreet color," was someone else's assessment.

"I wish John would spend some money on me," came a voice behind her as she continued to reveal the car. The large bow was around the front seat doors, so the car was left with both ends exposed and its midsection covered.

"Let me help you, honey," Jed offered happily.

Susan, speechless, nodded at him, but he was already cutting the ribbon with the Swiss Army knife he always carried. "There!" He stood back proudly as the ribbon fell to the floor and with it the tarpaulin.

It was a gray 740 turbocharged Volvo, fully equipped with air-conditioning, electric door locks, a burglar alarm, a tinted sunroof, a stereo AM/FM radio, a tape deck, and a built-in compact disk player.

Sitting in the driver's seat was Dawn Elliot. And she was dead.

V

"And I thought that the only thing I was going to have to worry about was if the caterers would show up on time."

Kathleen stopped pacing the floor long enough to look at her friend.

"How long are they going to hold us all here?" Jed asked now that he had her attention.

"Technically, they're not holding us," Kathleen corrected, her eleven years as a police officer making her knowledgeable. "They've just asked us down to the station to make our statements."

"Why couldn't they do this back at the house?" Jed asked. "This seems a little odd. I can't imagine what everyone thought."

"At least they followed your suggestion and interviewed the guests first," Kathleen said. "There's been an unexplained and violent death. A body appeared on your property. The police could have done most anything. I think that their decision to allow everyone to come down here to make statements was very humane."

"And gives them time to go through my house without interference," Jed said ruefully.

"That's true," she acknowledged. "But they haven't done anything out of line. And I think they've been pretty considerate of Susan."

Everyone in the room looked over at Susan at this mention of her name. She was sitting near a window, staring out, saying nothing.

"Who called the police?" Jed asked, to draw the attention away from his wife.

"I did."

"Of course, Kathleen. I should have realized that you were the only person who would have had the presence of mind under the circumstances."

"Well, I think someone else would have thought of it pretty quickly."

Her husband got up from his uncomfortable folding chair and walked over to a window on the opposite side of the room from Susan. "There don't seem to be any cars left in the lot. I think they've questioned everyone but us."

"You know," Jed began, joining him, "I don't understand why they let us all drive here. Didn't they think that the killer would get rid of the weapon during the trip?"

"Why do you rule out suicide?" Jerry asked.

"No weapon in the car. And it was pretty obvious that she'd been shot. If you kill yourself you don't have time to get rid of the weapon."

"There's been a lot of time to get rid of this weapon," Kathleen contradicted him. "That woman wasn't shot recently. I'd say it's been a couple of hours at least—maybe more. Anyone trained would see that. The police aren't concerned with weapon disposal—it's been done by now."

"Then, if the killing didn't take place at the party, why detain all the guests until questioned? Wait a minute. She couldn't have been dead in that car for very long. I drove that car into the driveway before breakfast this morning myself. I was tired, but I'd have noticed if I'd been sharing the driver's seat with a dead woman. Believe me."

"I do," Susan whispered from the other side of the room. No one heard her.

"The police had to question the guests. She wasn't killed in the car. But she was put into the car by someone who knew that the tarpaulin and ribbon were going to come off during the party—someone who planned that she would be found like she was. They need to know who that person is and if it's the same person who killed her," Kathleen said. "When did you put the car in the garage, Jed?"

"Before breakfast this morning. I picked it up at the dealer's last night and parked it overnight in the Hallards' garage next door. Then, this morning while the kids were feeding Susan breakfast in bed, I pulled the Mercedes and Susan's old Datsun out of the garage and drove the new Volvo in. I left the Mercedes in the driveway for us to take to the shore and put the Datsun back in Dan's garage. Their car was stolen in the city last week so they have an extra parking place."

"Did you cover it with the tarpaulin and the bow right away?" Kathleen continued.

"No. I did that tonight while Susan was showering. I didn't search the whole car, but I'm sure I would have noticed a dead body in the front seat! It wasn't there then, believe me. I wouldn't give Susan a car containing a dead body for her birthday intentionally, you know."

"I know." Susan whispered again. This time Kathleen heard her.

"I'm sure you wouldn't, Jed," Kathleen assured him, glancing at Susan. "Do you think we should leave her alone?" she continued in a whisper.

"Every time I go over she asks to be alone." The reply was also quiet. "Look, maybe she just doesn't want to see me. When the police come back, I'll ask if I can be questioned first. Will you see if she'll talk to you then? I hate to see her like this. And I don't know what to do."

Kathleen was perplexed by Susan's rejection of her husband during this crisis. It didn't seem typical of their relationship. But she agreed to his request. "I think they will want to see you and Susan last," she suggested. "This did all happen at your house—finding the body, if not the murder—and they're going to be most interested in the two of you, I'm afraid."

"I'll tell them how upset she is," Jed said. "Maybe they'll understand."

They may have understood, but, apparently unwilling to change their plans, Jed and Susan were the last questioned.

"Susan?" Jed could no longer leave her be when they were alone together; Jerry being in with the police, while Kathleen had already been questioned. "Honey? I'm sure sorry this had to happen on your birthday." He pulled another chair over to her and sat down. "I . . . I don't know what to say."

Susan could hear that he was near tears. She took a deep breath and turned from the window toward him. "I know this isn't your fault," she assured him, tears in her own eyes. She took his left hand in hers. "It really was a wonderful party, Jed. I know how hard you must have worked." She broke off, unable to continue. Her husband pulled her head against his shoulder, hiding his own face in her hair. They remained like that until the police came for them.

"Mrs. Henshaw?"

As Susan moved to respond, her husband instinctively pulled her to him. "Are you okay, honey? Can you go through with this?"

"I'm okay. I just want to get this over with. Don't worry."

"She'll be fine, Mr. Henshaw. We just need to get some preliminary information," the officer who had been coming in and out all evening reassured him. "You'll both be able to go home soon."

But things didn't seem quite so optimistic to Susan when she sat down in the room where her guests had been questioned previously. A very impatient duo of uniformed officers stood on either side of her, alternating turns firing off questions. And they didn't appear happy with her answers.

"So you didn't know you were getting the car for your birthday?"

"No."

"But you did know that you were going to have a . . . uh, surprise party?"

"Yes. I told you that. Kathleen Gordon let it slip a few

days ago. You've already questioned her. She must have told you about it.''

"When did you first see the body?"

"When I uncovered the car. That is, when Jed cut the ribbon for me and I pulled the middle of the tarpaulin from the top of the car.''

"And you recognized the body immediately?"

"I didn't know she was dead right away." Susan hesitated over this answer.

"But you knew that it was Dawn Elliot right away?"

"Oh, yes. I knew that.''

"You've seen her recently during her visit to town?"

"No. It's been years—three or more—since I saw her last.''

"But you recognized her right away?"

"Yes.''

"She was a good friend of yours?"

"No. Just a neighbor. She used to live around the corner from us.''

"But you recognized her pretty quickly after not seeing her for a long time.''

"Dawn is . . . was . . . a very . . . uh . . . remarkable-looking woman. It wasn't hard to recognize her. I think everyone did. Didn't they?''

Her question wasn't answered.

"Can you tell us anything else that might be relevant to our investigation of her murder?''

"No.''

"Then we'll question your husband. Right after that you'll probably be able to go home, Mrs. Henshaw. If you'll just wait for him in the lobby.''

It didn't take very long for Jed's interrogation, at least no longer than hers, but to Susan, with that 'probably' ringing in her ears, it seemed a decade. And then she remembered her children. The door that led to the room where Jed was being questioned was still closed, but she ran up and pounded her fist against it.

"Hey, you can't do that." The sleepy-looking redhead

who had been sitting idly behind a desk in the corner of the room protested her action.

"I have to talk to those men in there. I have to find out what happened to my children." Susan rushed from the door over to where the woman sat.

"Chrissy and Chad?" the woman asked, brushing her hair back out of her eyes.

"Yes! Yes . . . how do you know their names? Where are they? They're not here, are they?" Susan slammed her hands on the desk, demanding an answer.

"Hey, lady, I'm not a cop, but I'm official, if you know what I mean, and you better respect me. Get your hands off my desk, if you please." She stood up, revealing a chunky figure stretching against the seams of her uniform.

Susan, realizing her mistake, moved away quickly. "I'm sorry. I'm just upset. Do you know where my children are? Chrissy. And Chad," she reminded her of their names.

"Okay. They're your kids and you're upset. I understand. We get a lot of weird people in here, you know."

"I'm sure you do," Susan replied, clasping her hands behind her back and reminding herself to be patient. "You do know where my children are," she said, hoping the information arrived before she started screaming.

"Yes. They're at the house of a Doctor Dan Hallard. He lives at . . ."

"Thank you. I know the address. He's my next-door neighbor."

"Susan!" Her husband joined her in front of the desk. "It's all over, honey. We can go home."

"Well, it's not really all over, Mr. Henshaw." The officer who had come from the interrogation room behind Jed corrected him. "But we've removed the body and searched your home. I don't think we'll have to bother you anymore until tomorrow. I wouldn't worry too much about this, if I were you," he added, leading them to the door. "Officer Barnes will drive you both home. Good night."

Susan walked out into the chilly March night air, and pulled her coat closer around her.

"Oh, Mrs. Henshaw!" a voice behind her called out.

Susan turned as the officer's head reappeared in the light over the door. "Happy birthday," he called out.

FORTY PLUS ONE DAY

I

"HE REALLY SAID THAT? HE REALLY WISHED YOU A happy birthday?"

"Yeah. I couldn't believe it myself when I heard it, but that's what happened," Susan insisted, taking a deep breath and trying to find spring scents in the chilly air.

"Idiot!" Kathleen condemned him in absentia. "Must have been just what you needed. So how are the kids taking it all?"

"They're confused. They were both awake when we got home last night and that was well after one. And neither of them slept late this morning. Chrissy's friends have been calling since seven A.M. Heaven knows what they're hearing from their parents. Jed finally asked her not to talk about it on the phone. I thought she would blow up, but I think she was relieved to have an excuse to hang up. Chad was up in his room all morning, rearranging car posters on his walls. Jed helped him for a while; he was trying to give Chad an opportunity to talk about everything that's happened. And now Jed's taking both kids out to lunch at the diner. They all love it there. We're trying to keep things as normal as possible and that's hard with the phone ringing every few seconds."

"You're good parents."

Susan shrugged. "We try. And then something comes up like last night and we don't have any idea how to respond. Too much of parenting is just winging it." She bent over to pull up a piece of onion grass before continuing. "Let's go down to the stream. I want to see if the snowdrops are up."

The two women, who had been strolling from Kathleen's car around to the back of the Henshaw home, turned down the brick path to the stream at the end of the property.

"Snowdrops?"

"Uh-huh. I planted them years ago, when we first moved in. They're near the spot where the lilies come up in the early summer. Anyway, they usually bloom by my birthday. Yesterday I was too busy to look and, with that storm earlier this week . . . There they are! Look!"

"Susan! They're beautiful!"

"They are, aren't they?"

There were hundreds of tiny white caps spiking up through green foliage. They surrounded the willows and spilled down over the bank to the water. Susan and Kathleen stood silent, staring at them.

"I think I love them because they're so early. They come up in the snow and the mud and the misery of March and promise that spring really is going to come despite all evidence to the contrary," Susan said. There was an old wooden bench near the water and she pointed to it. "Want to sit down, or is it too cold for you?"

"No. I'm fine. Let's sit," Kathleen replied. "You know, this really is fantastic." She motioned to the flowers. "How many bulbs did you plant?"

"A hundred. And it took forever. We had just moved in and I wanted to do some gardening, but Jed had plans for formal flower beds in the backyard and wanted to work everything out on paper. But he didn't care about the land back here so I went down to that big nursery on the highway and bought a hundred snowdrop bulbs. I really didn't know what to buy, but when I saw all the bins of bulbs with their glossy pictures of daffodils and tulips, they reminded me of the flowers at the florists in the city. I wanted something that was definitely country and so I bought these.

"Planting them was a real thrill. Of course, it had to be done in the fall and it was chilly. Chrissy must have been four then and she ran all over the place and kept slipping on the leaves into the stream and I was sure she was going to catch pneumonia. And I was pregnant with Chad and bending over was uncomfortable. But I've never regretted a minute of it."

"It was worth it. This really is wonderful . . . almost magical," Kathleen agreed, looking around.

"Jed had an affair with her." Susan made the statement and then bent over and picked a stray flower growing near her foot.

"Jed . . . What?" Kathleen's voice betrayed her shock.

"Jed had an affair with Dawn Elliot." Susan didn't look up, seeming to concentrate on the tiny flower she was shredding with the tips of her nails.

"Susan." Kathleen didn't know what to say. She reached over and put her hand on her friend's arm.

Susan threw down the petal pieces and looked up, tears in the corners of her eyes, "I'm forty years old and it was my party and I can't believe this is happening," she said and, covering her face with her hands, she began to cry.

Kathleen let her. She had seen enough tragedy and grief in her years as a policewoman to know that sometimes the tears had to be released first. So she waited.

"I don't know what I'm going to do," was Susan's only comment.

"Why do you have to do anything?"

"What?" For the first time since her revelation, Susan looked up at her friend.

"Why do you have to do anything?" Kathleen repeated. "Let Jed tell the police about the affair—and I hope he did that already since you really shouldn't try to hide it from them."

"I don't know what Jed told the police."

"You didn't ask him?"

"No."

"Susan, why not?"

"Because he doesn't know that I know."

"He doesn't know that you know about his affair?" Kathleen asked, not believing it possible.

"Yes."

"You'd better start at the beginning—that is, if you want to talk about it," Kathleen said, not anxious to intrude.

"I guess I'd better. It's just . . . it's just that I thought it was all over. That I wouldn't have to think about it anymore."

Again, Kathleen was forced to wait for the crying to cease.

"Okay. I'm fine now." Susan inhaled deeply. "Really. I'd tell you about it from the beginning but I'm not really sure what the beginning was."

"When did you find out they were having an affair?"

"About four years ago."

"How did you find out? Susan, are you sure you want to tell me about this?" Kathleen asked, not comfortable asking so many questions.

"I don't want to even think about, but I'd better. It started four years ago. Actually, I don't know when they started sleeping together. But that's when I found out . . ."

"How did you find out?"

"I saw them going into a hotel room together."

"Here?"

"In the city. I was involved in a lecture series at the Metropolitan Museum of Art. Chad was in first grade and I had time to myself and I signed up for everything that year— cooking classes, another wine-tasting class, and some art appreciation stuff. Anyway, on days when I was in the city, I hired a sitter to be with the kids when they came home from school and feed them dinner and I drove home with Jed. Sometimes I met him for lunch and sometimes not. It depended on lecture times and on his schedule. Anyway, this particular day I'd been planning to lunch with a friend from the lecture but she hadn't shown up and, instead of eating in the cafeteria at the museum, I decided to go to Monique—

you know, the restaurant at the Bentley House Hotel. Jed and I had eaten there once or twice and it was good and so, on a whim, I went. Do you know, that was the first time I'd ever eaten alone in a restaurant?''

"Really?"

"Yes. Fine time to pick, too. Well, they gave me a tiny table in the back of the room where I wasn't too noticeable; a suburban woman alone isn't exactly something a restaurant is proud to display. So Jed and Dawn didn't see me.''

"They were eating there too?"

"They came in together about ten minutes after I sat down. They were so happy together, so obviously infatuated, that I knew right away not to leap up and greet them.''

"So you . . . ?"

"So I sat there and watched them flirt, and play with their food, and drink their wine. I just sat there," she repeated.

"But . . . maybe they didn't go to bed together," Kathleen offered, knowing that she was doubting her friend's intelligence.

"After they finished, they got up together. I collected my check immediately; the waiters had been trying to urge me out of the restaurant for some time and were thrilled to rush it through. I went out into the lobby and my husband and Dawn Elliot were getting a room. They were standing so close together that you could hardly tell where one person started and the other began—remember how we used to say that in college? Anyway, I stood there and watched them get into the elevator. I stood there in plain view, but they were too wrapped up in each other to bother to look up . . .''

"And? They went up in the elevator. What did you do?"

"I . . . I wanted to scream. I wanted to call the police. I wanted to start a fire or explode a bomb in the lobby. I wanted to rush up to their room and kill them both . . .''

"And?" Kathleen repeated quietly.

"I found the public phone near the ladies' room, and I called Jed's secretary and told her that I was sorry I had missed Jed, but that I wasn't feeling well and I was going to take the train home. And I did. I went home and called off the sitter, and picked up the kids at school, and talked on the phone, and fixed them dinner, and helped Chrissy with her homework. And, when Jed came home, I fixed him dinner and told him I thought I was coming down with the flu and I went to bed.''

"And you never told him what you saw?"

"Never."

"So, four years later he still doesn't know that you saw Dawn and him together that day?"

"No. It only lasted a few months. I'm pretty sure of that."

"Why?"

"Well, Jed acted distracted for a while. And stayed late at work and had to vanish back into the city for afternoons on weekends. All the classic tacky things. And then, one day he was back with us just like he used to be—not just spending time with us but concerned about us. And I heard that Dawn had left town and was teaching a class out West somewhere.''

"And you and Jed never, ever talked about it?" Kathleen knew she was repeating herself but she couldn't believe the answer she was getting.

"Never. Oh, there have been times since then when I thought it was going to come out. A friend would have an affair and we'd start talking about what would happen if one of us were involved with someone else. But the conversations have always stayed theoretical. I don't know how to tell him that I know and he's obviously decided not to tell me.''

"But Susan . . ." Kathleen didn't know what to say.

"Well, what could I say, Kathleen? 'Oh, Jed, by the way, I know that you had an affair with Dawn four years ago, but I forgot to mention it until now?' ''

"You trapped yourself into keeping the secret."

"Right. Not only did he deceive me, but I ended up deceiving him.''

"It sounds horrible."

"It was." Susan got up from the bench and started to pace near the stream. "I thought about it a lot at the time, of course. I used to wake up in the middle of the night with visions of the two of them in bed together. And I worried the next time Dawn came through town. But nothing happened. And, after a while I came to accept that it was over and . . .''

"And?"

"And that's all. End of story." She sat down again on the bench. "Until yesterday, that is."

"Not quite," Kathleen corrected her. "You were pretty upset to hear that Dawn was back in town. I couldn't have been the only one who noticed that."

"Yes. I guess I really hadn't dealt with my feelings as well as I thought I had. I always worry that something will happen when she's around again, but I'm pretty sure nothing has. When I heard she was back, a lot of the old hurt and anger returned. Oh, Kathleen, what am I going to do?"

"I don't know what you mean," Kathleen answered.

"How am I going to tell Jed that I know after all this time? Because we have to talk about it now, don't we?"

"Too bad you didn't decide to talk to him about it last night."

"I couldn't even think straight last night. I thought I would come home and go to bed and, after Jed had fallen asleep, get up and decide what to do. But Jed didn't fall asleep. At least he seemed to be awake whenever I was last night—you know how those kind of restless nights go. And this morning the kids were up early. And . . ." she broke off and kicked some pebbles in the water.

"And?"

"And I don't know what to say, anyway."

"You're worried about your marriage?"

"Yes. What else?"

"Susan, you better think about being a suspect in a murder case. You, or Jed, or both of you, I suppose." Kathleen watched her friend carefully, wondering what the reaction to this would be.

"I don't think that's the problem right know," Susan said and began to cry again. "Kathleen, I love Jed. I love him more now than I've ever loved him. How can I bring this up after all these years?" She stood up, suddenly angry. "And you know what I don't understand? I don't understand how he can go on deceiving me. He should have told me about it then and he should tell me about it now!''

"Really? What good would telling you then have done? He made a mistake; he didn't have to hurt you. But now is a different story. Now you two had better get together and have a talk.

"Susan, you can't have a good marriage if one of you is in prison. You're not paying attention to me: A murdered woman, a woman that you and your husband may both have reason to hate, was found in your garage last night. Susan, unless someone confesses to this crime, you or Jed are going to be major suspects in a murder case.''

"But unless Jed told the police about the affair, how would they know?''

"Well, he better have told them,'' Kathleen insisted. "Because they're probably going to find out.''

"How?''

"Well, you knew about it, didn't you? Someone else might have too and that someone else may have told the police.''

"I hadn't thought of that. I guess Jed and I had better have a talk.''

"Yes. I'm getting cold. Let's go back to the house.''

They got up and turned together, but it was Susan who first saw the man coming around the corner of her house.

"Who's that?''

"Looks like the police.''

They exchanged anxious glances and walked toward him.

II

"As I said, I don't know how long it'll be before you get your car back, Mrs. Henshaw,'' the police officer said, handing her a piece of paper. "Here's the receipt for it.''

Susan glanced down at the three-by-five sheet of tissue paper, a copy of the original document that he had filled out, the writing barely legible. "Thank you. Is that all you wanted?''

"Yes.'' He looked over at the shiny new car ignominiously being lifted by the dilapidated city tow truck and then back to her. "This would have been done last night, but the city tow trucks were all busy with a problem out on the highway. Why don't you two ladies go inside and leave everything to us?"

"I think you're right," Kathleen agreed, putting her arm around Susan's shoulder. "Let's go get some coffee. These men can take care of this themselves."

"Good idea. I really didn't get much to eat last night. Maybe there's something in the refrigerator." Susan opened the door to the kitchen while talking. She paused on the threshold, "Well, those caterers really cleaned up this place. I'm surprised that the police were so willing to let them go ahead and do it."

"It's not like Dawn Elliot was poisoned. I'll heat some water for coffee. What's in those large boxes over there?" Kathleen was glad to return to the normal things of life. Susan had to get herself together before talking to her husband.

"Look at this." Susan was peering into a bakery box. "There must be a thousand cookies in here. I wonder what's in the rest." She started going through the half-dozen similar boxes lined up on her counters. "My goodness. Cake and . . . is it baklava? Yes, it is! And tiny pastries and millefeuilles and chocolate truffles! Oh, Kathleen, it was going to be such a nice party!" she wailed.

"It was a nice party and . . ."

"I know, I know. I'm calming down. Let's eat some of this stuff. I must have burned a million calories in the last twelve hours. I deserve this."

"Great. Have some coffee. Jed must have made it this morning and left it for you." She looked carefully at her friend. "You're not going to start crying again, are you?"

"No. I have a problem with my marriage. We'll solve it. You know," she paused to pick out a tiny strawberry tart from one of the boxes. "I think a relationship has a life of its own."

"I don't know what you mean."

"Well . . ."

The phone rang.

"Let me get it," Kathleen offered, thinking of reporters or more police questions.

Susan, her mouth full of food, nodded.

"Hello?"

"Susan? Are you all right? You sound . . ."

"It's Kathleen, Jed. Susan's eating."

"It's Jed? Let me take it." Susan reached for the receiver. "Hi . . . Yes, I'm fine. They just took away the Volvo. They need it for evidence when the case goes to court. Kathleen can explain . . . You're kidding! But it was just fixed . . . No, no, don't call a cab, I'll come pick you up. Sure, the Datsun it still in the Hallards' garage, isn't it? Okay, in about fifteen minutes then." She hung up.

"Is that what I think it is?" Kathleen asked, swallowing a last sip of her coffee.

"The Mercedes is broken. It just stopped in the middle of the road. Jed called Triple A and says a tow truck's on the way. The dealer's maintenance shop isn't open on Saturday but it's going to be towed there anyway. Damn! They just worked on it. I hate it when this type of thing happens."

"So you're going to pick him up?"

"Yes. I'd better call Martha and tell her that I need to get into her garage."

"I'll go with you, if you'd like, but first I'm going to run to the bathroom."

"Fine." Susan reached for the phone.

When Kathleen returned, she was hanging up, staring out the window at the police car in her neighbor's driveway.

"They must be questioning the guests from the party all over again," Kathleen said.

"No, I just talked to Martha. The police are there because they were burgled last night. Martha's jewelry was stolen during the party. Let's get over there right away."

Kathleen, beginning to feel like she had fallen into her old life, followed quickly.

They could see Martha and her husband Dan sitting at the

kitchen table through the bay window that was set into the back of the Hallards' large Colonial home. A policeman was at the table with them and, sitting in the middle of it, surrounded by coffee mugs, sugar and cream, spoons and napkins, was a battered burgundy Italian leather jewelry box. It was empty. Susan and Kathleen entered without knocking.

"I bought the jade bracelet for my wife in Hong Kong when I was there with an international convention of gynecologists. That was seven years ago and it cost three thousand dollars then. I can't even imagine what it's worth now.

"Susan, Kathleen. Good morning. I . . ." Dan's phone rang. "If that's the Frankenthaller baby someone else in the office is just going to have to deliver it. Hello? Oh, yes. It's for you, Officer." He handed the phone across the table to the policeman. "Do you want some coffee?" he whispered to Kathleen and Susan.

"No thanks. We need to get my car. But, Martha, did you lose all your jewelry?"

"Everything," was the reply. "Well," she corrected herself, "not everything. I was wearing my engagement ring and my emerald ring and the emerald earrings that Dan brought me from his trip to Venezuela last year."

"And the pearls I bought you in San Francisco, too, remember," her husband completed the list.

"Oh yes, those too. I'm glad it was such a dressy party, Susan, or I wouldn't have been wearing so much."

"Where did the thief find the jewels?" Kathleen asked, instantly professional.

"In the wall safe in our bathroom. We had it installed behind the mirror over the sink. We never thought anyone would look there, but I guess we were wrong." She sighed.

"You don't have another safe somewhere in the house?" Kathleen asked.

"Not anymore. We used to have locked metal file cabinets built into the wall in the small room that Dan uses for his office next to our bedroom. Dan used to keep the medical files of his patients there. But they were broken into during a robbery a few years ago. The thief was probably looking for drugs. What he found was the jewelry I kept there, thinking it was a safe place.''

"And it was after that that you had the safe built?'' Kathleen asked.

"Yes.''

"Did it look like the burglar was looking for drugs this time?'' the policeman asked, interrupting his phone conversation.

"No,'' Dan answered. "I don't keep them around the house. Anyway, everything—including the files and medical histories of all my patients—is kept in my office at the hospital these days.''

"If you'll just hang this up for me, Dr. Hallard,'' the policeman interjected. "I gotta finish here and get going. Turns out that your home wasn't the only one broken into last night. I gotta check out . . .'' He looked at the list he had made during his conversation. "One fourteen Innsbruck Drive, Seven Franklin Place and Ten ten Forsythe Lane. Seems all three of those homes had problems last night.''

"I'll just . . . I'll just go get my car out of your garage, if you don't mind, Dan,'' Susan said quickly.

"No problem. It's open. Just help yourself,'' came the reply. "Now let me look at this list one more time, Officer.''

Susan didn't say anything until she had backed out of the garage and was driving down the long driveway to the street. "That's the Crabbes, the Logans, and the Bowers.''

"The addresses the officer recited,'' Kathleen stated, picking up on the conversation immediately.

"Yes.'' She steered the car around a corner and speeded up. "They were all at the party last night.''

"The plot,'' said Kathleen, "thickens.''

"I'll say. Do you think it had anything to do with the party or the murder?''

"I have a hard time believing that it doesn't have anything to do with the party. It sounds to me like a very organized group knew who was going to be out and when and swept through the deserted homes. Now whether that had to do

with the murder is something else. I don't see the connection.
There may be one, though.''

"How did they know they were going to be deserted?''

"What do you mean?''

"Well, Dan and Martha's kids are older and were bound
to be out on a Friday night, except for Charlie and he
was having a sleep over with Chad that night. In fact,
he was asleep in Chad's room throughout the whole party.
Chad was very disappointed. And the Crabbes have twins
at different universities in California. The Logans have one
child, but he just went to boarding school in Massachusetts
last fall and wouldn't have been home.''

"But the Bowers,'' Kathleen said. "They just got Missy—
no, she wasn't at home, was she?''

"No, she was upstairs in our bedroom,'' Susan said.
"Seems Gloria and Harvey got nervous about being so far
away from their baby at the last minute, and so they brought
her along. I think they may be carrying this perfect parent
bit a little far. I overheard Gloria talking about the possibility
of the welfare department making spot checks of their home,
but I can't believe that would happen on a weekend evening.
Anyway, they had called Jed and he agreed it was fine to
bring Missy along. I'm not so sure. Our bedroom smells like
baby puke. You know, though, if this was an organized group,
how would they know that the Bowers weren't going to be
home, since they decided to bring along the baby at the last
minute?''

"I don't have enough information to tell you anything,''
Kathleen said, truthfully enough, beginning to regret her am-
ateur status in the case. She certainly would have liked to
know more. "I think Jed can tell us something about this. If
the burglaries were organized to coincide with the party, as
it looks like they were, then they were organized by someone
with access to the guest list. And Jed would know who those
people were.''

"Well, there he is,'' Susan said, pointing to the man
standing on the side of the road, where a tow truck was

raising their Mercedes into the air. Her children stood nearby also. "I was planning to talk to him about Dawn, but . . ."

"Good idea, do that right away. In fact, why don't I take the kids out to the diner and you and he can have some time together alone? Susan," she added, as the car stopped, "the murder is more important than the burglaries."

"And my marriage is more important than both."

Kathleen didn't think this was the time to remind her that she wouldn't have much of a marriage if she or Jed were convicted of murder.

"Thank goodness, you're here. They're almost done, as you can see." He nodded to the men. "And the kids were getting bored and hungry. We never made it to the diner."

"We were just talking about that," Susan said. "Kathleen offered to drop us off at home and then take the kids out to lunch. You and I can eat some of the leftovers from the party."

"I want some of the cake," Chad chirped up from the backseat.

"We'll come back for dessert," Kathleen assured him.

"Okay. This wouldn't have happened to a Lamborghini Countach," he said to his father.

"It shouldn't have happened to my Mercedes," was his father's answer. Jed was looking at his wife curiously. He knew that Kathleen's offer was made for a reason.

"Speaking of cars, since the police impounded the Volvo and I'm driving the Datsun around, is it still insured?" Susan asked.

"Yes, I hadn't changed the policy yet. I wonder why the police needed the Volvo. Does this mean they found something in it that might convict someone of the murder?" he asked Kathleen.

"Who?" Susan was surprised to hear her daughter ask.

"Well, we don't know yet, do we?" Susan replied.

Chrissy leaned forward from the backseat. "Won't they think it's someone in our family?"

"Chrissy, what a horrible thing to say. Why would anybody in our family want to kill Dawn Elliot?" Jed said.

The Datsun, which had seen better days, rattled and puffed as it traveled down the road, otherwise everyone would have heard the classic pin drop after that question. Kathleen, sitting in the backseat between Chad and Chrissy, wondered if everyone needed to pay quite so much attention to the road ahead.

"We . . ." Jed began to say something to his daughter and then quit. "What's the police car doing at our house?" he began again.

"They probably want to ask more about the burglaries," Susan said. "Oh, Jed, we didn't have time to tell you. There were burglaries last night during my party."

"What?"

"I'm sure they'll explain."

Kathleen turned to the kids. "You two pile into my car and I'll tell you all about it on the way to the diner. It will be easier for your parents to handle this alone."

Jed and Susan walked up to the policemen waiting by their front door. So much for the serious discussion they were going to have, Susan thought to herself. Were they ever going to be alone together? Not that she wasn't relieved by this delay in their conversation.

Jed spoke first. "Can we help you?"

"We'd like to ask you and your wife some questions. I'm Officer Mitchell and this is Detective Sardini from the State Police. May we come in?" the younger of the two asked. He was an overweight, anxious-looking man.

"Of course." Jed hurried forward to unlock the door. Susan was surprised to see that her normally in-control husband was nervous.

They entered to the shrill scream of their burglar alarm.

"Damn!"

"Don't worry, Mitchell will call in," offered Detective Sardini, spying the phone near the stairs.

"Thanks. We haven't done that since the first week we had this thing installed," Jed explained.

"Happens all the time," Officer Mitchell assured them, dialing the phone and looking less amiable than his words.

"Could we sit down someplace?" suggested Detective Sardini, a tall, tired-looking man in his late forties.

"Of course," Susan leapt into her hostess role. "Let's go into the living room. Would you like some coffee or tea or something to eat?" she offered, thinking of the cartons in the kitchen.

"No, thank you."

"Oh, well, let's sit down then."

"That's taken care of." Officer Mitchell followed them into the room.

Susan repeated her offer of refreshment to him.

"Nothing," was the reply. Susan got the impression that he thought anything she offered him might be laced with poison.

"Are you ready to sit down and answer our questions now?" Officer Mitchell asked, leaning against the mantel and looking down at Susan and Jed.

"My wife was merely trying to be a good hostess," Jed objected.

"This isn't a social call," was Mitchell's response. He took a leather-covered notebook out of his jacket pocket and opened it to a page covered with writing. At the same time, Detective Sardini removed a small tape recorder from the bag he was carrying and, turning it to record, placed it carefully on the walnut burl coffee table in front of the couple.

"Don't we have the right to have a lawyer present if we're to be questioned?" Jed asked. And Susan could hear the anger in his voice.

"We're collecting information. Not accusing you or your wife of anything," came the irritating reply. "Not yet. However, if you feel that you need a law . . ."

"No, no, no. Let's just get on with it," Jed insisted.

"When did you begin to plan the party for your wife's birthday, Mr. Henshaw?" Mitchell asked.

"Well, I started thinking about it a few months ago—right after New Year's, I guess."

"When did it become public knowledge? When did other people know about it—the caterers, florist, the guests?"

"Well, the first person I talked to about it was Kathleen Gordon. She's one of our best friends and . . ."

"And when was that?"

"Actually, at a New Year's Eve party at a neighbor's house. It was after midnight and we were together in the kitchen and I told her that I had been thinking about a surprise party for Susan and asked her if she thought that Susan would like one."

"And?"

"And she said she thought it was a good idea. Kathleen was a big help in all of this. I had never given a formal party before and didn't know about things like how early you have to get hold of the caterers and things like that."

"So this Mrs. Gordon helped you from the beginning. Was she aware of the guest list?"

"Yes, we talked about how large a party to have and whom to invite. She was a big help."

"Did she know about the Volvo?"

"Know what?"

"Did she know that you were giving your wife the Volvo?"

"Yes, she did. I don't know what you're thinking, but you should know that Kathleen was a police officer—a state detective like Detective Sardini before she retired from her job and came to live here," Jed said.

"You're right, Mr. Henshaw. You don't know what I'm thinking," was the distinctly unpleasant reply.

Susan saw her husband grimace and started to speak. "I . . ."

"I'll get to you in a moment, Mrs. Henshaw. If you'll just be patient."

Susan took a deep breath and ground her own molars together.

"So when did you contact everyone, Mr. Henshaw? The caterers, and the florists, and the guests?"

"I called the caterers and the florists and also the liquor store the first week of January. Kathleen was sure that they should be contracted with immediately since we really wanted the party to be on my wife's birthday, and didn't feel free to change the date according to the availability of services. In fact, the florist we called originally was booked for a party on Friday night and two weddings Saturday and couldn't take the job. I was surprised how far ahead people make plans.''

''And your guests?''

''My guests?''

''When did you send out invitations to your guests?''

''About a month ago.''

''They were handwritten?''

''No, we had the print shop in town make them up, but they were hand-addressed.''

''You addressed them?''

''No, I was afraid Susan would run into them if they were in the house. Kathleen volunteered to address them at her house. And,'' he added, ''the responses went to her home also.''

''That doesn't matter,'' said the policeman, rudely, Susan thought. ''Who else knew about the party?''

''Anyone that any of the guests told about it. Or anyone that the caterers or the florists or anyone else who knew about it told,'' Jed answered, a bit impatient.

Officer Mitchell looked up from his writing to check the location of the recorder before he continued. ''How well did you know the deceased?''

''Dawn Elliot?''

''Do you know anyone else I might be asking about, Mr. Henshaw?''

Susan watched Jed's jaw tighten and, imperceptibly, moved a bit toward him before he spoke. ''She lived in Hancock and we saw her and her husband socially for a number of years. They lived just around the block, in fact. And, of course, we belonged to the same club—most everyone in town does—and Richard, her husband, and I played together on a mixed doubles team one summer. They were already living in Hancock when we moved in. And they moved out around three years ago in the spring, as a matter of fact.''

''Where to?''

Jed seemed surprised at the question. "I don't know."

"They moved to LA—Los Angeles," Susan interrupted.

"They've been living in LA ever since leaving here?" Sardini asked, in a voice kinder than that of his inferior.

"Well, that's where the Club has been sending their Christmas card for the last three years," Susan answered. "I know, because I was Club secretary one of those years and I've helped address cards other years. I think some people in town have been out to the coast and seen them, too. But they kept their house here in town—for visits, I guess."

"Have you been out to California in the past three years?" Mitchell returned to asking Jed his questions. "To the Los Angeles area?"

"Yes. Probably half a dozen times or more," Jed answered. "My agency does a lot of business of one sort or another on the coast, and I go out a few times a year. But I haven't seen Dawn Elliot or her husband."

"Is this the first time that they've been in Hancock since they moved? That you know of?" *Or are willing to admit* was the unasked question.

"I'd heard they had been in town. I just hadn't seen them."

"What did you think of Dawn Elliot, Mr. Henshaw?"

"Think of her?"

"Did you think that she was a nice person? That she was attractive? That she was . . ."

"Kind to children and small animals?" Jed interrupted a little sarcastically.

"If you like."

The smile on that man's face was definitely the nastiest she had ever seen, Susan decided.

"If you're asking me if I heard the rumors that she fooled around with men . . ."

"Married men?"

"Okay, married men, if you will. Then, yes, I heard about that. Everyone in town has heard about that. But I didn't think anything about it. This is a small town, Officer, and while everyone in it may not be as nice as can be, we all get along with one another."

"I don't want an argument, Mr. Henshaw, but I think we can assume that someone in town didn't get along with Dawn Elliot—and, in fact, killed her."

"It wasn't me."

"Did you sleep with her?"

"I'm very happily married, Detective Sardini. I didn't sleep with her."

Jed looked at his wife, but Susan didn't notice. She was staring anxiously at the policeman. Did he believe Jed? Why didn't the detective say anything? Mitchell turned from husband to wife abruptly.

"Do you believe your husband, Mrs. Henshaw?"

"Do I what?" She couldn't believe what he had asked.

"Do you believe that your husband didn't have an affair with Dawn Elliot?" he asked impatiently.

"I can't believe you're asking me that!" She spoke her feelings out loud, but she knew she had no choice about her answer.

"You're not answering me though, are you?"

That nasty smile. She'd like to kick him in the . . . "Of course I believe my husband, Detective. And you should too!"

"I'm investigating a murder, Mrs. Henshaw. I don't have the luxury of believing or not believing anyone. I have to find the truth."

"My husband is telling you the truth!" Susan stood up and shouted at the man. But he wasn't, was he? Jed was lying to the police. She put her hand over her eyes and sat down. What was going on?

"Susan? Do you feel all right?" Jed put his arms around her.

Susan didn't answer, but glared at the detective.

"Very dramatic, Mrs. Henshaw. I'll change the subject, since this one upsets you so much. Did you know you were going to get a surprise party from your husband?"

"Yes." Susan was furious, but knew she had to answer his questions.

"How did you find out?"

"Kathleen and I were having lunch together one day and she let the information slip."

"Did you know you were going to get a Volvo from him?"

"I had no idea that he was going to give me a car at all—any car."

"Well, I guess that's all," was the detective's surprising next comment.

"You don't want to ask us anything else?" Susan asked, trying to keep the relief out of her voice.

"No, but we'll be back. I would like to see the garage, though, if you don't mind."

"The car isn't there . . ."

"No, that reminds me of two more questions," Detective Sardini said, putting the recorder he had just picked up back down. "How did the car get from the dealer's to your house, Mr. Henshaw?"

"I drove it. I picked it up the night before the party—Thursday night—and I put it in the garage of our next-door neighbor, Dr. Hallard. Then, early the morning of the party, I brought it over here and put it in the garage. I put a blue tarpaulin and a big bow on it later in the evening, while Susan was showering."

"And at any time when you picked it up, or put it in your neighbor's garage, or when you brought it over here and decorated it, at any time, did you look in the trunk?"

"The trunk? No, I never looked in the trunk. Why do you ask?"

"Well, it would be nice to know how long the body was in the car, Mr. Henshaw," said Officer Mitchell. "That's all."

III

"I sure would like to get into the files they're keeping on this case," Kathleen said wistfully, putting the paint roller back in the tray. She and her husband were taking advantage of a free Saturday afternoon to paint the guest room of their new home.

"You regret leaving the department," Jerry said to his wife, his voice slightly sad.

"Never! I couldn't have stayed a detective and married you. And I think the security business is interesting," was the reply.

"Interesting?" He made his voice as noncommittal as he could: He'd seen how bored his bride was becoming and he'd worried about it. But it was up to her to come to her own conclusions. And to make her own decisions.

"A detective's life is difficult to blend with a family life and I worked in a different city. We wouldn't even have been able to live together!" Kathleen protested.

"I don't want you to give up what means the most to you," he reminded her, bending over to mop up some paint that had fallen on the oak parquet floor.

"I'm not! I didn't," she protested. "It's just that I want to help Susan and I don't have enough information."

"Can you call any old friends in Hartford?"

"Yes. I think I will. Or am I getting too involved?"

"From what you've been saying, it sounds like Susan and Jed are going to need all the help they can get."

"I wish you would talk to Jed and find out if he understands how serious this is. Susan's so involved in saving her marriage that she doesn't seem to think that being arrested for murder is possible."

"I still can't believe that Jed had an affair with Dawn."

"I thought everyone slept with Dawn," Kathleen said, hoping she wasn't going to hear what she didn't want to hear.

"Not really," was the mild reply. Jerry looked up at the wall they were working on. "Do you think this will smooth out? It's pretty streaked."

Kathleen stood back to get a better view. "No, that's the way it always looks before it's dry. Haven't you ever done this before?"

"Evelyn always had professionals in to do the work," he replied, thankful that he could talk comfortably about his dead wife.

"Well, when you're a cop, you can't afford to hire people

to do things that you can do yourself. And I like painting. I think the color's good, don't you?''

"A little light," he suggested.

"It'll dry darker," she assured him. "Listen, why don't we take a break and have some tea and it will dry and you'll see for yourself?''

"Good. How about a beer instead of tea? I'll get it.''

"Okay. Bring the roll of aluminum foil up from the kitchen and I'll wrap these brushes before they dry out.'' She started pouring paint from the tray back into its can.

When he returned, she had picked up some of the drop cloths and was busily resealing the cans.

"Thanks.'' She took the bottle from him and sat down in the large window seat on the opposite side of the room from the wet walls. Her husband sat next to her and, leaning back against the window, took a drink from his bottle. "It's looking worse, not better.''

"You forgot the aluminum foil.''

"Oh, damn . . .''

"I already wrapped them in plastic," she said, smiling at his mistake.

"You were asking about Dawn Elliot," he reminded her.

"You were saying that she hadn't slept with everyone.''

He smiled. "Well, not with me, if that's what you're wondering. Although she did offer. It was an offer she made to every man in Hancock," he added, when his wife didn't answer. "Not just me.''

"Yeah," Kathleen agreed absently, holding her beer up to the light as though studying it. "You didn't know about Jed and her?''

"No, but, you know, it makes some sense now that you've told me about it. You said it was four years ago, right? Well, about that time Jed was having a rotten time down at the agency. He was passed over for a promotion that he really wanted—it went to some hotshot from the coast. He even thought about leaving Raleigh and Rhyme for a time. Dawn Elliot would pick up on that and she might have used it to get close to him.''

"What was she like?"

"Dawn Elliot? Well, not your garden variety tramp, if that's what you're wondering."

"So what made her so different from any other woman who's working on sleeping with every married man in town?"

Jerry looked closely at his wife. "I don't really know. Maybe it's just that that's all you've heard about her."

"So tell me more. Tell me everything. It's going to take a while for the paint to dry."

"Well, she was supposedly an expert in her field . . . ."

"This is your idea of telling me everything? What's her field? What . . . ?"

"She was an anthropologist. I understand that she was on the faculty at UCLA. When she was here, she taught at NYU occasionally. She also had some sort of affiliation with the Museum of Natural History, but I don't know what. Dawn was one of these people who never explained anything, but jumped right in talking about what she's doing as though everyone had full background sketches. Anyway, her field was Anasazi Indians—you know, the ones in the Southwest— and she was always in and out of town, going on digs and conferring with researchers at other universities."

"Some life," Kathleen commented, having lived in this community long enough to know exactly how exciting and glamorous it must have appeared to the women staying at home raising their children or running small local boutiques.

"I think it really was. I remember her telling me at a party about the month she was snowed in at Chaco Canyon in New Mexico, about how the coyotes would come down from the hills and walk through the ruins in the moonlight."

Kathleen was remembering the arm that had fallen from the Volvo when Susan opened the door: tanned, slender, almost completely covered from wrist to elbow with bracelets of silver and turquoise. Then the short nails and weathered hand had surprised her. But it made sense in the context of how her husband was describing Dawn.

"She didn't have any children?"

"Not that I know of, at least none living with her or that

she would talk about. And I know that she and Richard didn't have any children of their own.''

''So she was married before?''

''I don't think so, but I don't know everything about her life so I wouldn't rule it out as a complete impossibility.''

''What's Richard like?''

''Not the deceived husband, if that's what you're thinking. He's an actor, a minor actor to be sure, but he seems to make a living at it. I see him from time to time in commercials: His looks make him the type to play the distinguished middle-aged doctor advising the TV audience to buy a certain laxative. He's not the sort of wimpy person who would ignore his wife's infidelities. But maybe he has such an overblown ego that it just doesn't matter to him. And, maybe, he has affairs of his own. I suppose they could have what used to be known as an open marriage.''

''Or maybe he's gay,'' Kathleen offered.

''Could be. Well, whatever.'' He shrugged. ''But if he had an extramarital sex life he didn't have it in Hancock—or he was more discreet than his wife. He traveled a lot for his work and she was always going off for hers—who knows what they might have worked out? I think that he's wealthy. He was always talking about his days in prep school and, heaven knows, they couldn't have afforded to live in Hancock on just the combined salaries of a professor and an unsuccessful actor. Anyway, I've always had the impression that there was money in his family and some of it was keeping the two of them. He grew up in Hancock. In fact, they lived in the house that he grew up in.''

''But you don't know for sure that the money was his?'' Kathleen asked, her police training making her interested in money from an unknown source.

''No, not for sure.''

''You said that Richard didn't seem like the wronged husband. What were they like as a couple? They sound very disparate, from what you've been saying.''

''Then I've been giving you the wrong impression. They were very much a couple. In fact, if you had been at a party of say twelve couples and everyone was talking to everyone else and mixed up, you'd have been able to spot the two of them as belonging to each other.''

''Really?'' Kathleen was interested. This wasn't what she had been expecting. Of course, looking like you belonged together wasn't everything, she reminded herself, knowing that her blond all-American good looks didn't necessarily blend with Jerry's advancing case of middle-aged spread. And they were happy.

''Well, you were pretty close to the car, so you know what Dawn looked like . . .''

''Not really. I didn't see much more than long reddish-brown hair and an armful of Indian jewelry.''

''She was sensational—very dramatic and sophisticated in a Western sort of way. She was one of those women who can wear clothes that are almost costumes—caftans, long, long skirts, scarves, and things like that—without looking absurd.''

Kathleen was beginning to get jealous.

''And,'' her husband continued, ''Richard is dramatic in his own way. Oh, he doesn't always wear capes or deer-stalker hats, but he does manage to give the impression of always being on stage. When the two of them entered a room, it was really an entrance. People tended to turn around and notice. And they were both very intense—always very involved in their conversations, very committed and verbal about something. They stood out in suburbia, I can tell you that.''

''I'll bet they did.''

''You know, the paint's beginning to even up. The color's not bad either.'' Jerry got up and walked across the room to examine the walls more closely. Checking for wetness, he ran his finger across the paint and then turned back to his wife. ''I wonder where Richard Elliot is right now.''

''And where he was when his wife was murdered,'' she added.

IV

"So you've been rehearsing this play for the last . . . what would you say? . . . the last three weeks?" The anchor-woman leaned toward her guest, a curious look on her face as if to emphasize the importance of her question.

"The last three and a half weeks, Janet. And not just in the daytime. We have worked on this night and day. Night and day," the guest repeated, leaning toward her.

Immediately, the perfectly made-up young woman swung around in her chair and beamed at the television camera. "Well, that's all we have time for today. Of course, we want to thank the talented Mr. Richard Elliot for his time and we'll be looking forward to seeing *The Calendar* when it is per-formed at the Little Playhouse on One hundred and first Street on April first, second, and third. We'll be back right after a commercial break with more information on that hostage situation over at the United Nations." Without even a nod at her "talented" guest, she leapt from her chair and moved quickly back to the anchor podium. A jeans-clad, long-haired young woman touched Richard Elliot on the arm.

"This way, Mr. . . . uh, sir," she urged him from his seat. "If you'll just follow me. We have a room where you can wash off that makeup." She brushed her hair back over her shoulder and walked off the set, expecting to be followed.

"Puerile trollop!" Richard Elliot flung the fabric of the cape he was wearing over his left shoulder and stalked off.

"What did he call her?" the young man standing behind camera one asked the floor director.

"Beats me, but she probably is one, whatever it is. Do you know . . ." And their conversation ended up where it always did—trashing their female colleagues.

Oblivious to what he had begun, Richard Elliot left the studio and walked into the fourth-floor hallway.

"I was watching in the green room and it looked good to me," his agent said, approaching him.

"That's because you love TV coverage. You'd be happy to

see me on the news in the middle of that shoddy hostage thing at the U.N.," protested Richard.

"Only if they mentioned your name, my boy. Only if they mentioned your name."

"That's about all that cretinous harlot did well. She ignored my part, she abused the very point of the play, and she had the nerve to tell all of America what she thinks of Broadway's current season. As though those money-grubbing producers of that whorehouse known as Broadway had any idea of what the theater is or can be. When I think . . ."

"Not all of America, just New York City and vicinity," corrected the other man.

"What?"

"Not all of America," the other man elaborated further. "This was a local show only seen by New Yorkers and . . ."

Richard Elliot stopped dramatically in the middle of their journey down the hall. "You mean I went through that for a mere few million viewers?"

"Well, if everyone watching in New York, New Jersey, and Connecticut bought tickets to *Calendar*, you'd have a pretty long run."

"Quality, not quantity," Richard Elliot said, displaying his willingness to use a cliché when appropriate. "And who ever decided to carpet the walls in this hallway? This place looks more like an institution for the mentally deficient than a television network!"

And, with that judgment still in the air, he marched off down the hall, his agent trotting behind.

They caught the first convenient elevator to the ground floor and moved quickly through the small lobby of the network and past the security guards, out into the building's concourse.

Two men, so obviously official that they had no need to wear uniforms, appeared from behind a pillar and accosted them.

"Mr. Elliot?" the elder of the two asked, reaching in the inside pocket of his navy sports jacket as he spoke.

"I don't sign autographs." Elliot waved him away.

"I don't collect them," came the reply. "I need to speak to you privately, Mr. Elliot. I'm Detective Sardini of the Connecticut State Police and . . ."

"Connecticut. My God, my wife is in Connecticut." He mopped his brow with a silk handkerchief. "Has something happened to Dawn? An automobile accident? A burglary? A . . . ?" He stopped, giving the impression that he could not bear considering any other possibilities.

"Could we go someplace to talk, Mr. Elliot?" Detective Sardini repeated. "Someplace private?"

Richard Elliot drew himself up to his full and not inconsiderable height and grabbed Detective Sardini by the shoulders. "I can no longer stand the suspense," he declared to the man, and, incidentally, to the many people rushing by on their way out of the building and to their homes. "Tell me here. I can take it."

"Maybe the coffee shop over there," his agent urged.

"Now! I must know now!" Richard Elliot's dramatic instinct, controlled throughout that boring interview boomed against the art deco brass work, slammed against the beige and brown murals that rimmed the room, and caused even the most blasé of New Yorkers to glance toward the four men.

"Your wife is dead, Mr. Elliot. She was murdered." Detective Sardini was robbed of the satisfaction of shocking this man that he had judged obnoxious when he had to watch him sink down to the marble floor, unconscious.

"He fainted, sir," the man with him said, kneeling down beside the body.

"Very astute, Mitchell. Very astute."

V

"You've reinterviewed everyone who was at the party last night?"

"No, just the people who reported burglaries during the party. That's why we needed to check out the guest list with you again. The local police knew who was here, but not who was invited,'' this same Mitchell was explaining to the Henshaws an hour later in the living room of their home.

"So you think the break-ins were planned to coincide with the party?" Jed asked, looking out the window, seemingly more interested in the wind that was beginning to blow through the trees than in an answer to his question.

"Of course."

"So the robber must have been someone who knew about the party," Susan cried out.

"Yes."

"Then . . ." she began excitedly.

"But everyone in town knew about your surprise party, Mrs. Henshaw," came Detective Sardini's quick response. "Even you."

"I don't see what my wife has to do with this." Jed Henshaw's angry comment shot out across the room.

"I was only pointing out that her party was hardly the secret it was supposed to be," came the mild reply.

"And you think that Dawn Elliot's death was connected to the burglaries?" Susan asked, watching the flames dance around her fireplace grate as winds rushed back down the flue.

"I didn't say that. I don't know how Mrs. Elliot's death figures into this. I can't make any assumptions at this point."

"But you're in town to investigate her death, not the burglaries," Jed insisted.

"I was sent here to look into the murder, yes. And in doing that I certainly can't ignore anything that happened at the party or . . ."

"You mean you think that she was killed during my party?" Susan looked up.

"Probably not, but we'll get the results of the autopsy tomorrow morning," was the obscure reply. "But, as I was going to say, we have to investigate every aspect of that night and, certainly, other crimes, whether related or not, fall into that category.

"We'll be going now," the detective continued, looking

meaningfully at his assistant. Mitchell, the man with either no first or no last name, took the cue and leapt to his feet.

"I'll see you to the door," Jed offered. "You stay where you are, Susan."

She nodded. "Good-bye, Detective and, uh, Officer Mitchell."

"Good evening, Mrs. Henshaw. We'll be seeing you again soon, I'm sure." Detective Sardini followed her husband and his officer out into the hall.

Susan had resumed staring into the fire when Jed returned. "Well, they're gone," he commented, sitting down beside his wife on the chintz couch.

"What do you think?"

"I think this mess is going to take a long, long time to straighten out. We'd better prepare ourselves."

"You think they suspect us?" She didn't look at him.

"Possibly, but I also think the local police thought that Dawn was killed long before the party . . ."

"And left inside my birthday present as a bad joke?" Susan interrupted.

"I don't know why she turned up here but, if she wasn't killed here, why should we be connected with this? And I can't imagine that they think we have anything to do with the burglaries. I . . ."

"Have the cops left?"

Chrissy had asked the question. She was standing in the doorway wearing a nightshirt bearing the likeness of four long-haired rock musicians whose faces were enough to give most adults insomnia. Her brother was standing beside her.

"What are you two doing?" Susan got up.

"We just wanted to know what the police were saying," Chad answered.

His parents exchanged glances. "Why don't we all go upstairs and talk about this?" Jed suggested. "Just let me put out this fire."

"Good idea. You two go get into your beds, and your father and I'll come up and we can talk a little," Susan suggested. "But not for long. Who knows what tomorrow will bring. We all need our sleep."

"Do you think the police are going to arrest you or Daddy for Mrs. Elliot's murder?" Chad asked.

"Of course not," his father answered quickly, smacking at the burning embers with a poker. "It's just that they're certainly going to be back to ask more questions and we want to be awake to help them with their investigation."

This time it was the children who surreptitiously exchanged worried looks.

VI

Driving to their motel, outside of Hancock on the highway, Mitchell finally gathered up the nerve to ask his superior a direct question. "You think one of the Henshaws is a murderer?"

"One of 'em. Or both of 'em," came the reply, as the car pulled into the motel parking lot. "It's too soon to tell. It's too soon to tell."

FORTY PLUS TWO

I

RECENTLY MARRIED, JERRY GORDON WAS DISAPPOINTED to awaken and find his wife no longer beside him: The other half of his king-size bed was empty. His disappointment turned to surprise when he discovered it wasn't yet 6 A.M. Well . . . one more moment of warmth and he'd get up and find her, he promised himself, rolling over and tucking an extra pillow under his head.

Two hours later, daylight was illuminating Kathleen's hair as she sat at their kitchen table, her coffee mug surrounded by legal-size pads of yellow paper. "Coffee's made and there are some bagels and lox if you're hungry," she suggested, not looking up from her writing.

"I missed you this morning." Jerry ran his hand through her lush blond hair.

"Hmmm." The response was one of inattention, not pleasure. Jerry decided he could use that coffee after all.

"You're going to go ahead and investigate Dawn's death, aren't you?" he asked, pouring coffee in a navy mug and heading to the refrigerator for some milk.

"And the burglaries."

"You think they're related?" The skim milk that Kathleen bought had turned his coffee a grayish brown instead of the dark beige that he preferred. She was convinced that it was better for his health and he was fairly sure the days of half and half were over.

"I don't know." She threw down her pencil in frustration. "I know that I can't leave them out of my figuring, but I don't see what they have to do with the murder."

"Maybe Dawn knew about the burglaries and threatened to expose the burglars and so she was killed," he suggested, trying to be helpful.

"Anything is possible. But Dawn wasn't killed the day of the party, you know."

"No, I didn't." He smeared cholesterol-free margarine on his bagel and leaned against the counter to talk. "How do you know?"

"The body was out of rigor mortis. She'd probably been dead for longer than twenty-four hours. I know," she paused to shuffle through the papers before her, "that she was alive on Wednesday. Gloria Bower told me that she talked on the phone with Dawn that morning and . . . My God! What time is it?"

"Eight-thirty. Why? What's wrong?"

"We've got to be at the Presbyterian church in an hour. Remember? The Bowers' baby—Missy—is going to be christened after the first service. We'd better get dressed and get over there." She was rapidly putting her papers in order.

Jerry took a large gulp of his coffee and hastily put the mug aside. "You're right. I almost forgot. We'd better hurry if we're going to be on time."

Kathleen paused on her way out the door. "Do you think, if we rushed, we could be there early?"

"Sure, but . . ."

"Everyone we know will be there," Kathleen explained, "and I might be able to find out more about Dawn and the burglaries and who was sleeping with . . ." Her voice became inaudible as she started upstairs.

II

"Chad was talking about something called a Vanden Plas all the way here," Susan told her husband as they walked into the prim Colonial vestibule of the Hancock Presbyterian church. "You sounded as if you knew what it was."

"A car."

"Then he's back to normal."

"It's the most exclusive of all the Jaguar sedans," her husband answered.

"He says it's the car Stephanie King's driving these days. She gave him a lift to school last week and he was very impressed with the fact that it has tray tables that fold down in the backseats," she said, wondering briefly if the same could be said of her new Volvo now stashed away somewhere in police custody.

"It's very luxurious," Jed commented, wiping his feet on the mat provided.

"Sound like an airplane and that's not so luxurious," she protested.

Jed laughed. "The trays are made of hand-polished walnut burl and the seats they extend from are made of soft glove leather. Very, very luxurious," he insisted.

Susan tried hard not to compare the description of this car with the Volvo he'd given her as he continued. "But what's important is that Chad's back to normal. I guess that talk we had with him last night did the trick."

"I hope so. But Chrissy's still awfully quiet. I suppose she's old enough to guess at how serious this could be for us."

Jed looked intensely at his wife but didn't say anything more.

"I guess we'd better go in now," Susan continued. "I think most everyone is seated already. Are Chad and Chrissy around?"

"Here behind you, Mom," her daughter answered impatiently. She and her brother were indeed right behind their parents, leaning against a wall and looking bored.

"How long . . ." Susan began.

"Well, now that we're all together, let's get going," her husband interrupted and hurried his family ahead of him into the narthex of the church. "Look, Kathleen and Jerry are over there. Maybe they've saved seats for us."

They never made it to the Gordons; about a third of the way down the aisle, Martha Hallard waved to attract their attention.

"Susan! Jed! I saved these seats. The kids can scoot in the pew in front. I need to talk to you," she added, quenching any idea Susan might have had about passing her by. Martha was very direct; when she said she had something to say it wasn't merely to pass the time. Susan nudged her husband ahead of her into the pew. Her children took the hint and slid into the spaces left open in front.

"Has something else happened? Did they find your jewelry or the person who did it?" Susan whispered beneath the organ music that had just begun.

"God, I wish," Martha began, then, remembering where she was, added, "that's a prayer, you know. I just wanted to know what Kathleen's doing. Did the police hire her to investigate the murder? Or did you and Jed?"

"No, of course not."

"Are you sure?"

Susan hesitated, taking the hymnbook out of the shelf in the pew before her. "Why do you ask?"

"Well, she's been running around here with a notebook asking questions about Dawn and your party and the robberies. If she isn't helping you or the police, what's she doing?"

"Good question."

The beginning of the service cut off any more talk and the minister's calm voice read through the service, apparently putting Missy to sleep as the transition from gentle cooing to silence indicated. Sympathetic to the baby's feelings, Susan's head began to nod. She hadn't gotten much sleep last night, what with worrying about Dawn and her husband and everything. Her eyes closed and she was just about to drift off when an unusual noise from the rear of the room startled her.

Susan turned, trying to track down the source of the sound. As far as she could tell, the disturbance emanated from the rear left side of the church. It sounded like an asthmatic cow and was getting louder. Even the front rows of the congregation were shifting in their seats. Susan exchanged looks with Jed, who had turned all the way around to look at the source of the noise.

"What is it?"

"I can't see anything. See if you can," was his reply.

Susan tried shifting her weight and looking over her shoulder as casually as possible. All she could see was that everyone behind her was also looking to the back of the room. But at what? Too many heads blocked her view.

"I can't see either," she whispered to her husband.

"It's Richard Elliot!" Whoever had made this discovery was too excited to keep it to herself; the announcement chimed out over the congregation. Possibly the only person present who didn't turn around and look to verify this statement for herself was little Missy, now completely asleep in her mother's arms.

"And he's crying," someone else added, only slightly more quietly.

"And so, ladies and gentlemen," the minister's voice rang out, calling his flock back to the matter at hand. Dutifully, heads faced front, but it would have been impossible to ignore the sounds, now louder than ever, and the minister speeded up the service as much as decorum would allow.

And Susan knew that what most people would remember about this morning was the sight of the baby's adoptive father spinning around and glaring in the direction of the noise, almost before Reverend Cox was finished.

"He sure looks mad," Susan whispered to her husband.

"Do you blame him?" responded Martha, having overheard her comment. "Here we're all together to celebrate Missy being adopted—which is really what this is: Why else would all these people turn up for a baptism ceremony?—and then Richard Elliot grabs all the attention for himself.''

"Well, his wife just died . . .'' began Susan.

"True. But Richard Elliot is just using that as an attention getter. You watch.''

But by the time Susan had pushed her way through the crowd, truly larger than usual for a baptism, Richard Elliot was no longer to be seen. She joined the line forming in the narthex to greet the Bowers, briefly wondering where Jed had gone. She'd thought he was following her, but they hadn't ended up in the same place. Probably with the kids, she decided.

"Some service. Jerry said the crier is Richard Elliot.''

Susan smiled at Kathleen. "It's the first baptism I've been to where someone cried louder than the baby.''

"I can't wait to meet him,'' Kathleen said.

"I don't see him,'' Susan replied, standing up on her toes to try to see over the heads of those around her. "I can't believe that he's left.''

Kathleen stared at her friend. "Susan,'' she grabbed her arm, "he's standing at the front of this line. It's Richard Elliot we're all waiting to see!''

"What? I thought this was the receiving line for Gloria and Harvey.'' She moved out of place and peered through the crowd ahead of her. Sure enough, Kathleen was right. There stood Richard Elliot, shaking hands while mopping the tears off his face with a gigantic linen handkerchief, flamboyantly embroidered with his initials. She wondered for a moment why he wasn't carrying one with wide black borders like a character out of Dickens. Probably couldn't find one on short notice.

"He's wearing a band around his arm,'' Kathleen whispered.

"No!''

"I'm not kidding. Get in front of me again and look.''

Susan did as she was told and, sure enough, Kathleen was right: Around his Harris tweed jacket, Richard Elliot had tied a piece of black fabric, the traditional crepe unless she missed her guess. "I can't believe it!" she said.

"Susan," Kathleen whispered in her ear. "I have to meet that man as soon as possible. Invite him to your house for dinner tonight," she ordered.

"What?"

"I said . . ."

"I know what you said," Susan began.

"Susan, I do have to meet him as soon as possible—and have a chance to talk to him. The only way I know for that to happen is for you to invite him and Jerry and me to dinner tonight. Do it! I'm going to go over and see the Bowers," she added, moving away. "Someone should pay them some attention."

The entrance of the Bowers reminded the group of their social obligations, and evidently enough people agreed with Kathleen for the line before Susan to shorten considerably. She soon found herself face to face with Richard Elliot.

"Richard . . ." she started, silently cursing herself for not having prepared something to say. She took his hand in what she hoped was a comforting manner.

"It was your car they found her in," he said, returning the gentle squeeze she gave him.

"Uh, yes," Susan agreed, wondering if that drew the two of them together in some way.

"I had always thought she would be found dead in some place more appropriate. An Indian ruin. A kiva, perhaps," he said, still not releasing her hand.

"I'm sure that would have been more appropriate," Susan agreed. "I can't tell you how sorry we are, Richard." She took a deep breath and, remembering Kathleen's request, continued, "Could you possibly come to dinner at our house tonight? Just something simple . . ."

"With a few intimate friends," he continued the planning for her. "Yes, Susan, I'd like that. I would very much like to see the place where they found her. I'd like that very much. I'll be there around five, if that's all right?"

"Yes," she answered, startled by his response. "The police . . . uh, the police impounded the car, but . . . you can see the garage if you want,'' she offered.

"I will find her aura there, I'm sure," he said and, giving her hand a final squeeze, moved along to the next person in his improvised receiving line.

III

"Just make something simple. After all, the man's bereaved, he shouldn't be eating like a horse," Kathleen said, walking up behind Susan, who was standing before the meat counter at the local grocery store, contemplating rows of identical pieces of animal carcass.

"I must not be hungry; nothing looks good. I cannot believe I let you talk me into doing this,'' Susan replied, ignoring the looks of the butcher, who obviously hoped she would make up her mind so he could help his other customers.

"How about a roast, maybe a . . ." Kathleen began.

"Good idea. A five-pound filet, please," she said to the man. "I think I saw some new potatoes on the way in the door and I can steam them and toss them in butter . . . and some of those French rolls from the bakery . . . and cheese and pâté before . . . crackers . . . a big spinach salad with toasted sesame seeds and raspberry vinaigrette . . . maybe all the candies and cookies and stuff left over from my party for dessert . . ."

"Susan, this isn't supposed to be the social event of the season. I just want a chance to get to know the man."

"Well, I invited him for dinner and I have to feed him something, don't I?" she replied, taking the package the butcher handed her.

"You don't have to . . . oh well, do what you think best." Kathleen gave up her argument, knowing that Susan easily put together a dinner that would have had her in a panic for days. "What I'm most interested in is getting him to talk."

"That won't be a problem. Richard Elliot loves to talk and, when he sees a woman with your looks, he'll be inspired to new heights of verboseness. Verbosity? Well, whatever. But you may not be able to get him to talk about what you want him to talk about. He has a way of taking over the conversation and running with it—in any direction he chooses, if you know what I mean.''

''Then we'll just see what he chooses to talk about—that in itself may tell us something. What are you looking for?'' she interrupted herself to ask as Susan stood in front of a display of French food, intently studying the labels.

''Walnut oil . . . maybe some of that canned goose liver pâté . . .''

Kathleen left her to her mumblings and wandered across the aisle to a magazine rack, picked up next month's *GQ*, and began thumbing through it.

''I think I have everything,'' Susan said, joining her. ''Oh, look, a magazine about Porsches. I think I'll buy it for Chad. He'll like it, and any reading is better than none.'' She threw the magazine on top of her groceries and headed for the checkout. ''Look at that. Sunday afternoon and only one checkout line open. We'll be here forever.'' She sighed and pulled her cart in behind the others. ''Do you think they'll miss us at the reception for Missy?'' she asked, turning to Kathleen and leaning against her cart.

''Frankly, they're probably glad you're not there. That way Missy can get some attention. When you're around, your party and Dawn's death tend to grab all the attention.''

''Thanks a lot. You haven't been helping all that much. Marty said you were running all over the church before the baptism asking questions about—actually I don't know what you were asking about. What's going on?''

''I'm investigating a murder,'' Kathleen answered. ''Oh, look. They're opening up another line. Let's get over there.''

''I think this one is longer than the original one was,'' Susan said, looking at the now shorter line she and others had just left. ''Oh, well, I always pick the slow one.''

''Everyone says that,'' Kathleen commented, picking up a *Vanity Fair*. ''But it can't be true. Someone must be in the shorter line.''

"Put down that damn magazine and start answering my questions," Susan insisted. "What do you mean you're investigating a murder? You're not on the police force anymore. You can't just take up an investigation."

"Why not?"

"Because . . ."

"Susan! Kathleen! I guess I'm not the only person who can't get organized today. I shop each Friday. I don't understand why I always run out of food before Sunday evening. Although I think it's having three teenage girls that does it." The woman who had called out to them stopped her cart as she swerved around a corner and, pushing her frosted-to-cover-the-gray hair off her forehead, rearranged the dozen or more packages from the in-store deli so they wouldn't fall onto the case of soda at the bottom of the substantial pile of groceries.

"I thought teenage girls were always dieting. I know Chrissy . . ." Susan began.

"It's not the girls. They live on yogurt and diet Coke. It's their boyfriends. Mandy's just started dating so it's not bad. The boys are still too shy in ninth grade to hang around much. But Jenny has three boys on her string and they rotate the days of the week that they hang out in front of my refrigerator. Monday it's Keith, Tuesday it's Brian, Wednesday it's Jeremy, and so on. And Cindy is the worst of all! She's dating Trevor Anderson and he's captain of the football team, lead downhill skier on the ski team, and he's just getting into hockey down at the Field Club. He's impossible. Food just vanishes when he's around. I think he eats through some sort of process of osmosis. My husband says that by the time he gets home from the city in the evening, the refrig is always empty."

"Poor Colin," Susan said, thinking of Maureen Small's husband. An ex-jock himself, she wondered if it was harder on him to find the cupboard bare, or to see in all these young boys his life as it was before middle-age struck.

" 'Poor Colin' nothing! Do you know what he told me the night before last?"

"The night of the party?" Kathleen asked quickly.

"Yeah, that's the night." Maureen pushed her hair back again, moved slightly closer and lowered her voice a fraction of a decibel. "He told me that he had an affair with Dawn Elliot! Do you believe that?"

"No!" That was Kathleen. Susan didn't know how to respond. Certainly, something like "Your husband? Mine too!" while appropriate, wasn't acceptable.

"Do you believe it?"

"How long ago?" Kathleen asked with what Susan thought was a lack of sympathy.

"Oh, years, that's probably why I'm so calm about it— that and the Valium I took before leaving the house."

"But when . . . ?"

"I can't believe the stupidity of that man," Maureen interrupted. "Here's Dawn Elliot dead as a doornail and never going to tell me about it and he does. You would think that seeing her dead would be a great relief. But not for Colin; now that no one is around to spill the beans, he does this trite confession scene. You know, the whole bit: I love you, but I strayed. Do you believe it: He actually used the word strayed like some little puppy who wanders off to pee in the neighbor's yard instead of a grown man who probably had to connive and sneak and plan to get into a neighbor's bed. Not that I only blame him. It was that bitch's fault too. After all, she wasn't driven to forget her inhibitions and fall into bed with Colin. He hasn't inspired that type of response since the Yale-Harvard game of '68. She'd go to bed with anybody. I'm glad she's dead! And I'm not the only woman in town who feels that way," she added, seeming to realize that gloating over someone's murder might be dumb, at least before the murderer was caught.

"Who else?" Kathleen was quick to ask.

"I'm not going to name any names," said Maureen quickly, moving off. "They're opening another line," she added, "I'd better get going." And, cutting off the cart of an elderly man, she made her way to the newly opened checkout number 5.

"That's interesting," Kathleen said. "It's just what we need to know."

"Kathleen . . ."

"What time do you want Jerry and me to arrive tonight?" she interrupted Susan.

"Around five or so? I thought . . ."

"I'll tell Jerry that I'm coming over to help you out early and I'll be there at four. He can drive over later. See you."

"Kathleen!" Susan called after her departing friend.

"We'll talk tonight. I have work to do!" Kathleen waved good-bye and headed out the automatic door.

"I . . ."

"If you're not going to move up, may I have your place?" asked a voice from behind her. Susan saw that the line had moved on, leaving her next to unload her groceries.

"I'm just starting," she assured the woman behind her and did just that.

IV

"Which do you like better? The 928 S 4 or the 911 Carrera Cabriolet?"

Susan peered at the pictures of the lima bean–shaped cars that her son was holding out to her. "They look pretty similar to me, Chad."

"Mo-om!" His voice rose and fell at least an octave and a half during the one word. "They're not at all alike. The 928 S 4 is the fastest production Porsche made. The Carrera Cabriolet is completely different: It's a convertible, for goodness' sake."

Susan rubbed her herb-covered hands together over the sink, the bright bits of green falling down the garbage disposal. "Just let me get the meat in the oven and I'll sit down and look at them more carefully," she promised.

Chad looked up from his magazine and seemed to notice what she was doing for the first time. "I don't have to eat that stuff, do I? I don't see why I should have to suffer just because you're having company."

"I don't think eating seven-ninety-nine-per-pound prime beef is suffering, Chad. But," she added before he could interrupt, "your father is going to take you and Chrissy to the deli for sandwiches before the company gets here. In fact, why don't you ask him to do that now?" she suggested, noticing Kathleen's car pulling into her driveway.

"You promised you would look at these cars," he reminded her. "Why did you buy me this magazine if you weren't interested?"

"I bought it for you, not for me. That's what buying presents is: Buying something that you think the person who is receiving it will like, not what the giver likes."

"Like Dad buying you the Volvo instead of the BMW 325i that he was drooling over," Chad agreed, sitting down at the table and spreading the magazine open at the pages he found interesting.

"The what?" Susan slammed the oven door.

"This great little BMW. A fantastic little car. It's sort of flashy—a convertible."

"And your father liked it?"

"Loved it," Chad agreed. "He really liked it in 'cinnabar red,' but I liked 'salmon silver.' Chrissy liked the 'alpine white.' I think maybe Dad thought you were too old for a convertible, though," he added. "Are you going to look at these? You said you would."

"Yes," she answered, trying to stay calm; it wasn't her son's fault that his father was a . . .

"Do you want me to take the kids downtown now? I'd better get going if you want me back to set up the bar," her husband suggested, sticking his head in the kitchen door. "And Kathleen's here," he added as there was a knock on the front door.

Susan didn't look up from Chad's magazine; her husband knew her too well to expose her face to him. He'd insist on talking and they really didn't have the time now if she was going to get this dinner ready. Kathleen's entrance gave her an excuse not to answer immediately.

"Hi." Kathleen walked in and, from her position, she couldn't miss Susan's face. "What's wr—?"

"Jed is taking the kids for sandwiches," Susan interrupted, not wanting any questions.

"Let me help you with this," Kathleen offered, slipping out of her fur, dumping it on a kitchen chair and grabbing an apron off a nearby hook. The apron proclaimed her to be forty and horny. She, noticing the inscription, removed it and, putting it back on, turned the words to herself. "I don't really want anyone to think I'm either right now," she explained.

Chad giggled appreciatively.

"Everything in the house seems to say something about my birthday. I have mugs, pencils, pillows, stationery, an umbrella—you name it—that tells the world I'm forty."

"The baby boom's getting older—there's a big market for things like that," Kathleen commented, washing her hands.

"We'll let you two manage here and I'll take the kids out. Anything I need to pick up?" offered Jed.

"No, just hurry back. I'll look at the magazine with you tonight, Chad," Susan promised as the males in her family departed.

"An umbrella?" Kathleen asked, grabbing a towel, and returning to the original conversation.

"That's not the worst," Susan said. "I didn't want to say anything with Chad here, but I also got bras, panties, and two nightshirts with what passes for clever sayings."

"Show me later. Let's get down to work." She sat down at the kitchen table, pushing aside a basket of homemade crackers.

"Down to work? I thought you were here to help me?" Susan said, looking around the kitchen. Wineglasses stood next to a rare Tomasi Amareone 1973; the roast, its outside crusted with freshly cut herbs, sat on a rack in a shiny rectangular pan; two bouquets of fresh flowers sat in the middle of the kitchen table; cheese and crackers were displayed upon leaves on straw trays.

Kathleen glanced at where she was looking. "Where did you get the leaves?" she asked, referring to this last item.

"The big rex begonia in the window in the study. I sure hope it isn't a poisonous plant." She unwrapped and added another goat cheese to the pile on the tray while speaking. "So, if you're not here to help with the food, what are you here for?"

"Information."

"This is beginning to sound like a broken record. Do you think you could wash the salad greens while you ask questions?" She motioned to the sink, full of leaves.

"Just as long as you let me tape-record everything."

"You brought a—" Susan stopped. After all, what difference did it make? And it might help her get dinner on the table. "Fine. Anything you say."

Kathleen rolled up her sleeves and, pressing the record button on the Walkman she'd brought, set to work. "I got two very interesting calls this afternoon. The first was from Martha Hallard. The second from Brigit Frye. Both Dan Hallard and Guy Frye were involved with Dawn Elliot."

Susan found the cheese knives in her drawer before answering. "I'd suspected Dan," she said, referring to her next-door-neighbor and gynecologist. "He and Martha have a pretty traditional marriage in some ways—I mean, he thinks of her as the perfect little woman and she thinks of him as the big strong man. Even though Martha is a power in the politics of Hancock and owns her own real estate agency, she's still very conservative . . ." She stopped talking and gathered her thoughts. "It's just that they have the type of relationship where I can imagine the husband going out and having an affair. Of course," she added, soberly, "it seems that Jed and I do, too."

"Except that Dan told Martha about his affair."

"He's more honest than Jed," Susan said sadly to the fork in her hand.

"No, he was so mad when Dawn dropped him that he exploded and told Martha about it."

"Oh?" Susan found her prurient interest aroused.

"Yes. Evidently he was so mad that he had to tell someone about it and he told Martha."

"He's not very bright," Susan said. "I've often wondered how he made it through med school."

"You go to him," Kathleen reminded her.

"Well, I started before I knew him well, and I hate to change doctors."

"Anyway. He had an affair with Dawn for almost six months about four years ago. In the spring and summer," Martha said.

"That was right before she and Jed . . ." Susan started. Had this woman gone in order around the block? she wondered. At the same time, she was slightly flattered that Dawn had had the sense to prefer her husband to Martha's. Oh, that was just sick! She put down the plates she held and turned to Kathleen. "Martha called and told you all about this?"

"You know Martha. She was direct and complete. She called and told me about Dan and Dawn, gave dates, explained how she knew about it, explained what she knew about it, and asked if I thought the police should be informed. Needless to say, I told her the same thing I told you: Tell them."

"Neither she nor Dan . . ."

"Saw fit to inform the police. Right."

"So I guess Jed and I aren't alone."

"I'm beginning to think that if everyone in town who hadn't told the police that they or their spouses had slept with Dawn Elliot were laid end to end they would look like the people we see every day in the summer lying around the pool at the Club."

"And are they going to tell the police?" Susan asked.

"Yes. I told Martha what I thought and she agreed. She and Dan were going to the police station this afternoon to explain everything."

"But it's different for them. They've already talked about it. They've already made their peace with each other over Dan's affair," Susan said.

"True. According to Martha, it's been so long that the

Mercedes he bought her for penance is ready to be replaced. I found myself wondering if, when she gets a new car, he gets a new woman.

"Is this done right?"

"What?" Susan asked.

"The salad," Kathleen explained. "Is this the way you wanted it?" She motioned to a large wooden bowl brimming with shiny lettuce and spinach.

"Great. Could we move this conversation to the dining room? I want to set the table."

"Sure." Kathleen grabbed her recorder off the counter. "Have Walkman, will travel."

"Take these bowls too, if you can. I can manage the silverware and the china is already out there. I assume," she continued, pushing open the swinging door between the kitchen and dining room with her foot, "that you told Brigit that she and Guy should tell the police about his relationship with Dawn, too?"

"They already did. In fact, that's what they were worried about." She put the bowls on the buffet at the side of the room and turned to look straight at Susan. "Brigit and Guy both told the police about Guy's affair with Dawn."

"When?" Susan was setting the places at the table and did not look up at Kathleen.

"Immediately after the murder. They drove over to the police station together and decided in the car that they would have to admit it. That's not the problem."

"Then what is?"

"Brigit says that Guy knows about two other men who slept with Dawn."

"So?"

"Those two other men didn't tell the police about their affairs—at least that's what Brigit says."

Susan froze, knives in her hand. "And?" She looked straight into Kathleen's eyes.

"And Brigit wanted to know if I thought she should go to the police with the information that Guy has. Well," she continued, "you can see her point. If the police think that only Guy Frye slept with Dawn, that makes him a prime suspect. If they know about the others it . . . well, it muddies the water somewhat.''

"Is Jed one of the men?" Susan asked.

Kathleen sighed. "I don't know. I asked who the men were but Brigit wouldn't tell me. She said something about not wanting to spread rumors.''

"That sounds just like Brigit. She not wanting to spread rumors. Baloney. She just wants to keep the information to herself.''

"That really doesn't sound like Brigit," Kathleen said gently.

"No, it doesn't, does it? Okay, what did you tell her to do?''

"I told her that she and Guy should confront the men he suspects and give them a chance to tell the police themselves. Actually, that way the police know and it does help Guy out of a tight spot and it looks better for Guy: He isn't just saying 'look, they did it too,' which could be construed as being too defensive.''

"Is that what they're going to do?" Susan asked, finishing up the place settings.

"I don't know. I really tried to get her to tell me who the men were, Susan.''

"I know you did," Susan assured her friend. "I'm not blaming you. I suppose Guy had told Brigit about the affair back when it happened?" she asked, trying to sound casual.

"Not really. She caught them together." Kathleen smiled.

"I don't think that's funny," Susan protested, remembering her experience at the hotel in the city.

"Actually, this is. You see, she ran into them at the desk checking into the Blackbird Inn up in Mountainville.''

"I still don't see why that's so funny," Susan repeated, the feeling she had gotten watching Jed and Dawn get on the elevator returning.

"Because Brigit was there with another man.''

"You mean . . . ?''

"It seems that both she and Guy like afternoon sex—with someone other than their spouse, at least in this case."

"Jed has always said that Brigit looked like a Norwegian sex goddess," Susan said, then started to think about what that might mean. "Kathleen, you don't think that she and Jed . . . ?"

"I think that you're going to have to talk about Dawn with him before you stop trusting him altogether," Kathleen replied firmly. "Anyway, it seems that Brigit and Guy have what used to be called an open marriage back before people got more conservative and worried about AIDS. They're pretty casual about each other's sex life—unless it ends up making them look like the major suspects in a murder case."

"I need the flowers for the center of the table," Susan said, moving a fork and straightening the napkin on which it lay.

"I'll get them," Kathleen offered, thinking that her friend needed to be alone.

"Thanks." Susan turned away and looked out the window. It was beginning to sleet. "What a miserable March this has been," she said, more to herself than Kathleen.

Her friend returned to the kitchen, knowing that platitudes wouldn't make Susan feel any better.

V

" 'A little fire is quickly trodden out; Which, being suffered, rivers cannot quench.' *Henry the Sixth.* Act Two or Three. I cannot remember at this moment. Ah, that tells of my grief, does it not? To forget the Bard. I ask you." Richard Elliot removed his hands from where he was warming them in front of the fireplace and, with a dramatic waving, spread them to the room in the form of an appeal.

Susan, who had forgotten her former neighbor's tendency to quote Shakespeare at any opportunity, no matter how inappropriate, smothered a smile and, like a good hostess, looked around the room at her guests. Everyone seemed to be well taken care of. And she'd been right when she predicted Richard's reaction to Kathleen. He was playing all his best lines to her like she was a critic, front row center.

"I think a fire is the only compensation for this miserable weather," Kathleen said, having realized that Richard didn't really care what anyone said to him, just that they listened to him.

"Truly," Richard agreed with her. "Many's the evening that my dear Dawn and I spent just staring into the fire, silent perhaps, yet in communion, if you know what I mean." He dropped his forehead down onto his hand.

Susan, thinking of all she had learned of Dawn's activities in the last few hours, considered the possibility that she had been too tired to do anything else. "You're going to miss her," she said aloud.

"Terribly," he agreed, glancing in her direction momentarily before returning his attention to Kathleen. "You didn't know my wife?"

"No, but I've heard a lot about her."

Susan, startled, waited for her next words. But Richard had again picked up the conversational ball and kept it.

"She was a remarkable woman. Remarkable," he repeated. "Our lives together had a simpatico that I think few couples ever achieve. And I loved her the very moment I first saw her. As the Bard himself would say, 'Who ever loved that loved not at first sight?' "

"Marlowe."

Richard Elliot pulled his attention from Kathleen and peered across the room at her husband, who had spoken. "Pardon?" The tone of the question implied an unforgivable intrusion.

"Marlowe," Jerry repeated. "It was Christopher Marlowe who said, or rather wrote that, not Shakespeare."

"I think not. Or, if so, he stole it from the Bard, of course. Many, many writers were guilty of stealing from the Bard." And Richard Elliot dismissed the correction with a brisk wave of his hand.

Jerry Gordon, who had entered his successful career in advertising equipped with a Phi Beta Kappa key earned while majoring in English lit at Stanford University, allowed the man his inaccuracies and accepted another Scotch from Jed.

"We weren't always together," Richard Elliot continued.

"Oh?" Kathleen began to pay more attention. So far she'd found Dawn's husband incapable of talking about anything but himself even while speaking of his dead wife: his bereavement being more significant than her death.

"No. We both had very demanding careers. Immediately after our marriage, I had to leave her to play Hamlet with a very small, dedicated, remarkably talented group of thespians in Raton, New Mexico. Now there are many who will go on and on endlessly about the rigors of the Broadway stage, but I know from personal experience that true theater dwells in America, in the small groups out in what some would call the sticks, who are tirelessly working on and perfecting their craft. You know, I was speaking to Richard Burton about this a few months before his death and, not only did he agree with me but, if he had lived, I'm sure you would have seen more of him in places like Raton."

"How interesting," Kathleen lied. "What did your wife do when you were away? I understand she wasn't an actress."

"No, Dawn marched to her own drummer and, in her own field, she was as well known as I in mine."

"What did she do?" Kathleen asked, wondering if he was capable of talking about anything besides himself.

"She was an archaeological anthropologist. Her field was the Anasazi and various aspects of ancient Indian life."

"She spent a large part of every year working on excavations in the Southwest," Jed put in.

"And teaching. She was on the staff at UCLA and she did research at one or two major universities periodically."

"Yes. She was at Stanford just a few years ago, wasn't she?" Jerry added. "I remember seeing something about it in one of the alumni letters at the time."

"I don't believe she was actually in residence in California. I think she was digging with a group of graduate students near Canyon de Chelly for the summer semester . . ."

"So your wife did a lot of traveling too," Kathleen commented and then hurried on before he could interrupt. "Why did you choose Connecticut as your permanent residence? It is your permanent residence?"

"Yes. It is also my spiritual home. I grew up in Hancock, and it nourishes me to return here once in a while. Dawn and I lived in the house that my parents lived in, you know. In fact, I still own it. I have it cleaned once a week and it is waiting my retirement, although, of course, that is a long, long way off."

"Really?" said Susan, who needed to say something. "How interesting. I wonder if you could tell us more about that at the dinner table? We'd better go on into the dining room if we want to eat a meal that is worth eating."

"Of course, of course. You'll be interested in my youth," he continued to Kathleen. "I've really led quite a fascinating life."

Susan rushed out to the kitchen to do the last-minute slicing of the meat, the stirring of sauce and the like. She knew that Jed would be busy at the table pouring the wine and tossing the vinaigrette with the salad. They'd done this so many times that it had become automatic and neither had to remind the other of what had to be done or when. When she returned to the dining room, she found that Richard Elliot had kept his promise and was telling Kathleen about his childhood. Jed was serving and passing around plates of salad. Jerry was taking rather large sips from his wineglass.

". . . even then I knew I was going to be an actor. You'll be interested in this, Susan," he acknowledged her presence. "Did you know that I starred in the first production that the Drama Club of Hancock ever performed?"

"When was that, Richard?" she asked, rather wickedly, knowing that he was adamant about keeping his age a secret.

"In 'my salad days,' " he replied. *"Antony and Cleopatra,"* he added, directing the reference rather pointedly to Jerry, "I assume you will agree that was written by Shakespeare?"

"Uh . . ." Jerry seemed startled by being addressed instead of his wife.

Kathleen took up the conversation. "Even I know that line. Have you ever played Antony? I'm sure that with your looks, you'd be perfect for the part."

"I thank you, my dear. But in the theater looks aren't everything, you know. I've played Richard, and I'm sure you'll agree that I'm not deformed." He smiled, assuming her agreement.

Susan thought his everlasting ego was as bad as a hump any day, but, naturally, kept those thoughts to herself. How had Dawn been able to stand being married to this man?

The meal continued. Midway through Jerry and Jed gave up any pretense of interest in what Richard was saying, and retreated into a discussion of some personnel problems they were having at the office. Susan poured the wine, passed the food, and interjected a "how interesting" whenever she felt it necessary. Kathleen held a look of rapt attention on her face that must have made her muscles ache. Richard Elliot spoke nonstop for almost an hour on the subject of himself and his life. He was having a wonderful time.

"You know," Susan finally said, as the man paused either to take a breath or to emphasize a point, "I'd like to borrow Kathleen to help me make the coffee and get dessert ready."

"Of course, of course." Richard Elliot granted his permission for the audience to leave.

"Jed must have been fascinated by what you were saying about the arts in Seattle," Susan pointedly put the conversational ball in her husband's corner.

Jed, looking slightly startled, picked up her hint. "Yes. I'd be interested to hear more about that, Richard."

"I'll be back soon," Kathleen said, more for Jed's sake than Richard's, although she addressed her promise to him. Grabbing the empty meat platter and a bread basket containing two forlorn rolls, she followed her hostess from the room.

"What do you think?" Susan whispered quickly, as the door swung closed behind them.

"That man is the worst egotist I've ever met. I'm sitting

there looking for clues to what his wife was like and all I keep thinking is why on earth did she marry him? Or, at least, stay married to him?'' Kathleen answered in the same tone of voice.

''Maybe because he was so busy emoting about his own life that he didn't notice what she was doing with hers?'' Susan offered as an explanation.

''I suppose,'' Kathleen said doubtfully. ''Whew. I think I drank a little too much.''

''Boredom can make you do that. Maybe the coffee will help.''

''I hope so. Make it strong. I don't think Jerry can stop yawning.''

''Jed, too. But they'll be okay. Two chocoholics like them will be thrilled when they see this.'' Susan pulled a handsome chocolate rectangle from a bakery box. ''I was going to serve desserts left over from the party, but thought this was a better idea.''

''Is that the double chocolate mousse cake you were telling me about?''

''Yup. It will help pay our husbands back for living through this evening. Put the teapot on the stove, will you? I'll get the rest of the dirty dishes off the table.''

Kathleen sat down at the table and, pulling her tiny recorder toward her, turned it on and dictated her thoughts about the evening thus far.

''Have you learned anything?'' Susan returned with her arms full of plates to ask. ''At least anything worthwhile?''

''I'm not sure I've heard a single fact all evening,'' Kathleen answered, taking half of the dishes from Susan and heading to the sink to rinse them. ''That man has made up the most incredible excuses for the fact that he hasn't had a decent acting job in his whole career. I think, in fact, that the most metropolitan audience he ever played to was at Hancock High however many years ago.''

''Well, he does play some of the smaller houses in the city,'' Susan said doubtfully.

''That type of playhouse has more rats than seats. You

open there and close three days later, after the reviewers have either ignored you or panned you and all your friends have seen the production. He's probably better off playing some small town in Colorado. You know,'' she stopped putting the dishes into the KitchenAid and turned to Susan, ''Dawn sounds like she was a very bright, successful woman—whatever you think of her sexual ethics—she must have noticed that she was married to an egocentric idiot sometime in the past twenty years. I can't see her staying married to him simply because he didn't notice that she was sleeping with everyone in sight. She could have divorced him and then lived her life as she chose to. She must have had some reason to want to be his wife.''

''Okay,'' Susan agreed. ''So what was it?''

''That's what we have to find out.''

Susan put Demerara sugar, cream, and thinly sliced lemons on a lacquer tray. ''I'll put these on the table and bring back the salt and pepper and anything else we forgot.''

''Hmmm.'' Kathleen didn't appear interested and Susan returned to the dining room. She wasn't gone more than a few minutes and Kathleen was still standing staring down at the dessert platter when she returned.

''Something's going on in there. Jed asked me what was taking so long—and we haven't been long at all. We'd better hurry back . . .''

''No!'' Kathleen seemed startled out of her inertia. ''Wait.'' She rushed over, leaned gently against the door between the two rooms, and listened intently.

''Damn. You would have a house so well-built that it has solid core doors,'' she said, moving back to the center of the room.

''Sorry. But I don't know what you're listening for—and Jed did seem to want us to return as quickly as possible.''

''I know, but it may not be boredom that he's trying to escape from. Something may be going on that makes him uncomfortable and we should find out what it is.''

''Kathleen, you're spying on Jed now too! That's horrible!'' And, pausing only to pick up the mousse cake, she sailed from the room. Kathleen, knowing that Susan had forgotten for the moment that nothing could be quite as horrible as being arrested for murder, followed, coffee and teapots in her hands.

She entered a silent room.

"Oh, good. I'll pour while Susan cuts the cake," Jed offered quickly. Kathleen put the pots before him and sat down in her place again, looking curiously at Richard Elliot. Why wasn't he talking? Why was he looking so . . . so smug?

"Richard was talking about the police investigation into his wife's murder while you two were in the kitchen," Jerry said slowly, as though hesitant to bring it up.

"Your husband says you were with the State Police at one time." Richard Elliot seemed to be interested in someone besides himself for the first time this evening. "Do you know this odd Detective Sardini?"

"We've met. Connecticut is a big state, but I think most of the State Police officers—especially the detectives—have met at one time. I've never worked with him, though. Why do you call him odd?"

"Well, he seemed so very conservative and unwilling to accept anything other than his own pedestrian life-style. I would think that a police officer would see so much of the world and be exposed to such unusual sights that he would be more open to differences in people."

Kathleen knew that, if he had seen some of the things that she had seen, he would understand why police sometimes took refuge in the ordinary, but she didn't try to explain. "Conservative? How?" she asked.

"Well, he asked about my relationship with Dawn and, when I explained—in passing, mind you, and I don't think it is so very out of the ordinary—that neither of us believed in monogamy, he acted as though I had thrown a bomb in my lap."

"A bomb?" Kathleen repeated, hoping for a more definitive description.

"Yes. First he was completely unwilling to accept that I wasn't jealous of the men that Dawn had gone to bed with.

He seemed to assume that I would have killed her for her infidelities. I told him I had played Othello but I didn't act like that in real life. Do you know, I'm not sure he knew what I was talking about. Appalling lack of education.''

''And then?'' Kathleen prompted, thinking she knew what the conversation had been while the women were in the kitchen.

''Then he wanted a list of the men my wife had relationships with. Can you imagine?''

Kathleen could. ''And what did you tell him?''

''I asked him if he wanted me to list all the men or just those on the East Coast. I cannot describe the look on his face when I said that.''

''Did he still want you to list the names of the men she . . . uh . . .'' Kathleen found that she was uncomfortable talking about this, too.

''Yes. He suggested that I start with the men who lived in or around Hancock. Can you believe that man?''

Susan wanted to reach across the table and smack him. Had he given the police what they wanted or not?

Kathleen asked the question. ''And did you give them a list of names?''

''That's just what I was telling your husbands, ladies.''

Kathleen looked at Jerry, hoping for a straight answer. Susan worked to keep her eyes off Jed.

''Richard and Dawn weren't monogamous, but they kept their affairs to themselves,'' Jerry explained.

''The only civilized way to live. There are ordinary people, I know that. But some of us must share ourselves with others, give of ourselves and our talents in very intimate ways. To do less would be to deprive the world of something very special. Don't you agree?''

The question was directed at Kathleen. Her husband, throwing liberal ideas into the wind, answered for her. ''Some of us believe in monogamy,'' he said, rather too loudly.

''Possibly. Possibly,'' Richard said, accepting the coffee and cake that were handed to him. ''But I can tell you all one thing. Some of the people in Hancock who say they believe in monogamy don't act like they do—not when they're alone with someone they're not married to.'' He looked around the table at his audience, a large smile on his face.

FORTY PLUS THREE

I

"Weeeeeee!!!" Thirty-nine fifth graders expressed their glee as the driver ran the schoolbus directly over another bump in the asphalt. Susan clutched the back of the seat in front of her, breaking a fingernail. She opened her mouth to curse and then thought better of it.

The bus careened into a pothole.

"Mrs. Henshaw? Mrs. Henshaw?" There was urgency in the childish voice, and Susan turned around in her seat to see where it was coming from. Her gaze rested on the ten-year-old girl seated directly behind her; the child looked a little pale. "Did you say something, Andrea?"

"I think I'm going to throw up."

"No, you won't," Susan said, her voice unnaturally sweet. "You're going to be fine," she insisted, taking the child's hand. "Let's get you to the front of the bus where it isn't so bumpy." She urged the girl from her seat and gently pushed her down the rocking and jerking middle aisle of the vehicle. "You'll feel much better there," she repeated, glaring over her shoulder at the boys in the rear seats, who, overhearing this conversation, were responding by making loud gagging noises.

"It's getting worse," Andrea informed her, halfway down the aisle.

"We're almost there. Here's Mrs. Lambert." They had arrived at the front seats where the two fifth-grade teachers were busy with papers and pamphlets. The one on top was titled 'Sharks: Friend or Foe?' Susan wondered if, after this trip to the New York Aquarium, she would know how a shark befriended one. In the past she had thought that the friendliest thing a shark could do was not attack her. But she had more pressing problems. "Andrea's feeling a little carsick," she informed Constance Lambert, her son's teacher. "I thought maybe if she sat up here . . ."

"Join the group," Connie Lambert replied, waving her hand at five little girls all collapsed in the first two seats of the bus. "Move over and make some room for Andrea, Maggie. It's much less bumpy up here. You'll feel better soon," she also assured the girl, despite five pale faces being evidence to the contrary. She turned her attention to Susan. "How's it going back there?"

Susan muttered something tactful about the behavior of the fifth-grade boys.

"You don't have to lie to me. I know they can be a handful—they are a handful," she corrected herself. "On the way back Ellen or I will sit with them, but we really need this time to get organized. Here." She gave Susan a handful of papers. "This is some of the information the aquarium sent. Maybe you'd like to look at it ahead of time."

A violent scream from the back of the bus attracted their attention.

"Johnny Campanelli!" The teacher identified the culprit.

"I didn't do anything," was the instantaneous response.

"He did too, Mrs. Lambert," a girlish voice insisted. "He . . ."

"I don't want to hear about it, Mandy." The teacher leapt to her feet and moved quickly to the children. Susan followed hesitantly. Not feeling remarkably successful in controlling her own two children, whom she could always ground without TV privileges as a last resort, she wondered what would motivate these children to listen to her. Mrs. Lambert provided her with an answer.

". . . and if Mrs. Henshaw tells me about any problems, I will send the people involved to the principal's office the moment we return to school. She's going to be taking down names. Understand?''

The children obviously did, even her son, who (having begged her to be the class mother who went on this trip with them) was glaring at her. She'd better not write down the names of his friends, he seemed to be thinking. Susan considered putting his name down on the paper the teacher had handed her and discarded the idea.

"I'm sure they'll be fine now," she assured the teacher, not believing a word she was saying.

"Of course they will be," Mrs. Lambert replied, equally doubtful.

Susan smiled at Connie Lambert in a manner she hoped was more confident than she felt and, as the bus hit another spine-shattering bump, the teacher bounced back to her seat. Susan started to say something to Chad, but he was huddled in the corner with another boy and studiously avoiding her eye. She gave up and shuffled through the pamphlets from the aquarium, considering her situation. Three weeks ago, when asked to chaperone the fifth grade on their class trip to the New York Aquarium, she had agreed (after the aforementioned pleading on the part of her son who was now wishing she was dead), even thinking that it might be a lot of fun. She'd been on this bus for almost an hour now and the fun was elusive, to say the least.

Yesterday, she'd almost called and excused herself, but she had decided the trip might be a needed distraction. Well, she thought, as the bus was passed by a very large, very loud truck, she hadn't thought about Dawn in at least ten minutes and that must be a record for the past four days.

Another loud blast sounded from behind the bus and she cringed. What was going on? Why was every truck on the road honking at a school bus full of children? She turned around in time to see a full dozen little boys motioning at every trucker on the road to yank their horn cords. She leapt from her seat.

By the time she had gotten the message that distracting the drivers of large trucks could be dangerous through to the boys, they were entering the parking lot of the aquarium.

"Now, no one is to move until the bus has come to a full stop and the doors are open. Everyone is to stay with his or her partner. Leave your lunches on your seats and we will collect them at noon and bring them to you. John, put down Kathy's backpack, and listen to me. We will be going first to the . . ."

Susan stopped listening. As the children filed off the bus, even the ones who had just moments before been complaining of motion sickness returned to their favorite preadolescent activity of flirting, pinching, and teasing between the sexes. Susan smiled at the group and wondered what Kathleen was doing.

II

"You know you're not with the department anymore, Mrs. Gordon, and Detective Sardini certainly doesn't have to share this information with you."

"I'm sure Mrs. Gordon is aware of that fact, Mitchell," the detective himself spoke, turning from his filing cabinets. "And she probably also knows that we wouldn't have agreed to meet with her unless we were planning to let her into our investigation—somewhat," he qualified his statement.

"I don't suppose it will help if I tell you that I believe that neither Jed nor Susan Henshaw had anything to do with the murder," Kathleen said.

"It would help if you'd tell me what they're hiding from us," was Sardini's immediate response.

Kathleen took it without blinking. "They've made their statements. If you think they're lying, why haven't you questioned them again?"

"I have to put up with Mitchell; please don't add to it by acting dumb."

Mitchell started to speak but Kathleen preempted him. "I've told my friends to be completely honest with the police."

Sardini looked at her solemnly. "Let's hope they listen," was all he said.

"You have the autopsy report," Kathleen changed the subject, looking pointedly at the pile of papers on his desk.

"Feel free." Sardini pushed the report toward her.

Kathleen took it without a word.

"I can give you all the vital information in a few words," Mitchell offered. "She was shot through the temple. The bullet entered through the left lobe and exited on the opposite side of the head. She was right- handed and so someone else must have fired the shot. Death was instantaneous. No bullet was found."

Kathleen nodded and read the three-page form that she had been handed. "I see there's no definite ID on the weapon."

"No, the gun was held to the head, as you can see by the report on the bruising and tearing of the tissue around the entry point. That's common in head wounds because the bone supports the skin against the weapon. But the bone was shattered at both entry and exit points so we can't be sure of exact calibre. It was definitely a handgun—probably a thirty-eight."

"She was killed the day before Susan's party."

"Within twenty-four hours of the party probably. Rigor mortis was just beginning to wear off. All the joints had been forcibly flexed. That was necessary to get the body into the seat of a car, of course. But it's likely that it was done to transport her between wherever she was killed and the car."

"The forensic experts list all the various fibers and dirt found on the body and clothing," Kathleen said, falling back into the impersonal manner of referring to corpses that she had learned during her career.

"And the interesting thing is that sand and small bits of seaweed and driftwood were found on her clothing and skin and hair on the left side of the body. She may have been killed at the beach or in someone's beach house because she certainly had contact with that environment at some point before or after her death," Detective Sardini pointed out.

"You've found nothing like bits of fiber from rugs in the Henshaws' or anything else that would connect the inside of their home with the body?"

"Nothing. But just because there's no evidence that she was killed in their house doesn't mean that they didn't take part in the murder. She was definitely found in their garage," he reminded her.

"I . . ." Mitchell started.

"We'd like some coffee, Mitchell," his superior interrupted. "And some danish from the bakery in town," he added, as the man headed for the coffeepot on a counter in the corner of the room. "You wouldn't mind driving over and getting us a selection, would you?"

"You don't think I'd be more valuable here?"

Kathleen was almost sorry for him, but she was glad he was going.

And going he was. "We'd really like that danish," Sardini insisted, ignoring him before he was out the door.

"What he was probably going to tell you is that we also took samples from the hotel suite in the city where she has been staying and we think it's unlikely that she was killed there. There were fibers from a synthetic rug in her hair—it's possible that she was pulled across a rug, most likely after she was dead, and they don't match anything we've found. They're not the same as the rug in the Henshaws' new car either. Of course, we really don't know where to look. We don't have a picture of where she was the last few days of her life. Not yet."

"No evidence of sexual activity in the few days before her death," Kathleen commented.

"None. Sounds like that was unusual in her life," he added, after a pause.

"Really?" Her voice was noncommittal.

"You're wasting my time." The statement was abrupt and his voice more cold than angry.

"Look, I'm not investigating this case because it's my job. I'm doing it because my friends are involved, are suspected of murder."

"And you're convinced they didn't have anything to do with the murder?" The question was asked calmly.

"Of course."

"Because you know them well enough to know that neither of them would ever murder anyone? Even considering the things you saw during your years as a police officer?"

"Unlikely people have committed crimes. I know that. Even horrible crimes," Kathleen agreed quietly. "But not the Henshaws. I'd stake my reputation on that."

"You left the force. It's not your reputation that we're dealing with here," Sardini reminded her. "And, if you're so convinced of their innocence, why aren't you willing to help us get at the truth? If they're innocent, it couldn't hurt them, could it?"

"In an investigation a lot of things are turned up, not all of them having a direct bearing on the murder. And some of those things can hurt other people," Kathleen answered.

"Okay, I understand. And I don't suppose you'll break any confidences," Sardini said, picking up an elastic band on his desk and wrapping it around a pencil aimlessly before continuing. "You've reminded your friends that they shouldn't lie to the police. And you don't know me very well, but I can give you my word that all I want is the truth and that I will spare anyone any pain that I can if only they will help me find that truth. But . . . ." He broke his pencil as if to emphasize his point. "But I will find it!"

"I'm sure it's not just the Henshaws that you're interested in," she reminded him.

"Certainly not. And I don't think that the Henshaws are the only members of this illustrious community that are lying—or might be lying," he corrected himself quickly.

Kathleen put down the autopsy report that she was still holding in her hand. "I know most of the guests at the party. I haven't lived in Hancock very long, but I was accepted quickly because my husband has lived here for years, and because Susan Henshaw and I are friends. This is a very nice community, Detective Sardini. A little conservative, a little, well, a little WASP, a little closed to outsiders sometimes, but a nice place to live. The people here aren't used to crimes like this. Oh, the men and some of the women commute to the city and they have contact with people who've been mugged or run into that type of violent crime themselves, but not here in Hancock. In Hancock, the biggest problem is theft: burglaries and, rarely, robberies. Last year there were two murders in Hancock, but they involved a small group of women and a relatively closed situation. You know enough about Dawn Elliot now to know that she was intimately involved in the lives of more than a few couples in this town. Her murder has dredged up feelings that a lot of people are having a hard time dealing with, but only one person murdered her . . ."

"Probably," he interrupted to suggest.

"Okay, but no matter how many people were involved in killing Dawn, more than one person is very upset about it," Kathleen finished.

Sardini shrugged. "So you're saying that—"

"That this isn't an easy murder to investigate, and one it would be easy to jump to conclusions about."

"And that's what you think I'm doing in the case of your friends? Well, I'm not. If I thought they were guilty, I'd have them in here right now instead of spending the time with you. I think they're lying to me about something and I know that the more lies told the harder it's going to be to get at the truth. I know the people here are upset and I know that you're in a unique position: You belong to this world and you belong to my world. And I have no reason to believe that your husband has ever been involved with Dawn Elliot, and that's not something I can say about many men in his group. You have access to information that I don't have. You don't want to violate the confidences of your friends. That's fine. You keep whatever information you have to yourself. But if you have more information than I do, then you damn well better find out who our killer is!'' He slammed his hand on the desk and looked up angrily as the office door opened.

"They had danish in the reception area,'' Mitchell explained his quick return.

"And it took you that long to find the way to the reception center in the same building we're in?'' his superior replied angrily, seeming to forget that the point of the errand had been to keep this man out of the way as long as possible.

"I have a lunch appointment,'' Kathleen said, rising from her chair. "I really don't need anything to eat and I should be going or I'll be late. Thank you for showing me the report,'' she added.

"Fine.'' Sardini waved his hand, dismissing her from the room and, seemingly, his mind.

Kathleen smiled her good-bye to Mitchell. As she stopped just inside the door to put on her down coat, she was aware of just how uncomfortable this interview had made her: The man was furious at her and she really couldn't blame him one bit.

III

"I adore sushi, don't you?'' Kathleen said, following the Japanese waiter to their table.

"I think I'll have something cooked,'' Martha Hallard replied.

"You don't like . . . ?''

"Never eat it. I was at an ob/gyn convention in San Francisco about ten years ago, before raw fish became popular, and spent an evening in a Japanese restaurant listening to a doctor who had lived in Japan talk about people getting worms from eating raw fish and meat. Great big long worms that filled their intestines and all sorts of horrible things. Of course sushi wasn't around much then, but I still never touch the stuff.''

"But, Martha, didn't Susan tell me that the first sushi she ever ate was at your house? Thank you,'' she added to the waiter who pulled out her chair.

"Thanks," Martha acknowledged the same service. "It may have been. That was years and years ago and the caterer assured me it was the latest thing, so I served it." She shrugged. "But I don't eat it."

"Well." Kathleen paused a moment to think about a hostess who would expose her guests to risks that she was unwilling to take.

"I don't smoke either, but I do put out cigarettes at my parties," Martha said, reading her thoughts. "Besides," she continued, "now that sushi's so popular, I don't serve it anymore." She picked up her menu and studied it.

Kathleen did the same. She was glad for the time to think. She had been to one of Martha's parties and had been highly impressed, knowing the kind of dedication that it took to put on such an affair. And speaking of affairs . . . now that she had gotten Martha to agree to meet for lunch, how was she going to bring up tactfully Dan's affair with Dawn? It really was much easier to be a policewoman; then everyone expected you to be blunt.

"Would you like a drink from the bar?" A young Japanese woman wearing a kimono appeared at their table.

"No, just some hot tea for me," Martha replied.

"The same for me," Kathleen agreed, the vision she'd been having of a cold Kirin beer with sushi vanishing. "And could we order now?"

The waitress agreed, and they placed their orders quickly and watched her rush off to the kitchen. Kathleen considered how to begin. "I didn't know you traveled to conventions with Dan," she started, thinking that at least they were talking about him and their relationship.

"No." Martha poured out the tea that had been placed before them immediately. "I find it hard to run a business and travel around the country at the same time. When we were first married, I did go with him more. I didn't have the agency then, of course. And he traveled less. That was before he was in a partnership and had other doctors to take care of his patients while he was out of town. And the kids were little then. It was great to hire a sitter to stay with them and get away. But now the two older kids are living away from home and Charlie's in school all day and I have a full-time job running the real estate office; I just don't have the time for it.

"And, frankly, I don't love a convention atmosphere: people getting together for drinks and dinner in mediocre restaurants or, even worse, the official banquets with speakers or awards given out. You cannot imagine how boring most doctors are when it comes to giving speeches. Of course, I never attended the meetings where the doctors give their papers. I'd probably have died of boredom."

Kathleen was sipping tea and thinking that she should ask after the older Hallard children. She didn't know very much about them. The son was in medical school somewhere in the Caribbean, she knew, and she seemed to remember that the daughter had announced her engagement at Christmas. "How are plans for the wedding going?"

"What wedding? Oh, I know what you're talking about," Martha said, seeing the look on Kathleen's face. "It's just that I'm not giving the wedding. My perfect Phi Beta Kappa daughter, my full scholarship to Yale for graduate work daughter, has decided that she is going to give the wedding herself. 'Just something small in the park,' she says. If she's so smart, how come she doesn't know that type of thing's been out of style since the sixties? I could kill her! Do you know that when she was born—that very day—I thought about the kind of wedding I would give her: outside on a warm spring day with daffodils in the flower beds and the magnolia trees blooming. We could have forced pots of lily of the valley for the tables. And used miniature narcissi to decorate the cake. In fact, one of the reasons we bought the house we did was because it has a perfect backyard for entertaining. And I planted those magnolia trees the week we moved in. Today they're just the right size. But she's going to get married in some park in New Haven with rusting beer cans on the ground and used condoms in the bushes! Disgusting!"

The arrival of their food stopped the tirade and gave Kathleen an opportunity to figure out how to turn the conversation around. She needn't have worried.

"You're interested in Dan's affair with Dawn, aren't you?" Martha asked, her mouth full of steaming noodles.

Now as much as Kathleen enjoyed sushi and, in fact, most oriental food, she had never developed much skill with chopsticks. Her takamaki dropped into her lap. She ignored it. "You're right. I'm worried about Susan or Jed being accused of killing Dawn. I'm not accusing anyone else. I just want all the information I can get in case either of them is arrested. You understand."

"Of course. In your position I'd do the same thing. And I am the logical person to talk to first: I know the community better than you do and, probably, as well as anyone else in Hancock."

Kathleen was relieved that Martha didn't appear to mind being considered as an alternative suspect. Again her thoughts were read.

"I don't worry about the police thinking of Dan or myself as a suspect, you know. In the first place, Dan was only one in a long line of conquests that Dawn made in Hancock. And there was no reason for him to kill her to hide their affair. I told you the other day that he told me about it at the time it ended. I wasn't going to get upset at this late date. Of course, it's different for the Henshaws: Jed never told Susan about his affair, did he?"

"You know?" Kathleen was in danger of finding her entire meal in her lap.

"Yes." Martha smiled ruefully. "Dan was so upset when Dawn dropped him that he had her tailed. Do you believe it? Just like a jealous husband. And the detective he hired found out about Jed right away. Dan told me, but I never mentioned it to Susan. She's not strong like I am. I don't think she could live with the idea that her husband was unfaithful. Some women have such old-fashioned, possessive ideas about marriage."

"And you?" Kathleen was hesitant to ask.

"I say if he wants to have fun out of the house, let him.

Then he leaves me alone.'' Martha speared the last piece of meat floating in her soup, put it in her mouth and then looked across the table at Kathleen. ''You're shocked? Well, people have different arrangements in their lives and this is one that Dan and I worked out long ago. Why do you think he brings me those wonderful gifts from his trips? Because he takes his secretaries with him, that's why. I benefit more than he does, is the way I see it. What the secretaries get out of it is beyond me. Dan is no great shakes in bed, I can tell you that. And he's never going to leave me and marry them either. Dan is very contemptuous of men who have midlife crises and leave their wives. And,'' she added before Kathleen had time to think it, ''why should he leave me? I give him all the freedom he wants and the home he thinks he deserves. He doesn't have to have a midlife crises. Any questions?''

Kathleen laid her chopsticks across her wooden tray, reached over, and poured herself another cup of tea. ''Does he always have his lovers tailed after the affair is over?''

''No.'' Martha paused, then reached for the teapot. ''Is this thing empty?''

''If it is, I'm sure the waitress will bring us another one,'' Kathleen murmured, knowing Martha was stalling for time, and letting her.

''No, it looks like some is left,'' Martha discovered, pouring the tea into her own cup, ''but I'll get her to bring us more the next time she passes.

''To answer your question: No, Dawn was different. Maybe she was Dan's midlife crises even if we didn't call it that. Dan thought he was really in love with that woman,'' she added, the first hint of bitterness in her voice. ''She was different for a lot of reasons. In the first place most of the women that Dan attracts are bimbos—real tacky and real dumb. I've always assumed that's the way he likes them. But Dawn isn't—wasn't—like that. Dawn was a classy lady: bright, sexy, independent. And he fell for her. The other reason Dawn was different was that she got tired of Dan before he got tired of her. *If* he ever would have gotten tired of her. She broke up the affair. I don't think it broke his heart, but he thought it did. I know it damaged his ego, hence the detective.''

"And when he found out that it was Jed she was sleeping with?''

"I don't think he did anything. At least nothing that he told me about. I don't think Jed knows that we know, but I may be wrong. You could ask him. I assume that it is Jed you have your information from?''

Kathleen chose to ignore the question. "Why do you think Dawn was attracted to Dan?'' she asked, knowing that it was an impertinent question.

"I don't know why Dawn was attracted to any of the men she slept with.''

"Who . . . ?''

"Oh, I don't know the names of anyone else. There were rumors from time to time when she was in town. Some of them must have been true.'' Martha shrugged her shoulders. "Maybe she was a nymphomaniac. Maybe Hancock bored her and she had to have something to keep her busy while she was here. Who knows? I've never understood how she got hooked up with Richard Elliot, for that matter.''

"You think it was an unlikely marriage?'' Kathleen asked.

"Definitely. But Dawn kept her opinions to herself. She didn't confide much about her personal life to any of the women I know. Or any of the men either. As far as her relationship with Dan was concerned, there were very romantic lunches and long sexy afternoons. But I get the idea that intellectual conversation wasn't one of the features of the day. Maybe she was different with Jed—or someone else.''

"And you think all she wanted from the men she had affairs with was sex?''

"What else? She and Elliot had all the money they needed, or at least they appeared to. She had her professional life, and it always seemed very fulfilling. She and Elliot didn't have kids, but I never got the impression that they thought that was much of a loss: They never made any sort of fuss over anyone's children and I know that Elliot considered children to be big scene stealers. And there's a man who doesn't tolerate the scene being stolen from him. He expects a lot of attention—somewhat like a child, if the truth be known. Maybe Dawn didn't have children because she was married to one. Who knows?''

"You didn't hate her?''

"How many people are stupid enough to admit that they hate someone who was just murdered—murderer unknown?'' came the logical reply. "I wonder if they have any red bean ice cream? The caterer was telling me that it's wonderful and we're having some of Dan's colleagues over in two weeks. I may as well check it out.''

The waitress came, another full teapot in her hands. She assured them that they would enjoy the unusual flavor ice cream and, promising to return with some, shimmered off in her flowing garment.

"I'd love to have been brought up in a country with a more dramatic national costume,'' Martha commented.

Kathleen, who had always thought that Martha's preppie style suited her admirably, was surprised and showed it.

"Oh, I have my own fantasies, too,'' Martha began and then stopped for the dessert to be placed before them. The waitress poured out two more cups of tea before she left and conversation could be resumed. "I've always been interested in other cultures. It wasn't Dawn Elliot's field exclusively, you know. Although I was interested in archaeology, not anthropology. And I was respected, even if I never got beyond the student stage. I had been accepted to do graduate work in England before Dan asked me to marry him.'' She tasted the ice cream, made a face, and put down the spoon. "I think I'll stick to crème brûlée for my party,'' she commented and then looked Kathleen full in the face. "That's not exactly true. I was accepted to do graduate work the day before I found out that I was pregnant with Dan's baby. He asked me to marry him all right. But if it hadn't been for my own stupidity, I never would have accepted him. And maybe,'' she paused, "maybe if I hadn't been pregnant, he never would have asked.''

IV

"Kathleen, Kathleen Gordon! Wait! You're just the person I want to see!" The voice came from behind and Kathleen, who had been about to unlock her car door, stopped and turned to see who it was.

"Maureen! Good to see you. Did you say you'd been looking for me? Anything I can do for you?"

"Yes. But I don't want to talk about it out here in the street. For one thing, we'll freeze to death, and, besides, it's private. Listen, there's a bakery just down the road with tables and chairs in one corner. Why don't we go have some coffee and a pastry and we can talk?"

Kathleen, without even a glance at the restaurant she had just left, agreed to the suggestion. That Maureen might have something to say about Dawn's murder was worth ruining her waistline for. And, if that wasn't what she wanted to talk about, Kathleen would change the subject and see that she did.

They were getting settled in the area of the bakery that had been decorated to resemble a café in France, as much as a ten-by-fifteen-foot space with a gray linoleum floor and no windows could be said to, before Maureen alluded to her reasons for wanting a meeting. "Like my new mink coat? It's my payment from Colin for sleeping with that bitch."

"Dawn Elliot?" Kathleen asked, wondering if any woman in Hancock owned anything that hadn't been a payoff for understanding the peccadilloes of her husband.

"I won't say that bitch's name. I just call her the bitch. We'll both know whom I'm talking about."

"You want to talk about Dawn?" Kathleen tried to keep the hope out of her voice. Here she had planned a day of talking with women whose husbands had slept with Dawn Elliot, and the one woman she hadn't been able to contact on the phone last night had just dropped out of the sky and into her lap.

"I don't want to; I have to. I feel, in fact, like all I've done in the past four days is talk about her. Oh, yes, we would like to order," she told the woman who had left her spot behind the counter to act as their waitress. "Coffee, and two napoleons and a small plate of your petit fours. And what do you want?" she asked Kathleen.

"Coffee and a napoleon," Kathleen said, wondering if they were going to be joined by someone else. She looked around for another chair.

"No one else is coming," Maureen said, seeing the look. "When I get upset, I eat."

"Well, it sure hasn't hurt your figure any," Kathleen said admiringly.

"Oh, I can eat anything and I don't gain weight," was the nonchalant response. "Here comes our snack. It looks good, doesn't it?"

It did, but Kathleen wondered if Maureen was truly upset over the discovery of her husband's affair with Dawn. Between her enjoyment of the new fur and the way she was plunging into those pastries, she sure was hiding it well. Was she sitting across from another woman who had an "arrangement" with her husband?

Then, her mouth full of the creamy filling from her second napoleon, Maureen burst into tears. "I cannot believe that he's done this to me," she wailed, oblivious to her surroundings. "I thought he loved me and all these years he's been lying to me."

Kathleen wondered if Dawn had been the only woman in Colin's life, but Maureen didn't give her time for questions.

"He keeps telling me that he loves me, that he's always loved me, that that bitch was some sort of abnormal episode in his life, that she bewitched him and he couldn't resist. Now you tell me what woman wants to hear that her husband found some other woman irresistible? None!"

Kathleen thought briefly of Jerry and agreed.

"He insists that she was the only other woman in his life, but how can I believe him? He could be deceiving me this very minute with some other woman, couldn't he? Couldn't he?" She repeated her question when Kathleen, who had thought it was rhetorical, didn't reply.

"I don't think . . ." Kathleen began.

"But this time I'll know. I hired a detective to follow him! He's never going to get away with anything else for as long as I live. I'm not going to be made a fool of again."

Kathleen, a little shocked at the vehemence of Maureen's feelings, forgot her mission of information-getting and made a suggestion. "Maybe you should separate for a while? Just till the hurt goes away."

"Are you out of your mind? You may not have any kids but I have three girls with expensive habits. Just their music, gymnastic, and skating lessons cost hundreds of dollars a month. And Colin and I have spent a fortune on private school tuition so that they can go to very expensive Ivy League colleges. I can't risk a divorce now, and separations always lead to divorces. I can give you lists of the couples we've known over the years who've had what they called 'trial separations' and are now divorced." She paused long enough to finish the last pastry and to ask the waitress for more. "He's not going to escape his responsibilities, I can tell you that. And I'm not stupid enough to go into a divorce court and gamble that I'll come out of it with the same life-style I have now. The woman's movement hasn't done divorced women a lot of good; I've watched what's happened to some of my friends and I know. A lot of women have to give up their homes and go to work! I'm not going to do that! I'm not going to be the one to pay for his mistake!"

"If you're not interested in evidence for a divorce proceeding, why are you having him followed?" Kathleen asked, sipping the last of her coffee.

"I'm interested in him knowing that I know what he's doing. I told him that I was having him followed! He won't dare have any fun with that detective around."

"When we ran into each other in the grocery the other day you said that Colin had confessed to having an affair with Dawn right after her death," Kathleen began, trying to return to the subject that interested her most.

"Yes. I thought at the time that he was crazy for telling me, but of course he had to." She bit into a petit four.

"Why?"

"Because he had to tell the police, of course. And he knew that they would ask me about it. Can you believe it? That's one of the worst things he's done to me: He had an affair with a woman who is murdered by God knows whom. Now we're both suspects in a murder case. I could kill him, I really could."

"I don't think this is the time to talk about killing anyone. As you said, we're in the middle of a murder investigation."

"There was no reason for me to kill the bitch. She's the one that broke up with Colin. She's the one who ended their affair."

"Really? Did Colin tell you that?"

"Of course. Oh, I've gotten all the details from him. I've insisted on hearing every little gruesome, sick moment of their affair, including how it ended."

Kathleen, who was dying to hear all about it, didn't know what to say. Luckily, it seemed no prompting was needed.

"What I can't figure out," Maureen continued, finishing her pastry and reaching for another, "is why that bitch picked Colin. There must be more interesting men in Hancock. I can name some myself." She seemed intrigued by that thought and didn't say anything for a few moments. "But anyway, why did she pick him?"

"When did it happen?" Kathleen asked.

"In the spring six years ago. It only lasted for a few months and then she left town. Colin thinks that she wouldn't have broken up except for what he calls 'the demands of her work'—my ass! The woman was a nympho! The police officer who interviewed me said as much! She would have needed someone else soon anyway."

"How did it begin?" Kathleen asked, hoping to hear a coherent story but not expecting one.

"They met in the city. You know—well, you don't know, but everyone else in Hancock does—Colin was working at *City Lights* at the time. You know, the magazine. Well, it was just beginning back then, and Colin was editor and publisher. It's hard work starting something new and the entire staff was working twenty-six hours a day or something similar. They were planning a cover article on American Indians in the city and Colin asked Dawn to do some consulting . . .''

"Did she have a reputation around Hancock that many years ago?''

"Sure. She had a reputation for as long as I've known her.''

"Then didn't you worry about Dawn and Colin getting together?''

"No. Colin is, well, Colin. I never thought another woman would find him all that interesting. I did think about her reputation at the time and I thought that she might get together with Derek Stiles. He was Colin's assistant at the time and any woman would have fallen for him: good-looking, talented, incredibly sexy. But the bitch had the bad taste to fall for Colin. I cannot believe her.

"Anyway,'' she continued her story after finishing the last pastry and putting down her fork, seemingly replete. "They fell in love over the proofs of an article on Indians in the construction unions. At least that's how Colin puts it. What he really means is that they were screwing on the floor of his office—because the magazine was too new and too poor to afford couches then—every time they got a chance. And that was the year that my mother had her stroke and so I was flying out to Indianapolis, where she lived before we put her in the home, every few weeks. And when I was there, they were together. Colin had it all worked out: The magazine had a small suite at the Waldorf that they used to try to impress potential advertisers when they came to town and Colin sometimes spent the night there when he was busy. He usually stayed there when I was gone because it was easier than commuting. So I would call him there at night to tell him that my flight had arrived all right and about my mother, and all the time Dawn—I mean that bitch—was lying in bed next to him!''

"Surely not all the time. What about Richard Elliot?''

"What about him? He never counted for much. Besides,

he was probably giving an immortal, unforgettable perfor-
mance of Hamlet in some distinguished little theater in the
suburbs of Buffalo. Can you believe that man?''

''No,'' Kathleen said, not sure what man she was referring
to, but thinking it applied equally to them both.

''Neither can I.'' She looked longingly at the case of
pastry.

''You're not going to have another?''

''I'd love to, but I think I'd throw up. Damn!'' She
slammed her hand on the table. ''I wish I hadn't quit smoking! I suppose it's a little early to start drinking?'' she asked
wistfully.

''I think alcohol on top of all that sugar would guarantee
you throwing up,'' Kathleen said. ''Maureen, when we ran
into each other the other day at the store, you said something
about other women in town being glad Dawn was dead. Do
you know that she slept with other men? For sure, not just
innuendo.''

''I'm sure. In the first place, that bitch told Colin that she
had an affair with Harv Bower . . .''

''You mean Harvey Bower? Missy's father? Do you know
if his wife knows?''

''No. But I don't think that it has that much to do with
Gloria. She and Harvey weren't married at the time. Harvey
was married to a woman named Samantha. But Samantha
died years and years ago—of cancer—so that couldn't have
anything to do with Gloria and Harvey's relationship.

''I also think that Dawn slept with Guy Frye. They were
interviewed by the police before we were and I saw them
after their interviews and they were furious with each other.
It could have been something else, of course, but . . .''

''You're right, it could have been something else,'' Kathleen agreed, doubting it.

''I have to get going. I'm going to be late to drive Cindy
to her SAT review course. I'm glad I talked to you. I'm
feeling much better.'' She stood up and straightened out her
short straight skirt. ''Maybe just a little fatter, though.

"Say, where's Susan today? How's she taking all this now that everything seems to be settling down?"

"She's on a class trip with the fifth grade to the New York Aquarium. She's probably having too good a time to even think about the murder."

"I hope so," Maureen agreed, placing money on the table for the tab and a minuscule tip. "What a lousy thing to have happen on your fortieth birthday. As if being old isn't trouble enough!"

V

"Well, at least we're coming back home with the same number we started with," Connie Lambert sighed, wearily dropping down on the seat beside Susan. "My feet are killing me. And these shoes are two years old."

"I know what you mean. My whole body aches," Susan said, wondering if coming home with the same number they began with was such a virtue. There was one obnoxious little boy that she would love to have accidentally dropped into the shark tank.

"Now you know how it is to be a teacher," Connie Lambert was saying.

"Look at that Lamborghini Countach 5000! Twelve cylinders, 5.2 liter, fuel-injected engine. It can go 185 miles an hour!"

Susan heard the enthusiastic voice of her own son.

"He sure knows a lot about cars," his teacher commented.

"It would be nice if he spent as much time on schoolwork as he does with his foreign car magazines," Susan replied.

Connie Lambert smiled understandingly. "Well, at least he's reading something. It would be a help if he could incorporate fractions into that bright head of his along with all that information on speed and engine size."

"I agree. I think, though, that the kids must have learned a lot on this trip. I did. I had no idea that starfish have five sex organs."

"Neither did I. And I'd love to know what Johnny Campanelli thought about it. He had all of the boys in stitches with the comment he made. Probably just as well that I was too far away to hear it."

Susan, who hadn't been, agreed. "And the display is really much better than I remember it being. Of course, the last time I was there Chrissy was younger than Chad is now so it's had a lot of time to improve."

There was a loud cry from somewhere in the bus and both women winced. "Don't worry. Ellen's back there. She'll find out what's going on and take care of it.

"So what are the police saying about what happened last weekend at your house?" the teacher asked, not mentioning the nature of the event in case any children were listening.

"Nothing to us. You know about the break-ins and burglaries that happened during the party?"

"The article in *The Hancock Press* talked about them. Do they think that the two, or, I guess five, events were connected?" she asked, remembering that there had been four reported burglaries.

"I think it's still too early for them to be sure about that. At least that's the impression I got," Susan answered.

Before she had a chance to elaborate, they were joined by Andrea, who had left her seat and staggered down the aisle. "I think I'm going to be sick, Mrs. Lambert."

VI

Kathleen had asked Brigit Frye to meet her in the bar at the Hancock Inn at four; the impromptu meeting with Maureen had made her late. But Brigit Fry was even later. "Just some seltzer and a wedge of lime, Barnard," Kathleen said to the bartender. "I'll be sitting at the table near the window. Could you have someone bring my drink to me? Oh, and I'm meeting Mrs. Frye, if you see her come in . . ."

"I'll send her right over, Mrs. Gordon. Would you like something to eat with your drink?"

Kathleen started to refuse until she remembered her guest.

"Good idea. Anything that looks good to you." She smiled warmly at the man and went over to her seat. This was one of the best things about living in Hancock: Although a suburb, it was still enough of a small town for everyone to know everyone else.

Kathleen was the daughter of a cop, a city cop who had made his home in Philadelphia. Cops didn't live in Germantown or on Rittenhouse Square; her father made just enough to keep his family in a falling down rented house too close to the slums in West Philly. But it was close enough to the University of Pennsylvania for her to see her way out of the lower middle class life she'd been born into. She'd always been good at school; an academic scholarship and four years commuting from her parents' home had gotten her a degree in public relations and the chance at something different from her parents' life.

But her father's untimely death just four days before he was to retire had forced her to look more closely at what she was working so hard to leave. He had died trying to save a four-year-old boy from a vicious attack by a street gang that had a grudge against his teenage cousin. Kathleen saw for the first time that her father had, in his own way, been trying to change what was wrong with the world. And that the attempt shouldn't stop with his death. She'd signed up for the tests, passed them, and was in training to be a police officer in New York City before her friends or family could talk her out of it. And she'd never regretted it.

Her first husband had been a cop who hadn't been able to live with the agony of the job, dying drunk in an auto accident. But Kathleen had worked on, moving up in her department, and then moving across state lines to become one of the Connecticut State Police's detectives. Until meeting Jerry, she had never thought of leaving the department. And she didn't think that she regretted her decision once she had. But was she investigating Dawn Elliot's death for any reason other than to protect her friends?

"Are you okay, Kathleen?" The worried voice of Brigit Frye interrupted Kathleen's reverie.

"Just thinking over my life," Kathleen answered honestly, smiling up at her guest.

"That's one way to spend a dreary March afternoon. How I hate this month! Every year I think spring comes in March and every year it comes in late April. You'd think I'd learn! So how are you?" Brigit Frye asked, sitting down and flinging her handwoven wool coat off her shoulders and onto the chair.

Kathleen stopped a moment and considered Brigit Frye, a northern beauty. From her short pale, pale blond hair, blue eyes, and creamy skin to her almost aggressively bony frame, she was a woman most people would look at twice. And many men would follow up with a third glance. She was dressed today, as she usually was, with artistic flair, certainly more creatively than most women in Hancock. Kathleen appreciated that Brigit was the only woman she had talked to today who was wearing some outer covering other than fur, but she doubted if the coat now falling off the chair behind Brigit's broad shoulders had cost less than some of its hairier cousins.

"Why are you thinking over your life? Is something bothering you? Anything I can do?" Brigit leaned across the table, a concerned expression on her face.

"I . . ."

"Would madam like to order?" the waiter who had brought Kathleen's club soda and food asked.

"Yes, she would, Charles." Brigit smiled up at him. "I'd like a Kir, light, and some of those things." She waved at the platter of mixed appetizers. "Oh, and also a basket of breadsticks and cheese straws, please. And some smoked trout, if you have any."

The man hurried off to get her food and Brigit smiled at Kathleen. "Guy is staying in the city tonight. They're involved in some serious last-minute negotiations and he won't be home for days. This'll probably be my dinner."

"This will sound stupid, but I don't know what Guy does," Kathleen said, picking up her seltzer and taking a sip.

"You mean besides having affairs with women who are

subsequently murdered?'' Brigit asked, a smile, not entirely sarcastic, on her face.

"I . . ."

"He's a lawyer who specializes in negotiating union contracts. He usually works on the union side,'' she continued, ignoring her own previous statement.

"So, if he's staying in the city, this must be an important time in the negotiations?''

"Not necessarily. Oh, he would say it is, but I've lived with it all so long that I don't get very excited anymore. Every negotiation starts out with a very strange combination of threats and hope, slogs along for a few weeks, or months, or, in one memorable case, years, and then ends up at the last minute with a crisis. It's all garbage to me. But Guy thrives on it. And that's not what you want to talk about. Oh, thank you,'' she added, as her drink and food arrived.

"You're interested in Guy and Dawn, aren't you?'' Brigit picked up a piece of fish on her fork, dipped it in the cup of creamy sauce provided, and put it in her mouth. "I heard you were investigating the murder and I don't mind talking about it. Guy and I have a very open relationship. We have for years. Although, with Dawn, he broke the rules.'' She sipped her drink.

"The rules?''

"Yeah, it sounds strange, doesn't it? You and Jerry haven't been married long enough for you to understand probably, but . . ."

"I was married before,'' Kathleen interjected.

"Really?'' Brigit was obviously not terribly interested. "Then maybe you will understand.'' She sounded doubtful. "Well, Guy and I haven't had an easy marriage. Maybe we never should have gotten married in the first place, but by the time we discovered that we'd had two children and the third was on the way. Probably we would have had a hard time being married to anyone; both of us need more excitement than life in the suburbs, three kids, and a dog provide. Anyway, the time I'm talking about was years ago. We went to a marriage counselor and she suggested an open marriage:

They were all the rage in 1974 and we figured, why not? And it worked. We both sleep with other people and we're happier and our marriage is stronger.''

"You mentioned rules? The one that Guy broke when he slept with Dawn?''

Brigit was holding a cheese straw, concentrating on spreading it with butter without breaking it, and didn't answer immediately. "When we agreed to the open marriage . . .'' She paused to sip her wine. "We agreed that certain rules apply and one of those rules is that we don't have affairs with people we both know. It makes things cleaner and neater.''

Kathleen thought that was an interesting description, but didn't question it. "So, since Dawn was a friend and neighbor . . .''

"He should have stayed out of her bed, yes. Especially since it is much easier for him to find people than for me. After all, he works in the city and his job puts him in the middle of a new situation and new co-workers every few months. I have a harder time of it. I have to keep taking courses and going to meetings of the writers group I belong to in Hartford and hoping that I will run into someone interesting.''

"I can see that it would be a problem, at least more of a problem for you than for Guy.''

"Well, you meet more people negotiating contracts than free-lance writing, that's for sure.''

"Did the affair end when you saw the two of them together? At the inn that afternoon that you told me about two days ago?''

"No. I was mad then, but involved with a wonderful professor at Yale who writes mysteries in his spare time, and I didn't bother to make much fuss. Dawn broke the affair off fairly soon after that: She went back out West to do some work. I think maybe Guy thought that she would resume their relationship when she was back in town, but she picked up some other man the next year.''

"Do you know who?''

"No. I do know that she was involved with Dan Hallard and Jed Henshaw at different times."

Kathleen had been waiting all day to hear this and she didn't know what to do now that she had. "Why those two men?" she asked, trying to make it sound like her other questions.

"Well, Dan and Guy have talked about Dawn. I don't know how the subject came up. Dan and she were together after she and Guy were together. I assume one of them mentioned it to the other casually, you know, locker room stuff. You know how men talk."

Kathleen, who had been involved in racquetball and aerobics classes for years, doubted that men could possibly talk more about their conquests than women did.

"That's really the reason that we agreed originally to the rule that neither of us would sleep with a neighbor or mutual friend: Our therapist pointed out that no one wants to hear his or her spouse talked about in that type of situation. Anyway, Guy talked with Dan and then he told me about it."

"And Jed?"

"Guy told me about Jed, too, but he didn't tell me how he knew. He also told me not to tell anyone that we knew." Brigit casually finished off her trout and then her Kir. "Where is that waiter? I'd like another one of these." She motioned to the drink.

"I see him," Kathleen exclaimed, waving at the man. "He's coming over."

Brigit ordered a refill while Kathleen tried hard to wait patiently for an explanation. "I don't understand," she said, as soon as they were alone.

"I don't either. Guy told me that Jed Henshaw had an affair with Dawn Elliot and he told me not to tell anyone and to be sure not to let Jed know that we knew. But he didn't tell me how he knew."

Two questions occurred to Kathleen; she asked the more innocuous one first. "Why does he think an affair took place?"

"I don't know. He didn't tell me, but there's no mistake.

I asked him if he was sure. You know, Jed and Susan seem so together and I really was surprised—as much as anything surprises me these days.''

"Did you tell the police?" Kathleen asked, hoping for the right answer.

"Well, Guy insisted that it would be a foolish thing to do, that if we told on someone else the police would just suspect us more, but I think he's wrong. So," she paused to shrug, "I told them. Guy doesn't know.

"Now look, I know what you're thinking. I like Susan and Jed as much as anyone, but I'm not going to have Guy and myself suspects in a murder case and then hold back information that might clear us. You know the murder took place in the Henshaws' garage. If the police are looking into relationships with Dawn then they might as well start there first, especially if Jed was involved with her, too.''

It was a nasty thought, but Kathleen found it hopeful: Maybe Brigit had good reason to deflect possible guilt away from herself and her husband. And at least now she knew that Detective Sardini knew about Jed and Dawn. She also knew that there were going to be questions about just why Jed had hidden that knowledge from the police. Sardini probably wouldn't care that Jed had been trying to protect his wife and his marriage—a murder investigation didn't leave much room for sentiment. But Brigit was waiting for a response.

"Do you think that Jed and Dan were the only two other men in Hancock who had affairs with Dawn?" Kathleen asked, finishing her seltzer and thinking about a real drink.

"Probably not. Dawn was always hinting about the men who liked her. There probably were others.''

"I just met Richard Elliot a few days ago," Kathleen began. "Do you think that he and his wife had an open marriage like yours?"

"Well, certainly not like ours. At least they weren't following the same rules; it looks like they didn't care about getting involved with friends. And, for that matter, although we all heard rumors about Dawn, either Richard wasn't as sexually active or else he was more discreet; no one ever heard anything about him. I don't think he ever made a pass at anyone I knew. At least I never heard anything about it. Maybe he's . . .''

"Isn't that just like you, Brigit Frye, sitting around gossiping. And to think that I've considered you one of my closest friends. I cannot believe what you've done. And I'm certainly not going to forgive you, I can tell you that!'' Gloria Bower's angry voice broke into the discreet murmur that had made up the noise in the bar until her arrival. The patrons, clustered around small tables like Kathleen and Brigit, were too well behaved to look around at the disturbance.

"Gloria, what are you talking about?'' Kathleen stood up and grabbed her by the arm. "Sit down and relax, there must be some misunderstanding here. If we all talk about . . .''

"There's no misunderstanding here. We've been friends for years, but if you think I'm going to ignore the fact that my friends are sitting around and talking about me, you're crazy. This is the wrong time in my life for people to be spreading rumors about me and I'll get you for it, Brigit Frye! I'll get you for it!'' Gloria spun around and stalked out of the room, oblivious to the tinkle of glass as her mink swept over a small serving table.

"I cannot imagine what she's so upset about. Having a small baby around and not sleeping through the night must be getting to her,'' Brigit suggested, watching a bevy of waiters scurrying around to pick up shards of glass from the shiny waxed floor.

"Maybe,'' Kathleen said. Her voice was noncommittal.

VII

"You remind me of Santa Claus,'' Susan commented, looking at her passenger as she drove the car through the rush hour traffic.

"Santa Claus?'' Kathleen asked, thinking of her full stomach.

"You know. Making a list and checking it twice.''

"Cute. Richard Elliot quotes Shakespeare and you quote Christmas carols," came the sarcastic reply.

"Or maybe he was really quoting Marlowe?" Susan continued her teasing.

"So Jerry insists," Kathleen answered, stuffing the notebook in which she had been writing into her large leather purse. She picked up a well-worn paperback from the seat between them and glanced at its title page. "Dr. R. Doubleday Sterling," she said, reading the author's name. "Jerry's friend from Stanford says that he calls himself Day. I'm glad he's in town. It will be interesting to hear more about Dawn's professional life."

"I hope he's not going to be late," Susan said, pulling her car into a miraculously empty parking space about a block from Columbia University and looking up the street. "There's the restaurant. Let's go in and see if he's waiting."

Minutes later they were seated in a booth, peering around in the dark interior of the sleazy restaurant. "What else did Jerry say about him? How did he get his name anyway?" Susan asked, moving her feet away from something gummy that was gluing them to the floor under the table.

"He called an old friend in the English department at Stanford, who called an old friend in the anthropology department, who traced the man who worked the closest with Dawn. It was no big deal. I'll bet the police have talked to Dr. Sterling already."

"Excellent guess. They have. In fact, they've spoken with me twice. They seem to be unable to accept what I tell them about Dawn. They keep asking the same question: What was she like? And when I tell them they don't accept the answer, but continue to repeat the question."

Susan and Kathleen looked at the man standing before them. He wasn't quite six feet tall and was very overweight. His shiny polyester pants, unironed oxford shirt, and worn Harris tweed jacket proclaimed him to be a professor, and his ink-stained fingers, disgraceful briefcase, and esoteric puffs of hair sprouting over his ears and beneath the glow of his bald head confirmed the judgment. His smile was genuine, friendly, and intelligent. Both women liked him instantly.

"You're Dr. Sterling!" Susan exclaimed.

"Please call me Day," was the reply. "May I sit down?"

"Of course." Susan scooted over on her bench, trying to ignore the ripping sound her skirt made as it caught on a long splinter.

A smiling waiter hurried over. "Professor Sterling? It is you, isn't it?"

"It certainly is." Professor Sterling returned the beam. "I always come here when I'm in town, don't I? The best blintzes in the world!" he announced. "Three orders of cheese blintzes and three glasses of seltzer. Have either of you ladies eaten here before?" he asked, appearing to be unaware of how unlikely that was. "No? Well then, you're in for a treat. The blintzes are heaven. Absolute heaven."

Kathleen worked to keep the smile on her face. She certainly wasn't hungry, but the waiter had rushed off to the kitchen leaving them alone and she was anxious to get to work.

"We were glad to discover that you were in town, Professor Sterling," she began.

"I am too." His expression changed. "I am going to be able to attend the funeral of my great friend, Dawn Elliot, and to say good-bye properly. It will be a small consolation but an important one. When one studies anthropology, one cannot help but believe that these small ceremonies of life are in many ways as important as anything we have."

"You and she were close?" Kathleen asked, hating to pry but knowing she had to.

"Yes. I loved her. Oh, not like that!" he corrected himself as Susan's eyebrows crept half an inch up her forehead. "I did love her but we were not lovers. I think in some ways what we had was more special than that. You see, we worked in the same small area of archaeological anthropology: the Anasazi Indians. I am interested in their travels, their trade routes and migrations from the northern plateaus into the canyon walls and then down into the canyons themselves.

Dawn's work was more in the social development and the communications between the various groups of peoples living at the same time. But we were both, of course, intensely interested in knowing why these talented, resourceful, and peaceful people died out, or where they migrated to after they left the cities in which they had lived for hundreds of years. We both cared deeply for our subjects and we spent a lot of time together in the field on research as well as in libraries and on consultations with various colleagues.''

"So you were close."

"Very. Anthropology is like many scholarly pursuits: Each step toward the truth is tiny, almost infinitesimal and usually unseen by anyone but those closely involved. Frequently, the comradeship is very deep. Dawn and I had a very special relationship, and I will miss her very much.''

This intense and dignified statement was interrupted by the arrival of the enthusiastic waiter presenting each of them with large platters containing six gigantic cheese blintzes, a pint of sour cream, still in the plastic container in which it had been sold, balanced on each plate. Professor Sterling brightened considerably.

"Wonderful, wonderful. Eat, eat, both of you,'' he urged, dumping the entire pint of cream on his plate and smearing it across the blintzes with one sweep of his knife. "We'll eat these as a tribute to Dawn Elliot. If she were here, she would order two plates of these blintzes and she would eat every morsel.''

The two women exchanged glances and, ignoring the garnishments, put their forks into the warm, crisp, and creamy food. In minutes, both were duplicating the enthusiasm of their host, and Susan was spreading sour cream as though she couldn't live without it.

"These are fantastic,'' Susan enthused, her mouth not quite full.

"You didn't think they were going to be, did you?'' There was a gleam in the professor's eye.

They all smiled at each other and continued eating until there were three clean plates on the table and three empty glasses beside them. "Now we have something in common, now we're ready to talk about my Dawn," said Day. "But I don't know what I can say about her except that she was an extraordinarily hard worker, a dedicated scholar, and a very special friend. She was beautiful, yes. And intense, very intense about anything she was involved in, from her work to her relationships with people. What else do you need to know?"

Kathleen moved her plate to one side and put her elbows on the table. "The problem is that we are beginning to get two different pictures of Dr. Elliot. At least I am—although I'm the only person involved in this who didn't know her."

"But Kathleen is right," Susan agreed. "I knew Dawn in Hancock and she wasn't at all like the person you're describing . . ."

"I think if you examine your assumptions, you'll find that the statement you just made was incorrect."

"Pardon?" Susan had once had a professor in an Intro to Philosophy course her freshman year say much the same thing to her. She still didn't know what it meant.

"Did anything you saw in Dawn while she was in Connecticut contradict the description I'm giving you? Did you see that she wasn't dedicated to her profession? That she wasn't intense about her work? That she wasn't a hard worker?"

"No," Susan admitted.

"Then possibly you didn't know everything about her, possibly you only saw one side of her personality," Day suggested quietly.

"But her marriage . . ." Kathleen began.

"Ah, yes, that bombastic fool Richard Elliot. I've often wondered about him myself. And about his place in Dawn's life." He paused. "To tell you the truth, I've never understood why Dawn married that man. He's certainly the most pompous, egotistical, verbose failure I've ever met. And, while I can accept that she fell for his charm or something when she was a young girl, why stay married?"

"Perhaps she had religious beliefs that precluded divorce?" Kathleen suggested.

"No. Anthropologists, who study the myths that societies make up for themselves in order to understand and cope with the unknown, are just as willing to believe the myths of their own world as any other group, but I don't believe that Dawn incorporated either a Roman Catholic or a puritanical disdain for divorce in her life."

"Did you ever ask her?"

"I believed Dawn to be capable of making such decisions about her own life and I dislike prying, so I never asked. But once she told me—this was years ago when we were together digging beneath the chaparral of northeastern Arizona—that Hancock was her penance."

" 'Her penance?' Do you know what she meant?"

"I didn't ask. She never said her husband, but Hancock. I assumed that she meant the time she spent there, but I could be wrong. And I certainly have no knowledge of what she might be performing penance for."

"Did you see much of Richard Elliot during the time that Dawn was working?"

"Rarely. He was hardly the type of man who was happy in the primitive conditions that we lived in while on digs. He preferred the Plaza Hotel to adobe shacks or tents. In fact," the professor chuckled to himself, "I remember well the first time he ran into a snake in his sleeping bag. It wasn't a rattler, merely a harmless saddled leaf-nosed snake looking for something worth eating. The man went crazy: screaming and hollering and misquoting Shakespeare for hours and then, instead of getting back to the business of living, he borrowed one of the Jeeps that the group owned and took off for Santa Fe and what he called civilization. We all had a hard time hiding our disgust with his behavior from Dawn. No one blamed him for being surprised and scared, mind you. It's just that he insisted on making such a fuss and he quit so easily."

"This was recently?" Kathleen asked.

"No, no, years and years ago when they were first married. I don't think he was ever on a dig after that. At least none that I know of. Of course, when we were in more urban locations he often showed up. Especially when we were involved in conferences and symposiums in Europe.''

''And did he fit in better then?''

''Not a bit. Well, he didn't go off and leave in a huff but he did bore everyone to distraction talking about himself and his nonexistent career.''

''And Dawn? How did she take this?''

''You mean how did she act?''

''When he was standing around talking about himself, ignoring the work that his wife and the rest of her colleagues were involved in,'' Kathleen amplified.

''She . . .'' He paused and scratched his bald head. ''I almost said that she ignored it, but she didn't. She lived her own life and he lived his—even when they were in the same room. And, you know, I never heard her say a disloyal thing about her husband. Nor would she allow anything against him to be said in her presence.''

''Was she involved with men she worked with? Romantically?'' Kathleen asked.

''Not that I know of. If there was anyone, she was very discreet about it. As far as I know, she was completely faithful to that idiot of a husband,'' came the surprise answer.

''Do you think she loved him?'' Susan asked, thinking that Dawn sounded like she was living two separate lives.

Day sighed. ''I can't imagine that she did. He was simply not worth half of her, and Dawn was a woman who knew her own worth. But, if she didn't love him, why did she stay with him?''

No one answered the question because no one knew the answer.

FORTY PLUS FOUR

I

KATHLEEN AND JERRY WERE CONTINUING THE CONVERSATION that had ruined their chance for romance last night.

"Look, I'm meeting Jed for lunch—and I had to cancel an important meeting to get that time today—but I am not going to press him for any details about Dawn or what he's told the police or . . ." He stopped and took a large bite out of his bran muffin.

"If you're not going to bother to find out anything, why are you lunching with him?" Kathleen poured herself a cup of coffee and replaced the pot on the stove with a slight bang.

"Look, to you this is an investigation, to me it's trying to help out an old friend—"

"Just because I haven't known the Henshaws as long as you—" Kathleen began, her voice angry.

"I'm sorry. We went through this all last night, Kath. You do what you have to do and I'll do everything I can to help." He reached out to pick up the wall phone; its ringing had interrupted them. "Jed, good morning . . . Sure, I'll be leaving in about ten minutes. I'll pick you up at your house, okay?" He listened a moment more before laughing and hanging up.

"That was Jed?" Kathleen asked quickly.

"Yes. The Mercedes is still at the garage and since Susan needs her car for something else today, he asked if we could drive in together. You remember that we have that big banquet tonight, don't you? Did you get . . . ?"

"Your tux was pressed at the cleaners yesterday and everything is hanging by the front door."

"Studs?"

"I said everything, didn't I? I don't think you have any faith in me," she added, laughing.

"I . . ."

"I know," she interrupted. "I don't take it as an insult. Have a good day, and a good dinner tonight. You know," she added, "you're going to be spending an awful lot of time with Jed today. You should be able to find out something."

"I certainly did marry a persistent person, didn't I?" he answered, also smiling.

"Yes, you did."

II

"You would think that spending forty-seven thousand dollars for a car would be some sort of guarantee that the damn thing would work two days in a row, wouldn't you?" Jed stuffed a black jacket into a garment bag as he spoke.

"Jed, that's going to be all wrinkled if you don't straighten it out," Susan protested without much enthusiasm. She always had mixed feelings about social office functions to which wives weren't invited. Part of her resented seeing her husband all dressed up going off to eat, drink, and be merry without her. But she had been to enough dinners in the ballrooms of New York hotels to know that the food was fancy and mediocre and the speeches usually full of in-jokes and self-congratulations. So much for being merry.

"You have a busy schedule today?" Jed asked, wrapping a silk cummerbund around a matching bow tie and adding it to the garment bag.

"Sort of. The first of my new aerobic classes is today. And I still have to buy a gift for Missy. I went to the book shop last week to get something and came out empty-handed because of the storm and all and . . . ." She didn't stop talking as much as she just dwindled off, thinking that her activities sounded trivial compared with her husband's.

Jed may have thought the same thing; he didn't seem to be paying much attention to her answer. "Have you heard anything from the police?" he asked, zipping up the bag.

"No. Yesterday I was on the class trip, of course, but I turned on the answering machine and they didn't call and leave a message. Although one or two calls were just people hanging up. I don't think the police would do that, do you?"

"I doubt it."

"Well, then I haven't heard from them. Do you think I will?"

"I don't know." Jed took a deep breath. "Susan, I'm going to talk to a lawyer. In fact, I have an appointment this afternoon with Andrew Weeks. He has a practice in the city. He's very well thought of, I understand. His brother was at Yale with me."

"Why don't you just call Bob O'Malley? He closed on the house and did all the work on our wills and everything."

"Andrew Weeks is a criminal lawyer, Susan," Jed said quietly. "Now, I don't want to worry you, but I think we should be prepared for anything that might happen. Dawn was found in our garage, after all."

"You think . . . ?"

"I don't think anything. I'm just being careful. Now don't worry. Go ahead and take your aerobics class and go to . . . uh, whatever meeting you were going to. I'll give you a call after I talk to Weeks." Jed heard the friendly honk of Jerry's car, grabbed the bag and his briefcase, and headed for the door.

"Have a good day," Susan said.

Jed turned back to her with a smile on his face. He kissed her quietly. "You thought I was going to forget, didn't you?"

She smiled up at him. "No," she lied.

She kept a smile on her face until he disappeared into

Jerry's car and then she rushed to the phone and dialed. It was answered almost immediately.

"Kathleen, Jed has an appointment with a lawyer in the city today! A criminal lawyer!"

"Good," was the response.

"Good?"

"Yes. Look, he's not going to hire a lawyer and then lie to him about his involvement with Dawn, is he? And the lawyer will suggest that he tell the police about it, and then we'll get past that hump in all of this. That is, he'll give him that advice if he's a good lawyer. He is, isn't he?"

"Well, his brother went to Yale," Susan offered as credibility.

"I suppose that says something," Kathleen agreed, not knowing what. "Are you going to miss class this morning?"

"Of course not! I'm dedicated enough to make it to the first of any series of classes," Susan replied.

"Then hadn't you better get going? The Club's fifteen minutes from your house and the class starts in twenty."

"You're right! I'd better hurry. See you there!" Susan hung up without waiting for a reply. She ran upstairs and pulled a shiny new leotard from one dresser drawer and matching tights from another. She grabbed some warm boots and heavy socks. Her Avias were in her locker at the Club. She was stuffing everything into a bright green duffel bag that had "Forty and Fabulous" printed on one side when the doorbell rang. Mrs. Annie! She'd forgotten it was one of the two days a week she showed up to clean. Susan ran to the kitchen to let her in.

"Mrs. Annie! I'm late for my aerobics class. You know everything to do, don't you?"

"After all these years, of course I do, Mrs. Henshaw. You just leave everything to me and I'll have this house clean by three." The woman went over to the small TV on the kitchen table and turned it on while talking.

Susan, who knew that she would return to a house where every television was turned on in every room, headed for the door. "Well, I'll be back before then. And I'll be at the Club for the next few hours, if you need me." Putting on her coat, she hurried into the freezing garage to get her car. A quick glance around reassured her that no ghosts were present, but she climbed into the Datsun as quickly as possible. It started up right away even on this cold morning. She was out of the garage in minutes. Backing down the driveway, she pushed gently on the brake, not wanting to hit the patch of ice that always formed at the end of her drive at full speed. Traveling so slowly, she was able to see the black Jeep, with its identifying smashed side, pull away from the curb and turn the corner opposite to the direction she was heading.

III

"Did you get the license number by any chance?" Kathleen asked, pulling her long blond hair back and fixing it with the large tortoiseshell barrette that she had just taken from the locker reserved for her in the Field Club women's locker room.

"No, but didn't you write it down after the accident?" Susan answered, pulling on her leg warmers and trying to remember that she shouldn't hate Kathleen just because she had a great figure.

"Yes, but I lost it," Kathleen admitted. "I thought I had put it in my glove compartment, but when I looked for it on Sunday to get all the information together for my insurance company, it was gone. So I must have put it someplace else."

"It will turn up," Susan said.

"I hope so, my insurance company isn't going to be happy until it does."

"The class begins in three minutes, ladies. Please hurry, we're starting seven minutes late as it is," a voice called in the door of the room.

"Three minutes? Seven minutes? What sort of time freak is this?" Susan muttered, double-knotting her shoes.

"New teacher," came a voice from behind the bank of lockers.

"Gloria? Is that you?" Susan called back.

"Sure is." Gloria Bower appeared in their aisle, carrying a broken blue barrette. "Look what happened," she said. "Anyone have an elastic I can borrow to keep my hair out of my eyes?"

"I have a whole packet of those things here," Susan said, reaching into her locker. "I always wonder how they get lost. It reminds me of those *Borrower* books I used to read to the kids when they were smaller." She handed a cellophane bag to her friend. "Here. Take a few." She looked up smiling as she made her offer and discovered that Kathleen and Gloria were exchanging uncomfortable looks. "What's going on?" she asked.

"Kathleen was present when I made a fool of myself yesterday afternoon at the Inn," Gloria said.

"You did what?" Susan asked, thinking about spilling drinks, or upsetting plates of food or, possibly, getting drunk in public. She discounted the latter in Gloria's case; Gloria was too careful, too conservative to lose control in public. It must have been some sort of embarrassing accident that she was talking about.

But Kathleen knew better and she wanted to know more. She waited, a noncommittal smile on her face, hoping that Gloria would continue. But they were interrupted again by the voice of the class instructor.

"Class beginning, ladies. Everyone on the floor for warm-up exercises!"

Kathleen and Susan slammed their lockers shut and followed Gloria, still making two pigtails of her hair, from the room.

They joined a couple dozen other women on a large gymnasium floor in a room originally designed for indoor team sports for children, but altered by adding mirrors at one end about ten years ago when the exercise class craze had begun.

"Everyone line up. You know the routine, ladies!" called out the instructor.

And they did "know the routine," Susan thought to herself, looking around the room. Everyone here had taken more than one class over the years; most of the women had taken many. The room was crowded, as this was the last series of classes before the start of summer. Susan wondered how many of the women here had tried on their swimsuits before signing up for class. Of course, there were a lot of tan women who had returned from winter vacations to the islands, and who probably had a head start on their exercise program. But the instructor was issuing orders and she'd better pay attention.

"Three steps left . . . turn . . . face the back of the room . . . three more steps left . . . I said left, ladies . . ."

Susan had to concentrate to follow the directions and she didn't hear the first time Gloria said her name.

"Susan, I need to talk to you!" The insistent hiss came from behind her.

"After class?" Susan offered, turning right instead of left and bumping into the woman next to her who was correctly following directions.

"Now!" came the reply. "What did Kathleen say to you about yesterday?"

"Clap hands above your head . . . high up . . . stretch . . . ten times and now five times on each side, ladies."

Susan had to wait until the noise had subsided to reply. "Nothing. She didn't mention it. What happened?"

"Knees up nice and high and elbow to opposite knee, ladies . . . then turn in a circle twice . . . and twenty steps in place . . . knees nice and high . . ."

Susan tried to get Kathleen's attention and failed. Kathleen was working hard, knees as high as they would go, arms waving, long ponytail bobbing in time to the music. No wonder she looks better than I do, Susan thought, again losing track of the instructions and traveling in the opposite direction to the rest of the class.

"Now, ladies, we're going to repeat the whole routine. I think that most of you have gotten it. The ones that are having an extra bit of trouble" (here she looked straight at Susan) "can just follow along as best they can. Now . . . three steps left and turn . . . Yes, what is it, Mrs. Grey?" she interrupted herself as the Club switchboard operator appeared in the doorway.

"I have a message for Mrs. Susan Henshaw."

Susan left the line quickly and hurried over to the woman. "What's wrong?" she asked anxiously, thinking of her husband in an automobile accident or maybe a heart attack—or arrested.

"Hancock Elementary called. Your son, Chad, is in the nurse's office with a fever of a hundred and two degrees. They think you'd better go over."

"Susan?" Kathleen came up behind her.

"It's okay, Kathleen. Chad's sick at school and they want me to pick him up."

"Oh, I thought that something terrible had happened."

"No, probably just another case of strep throat; he gets it every single time someone breathes near him. Listen, call me later, will you? I want to hear about everything with Gloria."

"So do I," Kathleen agreed. "I'd better get back to class, but I'll call you afterward."

Susan ran back to her locker and got her coat and purse. She left the Clubhouse without bothering to change and drove quickly over to school, lecturing herself for not paying more attention to her son's health at breakfast this morning. The school was on the other side of town, but Hancock wasn't large and she was in the nurse's office in less than fifteen minutes.

"Hello. I got a call that Chad was sick—had a fever," she said, entering the small office near the gymnasium.

"You must be Mrs. Henshaw." The tall efficient woman in the white uniform of her profession came to the door to meet her. "We called about forty-five minutes ago and your housekeeper said you were out. I'm glad she found you so quickly."

Susan thought briefly that the timing meant that Chad must have gotten sick almost as soon as he got to school. "He seemed all right at breakfast," she began.

"Well, these things come on quickly," Mrs. Robinson

said diplomatically. "The spots are just beginning to show up now."

"Spots? I was told he had a fever. I was thinking strep throat again."

"I think you'd better start thinking chicken pox, Mrs. Henshaw, because that's what he has."

"Chicken pox?" Susan repeated weakly, remembering the cold compresses, calamine lotion, and scabs that she had lived with before.

"Yes, chicken pox, and it looks like it's going to be a doozy of a case. Has Chrissy had it?"

"Yes, when she was a baby," Susan replied. "Chad wasn't born yet."

"Oh, too bad; it's easier when the whole family can get it over with at one time. But sometimes these things just don't work out," she concluded briskly.

"Where is Chad?" Susan asked.

"Right here. His teacher was bringing his coat and he went out in the hall to meet her," the nurse replied, as the child walked back into the room, carrying not only his coat but a pile of schoolbooks.

"I'll carry those, Chaddy," Susan said, taking the books from him with one hand and helping him put on his coat with the other. "I don't see any spots," she said.

"Look. Here and here," the nurse replied, pulling the child's too-long hair off the back of his neck. "And when he takes off that shirt, you'll see that he's full of them."

Susan recognized the telltale spots and sighed. "Well, I guess we'd better be getting home and calling the doctor. Thank you very much. Let's go, Chaddy."

"Stop calling me that!" the child insisted angrily.

Susan and the nurse exchanged looks. Susan's said that her child would never talk that way to her except when he was sick. The nurse's look indicated that she doubted it.

Susan and her son hurried through the cold to the car. "I think I'm freezing," Chad said, wrapping his arms around himself and reaching over to turn up the heat.

"We'll be home quickly," his mother assured him, reaching out and feeling his forehead. The child was burning up; she pressed down on the accelerator and the car speeded up. They made it into her garage in record time. On the door to the kitchen hung a note with her name on the outside.

"What is it?" asked Chad, stopping and leaning against the side of the garage.

"It looks like Mrs. Annie's writing," Susan began, opening the letter. "Oh, it is. It says she got a call from home and her daughter had an emergency and so she's left for the day . . ." She noticed her son's position against the wall. "Chaddy, I'm sorry to leave you standing out here. You'd better get to bed and I'll call the doctor right away."

"Bed? Can't I lie down in front of the TV? I'll be bored in bed," the child protested.

Susan took one look at his flushed face and knew he would be asleep soon no matter where she put him and made a quick decision. "The den isn't ready to be a sick room. Get into your pajamas and you can lie in my bed and watch TV. Okay?"

"Okay."

When they got to her bedroom, she helped him out of his clothes and into the sweatpants and T-shirt he wore for pajamas, Chad being too sick to remember his recently acquired modesty. She tucked him into her bed, giving him a dose of Tylenol, and, placing the remote control in his hand, she left him alone. She called the pediatrician first and, after the predictable discussion of fevers and antihistamines, she hung up. A knock on her front door pulled her back downstairs. She was more than a little surprised to find Mitchell and Sardini waiting for her.

"We have some questions for you," Mitchell said.

"Hello, Mrs. Henshaw. My young friend here makes it sound more ominous than it is. We would like to look around your home and ask you a few—a very few—questions. You may refuse or ask for a lawyer present, of course."

"No, that won't be necessary. Just let me tell my son what I'm doing. He's upstairs. Why don't you wait in the living room?"

"Excellent." The two men did as she suggested and Susan ran back up to her son. He was asleep, but her hand on his head told her that the fever was still raging. She covered him lightly, turned off the TV, and hurried downstairs.

"Have you checked to see if any of your jewelry is missing, ma'am?" Mitchell surprised her by asking.

"My . . . ? I don't think so, but I could check," Susan offered, remembering her hiding place for jewelry and blushing.

"Have you looked at it since your party?" Sardini asked.

"No. Do you want to come with me while I check?"

"If we could." Sardini got up from the couch.

"I haven't seen any signs that anyone has been in the house," Susan added.

"Let's check anyway," was his response.

Both men followed her into the master bedroom. Susan glanced over at the bed and saw, with relief, that Chad was still asleep. Neither man said anything, nor seemed surprised when she led them into the large connecting bathroom. Susan knelt on the handpainted ceramic tile floor and opened the door to the cabinet under the sink; she removed a large-size Tampax box. Standing up, she covered the counter top with a fluffy towel before opening the box and dumping out its contents. A half-dozen little leather jewelry boxes and one or two made of cardboard fell onto the towel. Susan opened them all and searched through the various sparkling contents. "Everything seems to be here," she said finally.

"You keep your jewelry in a Tampax box?" Mitchell was amazed.

Sardini was grinning broadly, but said nothing.

"I thought it was one place no one would look," Susan explained. "I used to keep it in the safe deposit box but this is more convenient. We kept meaning to get a home safe, but just never got around to it." She replaced everything as she spoke.

"Probably as safe as most places," Sardini agreed.

The three of them left the bathroom. This time Susan went

to the bed and felt her son's head again. He seemed cooler; the medicine must be working.

"Home sick from school?" Mitchell asked.

"Yes. I was at my aerobics class when the school nurse got a message to me that he needed picking up," Susan answered, leading the men back downstairs.

"How did the school find you at your class?" Sardini asked, taking out the notebook he had been writing in before they went upstairs.

Susan explained how the call had been forwarded by her cleaning woman and began to tell how she had found the note from her telling about the emergency departure.

"Have you seen anyone suspicious around?" Sardini asked.

"No, I . . ." she began and then remembered the man in the dented Jeep that she had seen waiting outside her house just a few hours ago. She told them about it.

"That's very interesting, Mrs. Henshaw."

"Really?" Susan asked, wondering how significant it could be.

"Yes. You see, we put Mrs. Elliot's name through the Department of Motor Vehicles' computers—just standard procedure; we didn't think that she had committed a crime. And what popped up was an accident between your friend Kathleen Gordon and a black Jeep. The Jeep is registered to Mrs. Dawn Elliot."

"Mom, I feel so sick," came a voice from the top of the stairway. The men and Susan turned around in time to see her son lean against the banister and throw up.

IV

"So a man driving Dawn's car was hanging around my house," Susan said, pouring out some steamy tea for Kathleen. The two women were sitting at her kitchen table discussing recent revelations.

"Susan, how many times have you seen him today?"

"Just once, this morning."

"And before that?"

"Just the time you hit him," Susan answered.

"Well, I was telling Jerry about the accident, and do you know what he said? He said that he thought the man with the Jeep came to the door during your party."

"What?"

"Jerry opened the door for some late guests and this man was there asking about for someone's house. Well, Jerry didn't know the people he was asking about—and, remember he's lived in Hancock a long time and knows a lot of people—and the man went back outside and drove off in a black Jeep with a bashed-in side."

"So, if it's the same man, he was around that night. But why? Maybe . . ." Susan got excited at her thought. "Maybe he killed Dawn and was putting her in the Volvo."

"And then came to the door to draw attention to himself? I doubt it."

Susan sat back and sighed. "Then what?"

"I don't know. But he must fit in here somewhere," Kathleen said. "I think I need to spend some time with a pencil and paper."

"I know you're doing all this to help Jed and me, but I wonder if I could ask you for another favor?" Susan said.

"Sure."

"Would you go upstairs and sit with Chad? He's still sleeping, but I know he's going to wake up and I need to go to the drugstore and pick up the calamine lotion and more Tylenol."

"Of course. I'll go up to your room and work on my lists."

"You have had chicken pox, haven't you?" Susan asked.

"Sure have. There's even a little triangle of scars on my stomach to prove it. Don't worry about anything. Chad and I will do just fine."

"Well, here's the pediatrician's phone number, in case you need it."

"We'll be okay," Kathleen repeated. "Go do your errands." She took a tiny gold pen and a large leather notebook from her purse and started upstairs. "Oh, Susan," she called back to her, "have you heard anything from Jed? About his meeting with the lawyer this morning?"

"No, I think it was this afternoon. He may call while I'm out, but I don't think you should . . ."

"I won't tell him that you mentioned it to me. I'll explain about Chad, though," Kathleen said, guessing at what Susan had been going to say.

"Great."

The Datsun rattled out of the driveway for the second time that day; Susan turned it in the direction of Hancock's small commercial district. She was lucky, quickly finding a parking space. She locked her tiny car and put a quarter in the parking meter in front of the florist's cheerful window. Maybe she'd stop after her errands and buy herself a bouquet of spring flowers; the ones left over from her party were beginning to look pretty sad. Maybe some of those deep purple tulips and white freesias for the living room coffee table. Well, she'd decide later. She headed for the drugstore.

"Well, you're certainly looking very athletic," came a voice from behind the wicker shelves of hair products. Hancock's strict zoning laws didn't extend into its shops, but there were unwritten laws that standard chrome and glass fittings were slightly beneath the town's standards.

Susan, startled, looked around.

"Your leotard," explained Martha Hallard, pointing to Susan's pink Lycra-encased legs shining from below her coat.

"I'd forgotten all about that," Susan admitted, taking the largest bottle of calamine lotion that the store offered off the shelf.

"I don't suppose that's for poison ivy at this time of the year."

"Chicken pox," Susan replied, getting some Tylenol liquid also.

"Oh, no. Dan told me that there were some cases around, but I was hoping we wouldn't have to go through another round of that disease this spring."

"Hasn't Charlie had it yet?"

"Years ago, but it's so difficult to get anything done once a real epidemic gets started. No one can make it to meetings; everyone's either tired from being up at night with their kids, or else bored to death after staying at home with them. And March is a rotten month anyway. The doldrums or something. I heard on the radio that another storm is coming in tomorrow. And the snow from last Friday still hasn't melted. I hate this weather."

Susan, who had always thought of Martha as very self-disciplined and unlikely to be affected by anything as minor as the weather, was surprised to hear this. "What are you working on now?" she asked, knowing her neighbor always had a committee or two busy with a community project as well as running her house and real estate business.

"Very little," came the surprising reply. "Did you hear that the police found my jewelry?" she asked, changing the subject.

"No, how wonderful! Where was it? That means they must know who the burglars are."

"I don't think so."

"Then how . . . ?" Susan began.

"It was found in the possession of some fence up in Hartford. As I understand the story, the police acted on an anonymous tip—sounds like a movie, doesn't it?—and they found everything that was stolen that night in this guy's apartment. And get this: It had been mailed to him from New York City. No return address, just the cancellation stamp to tell them where it came from. The fence says he has no idea who sent it. That a box arrived yesterday in the regular mail and, when he opened it, he was as surprised as anyone to find that it contained valuable jewels."

"No one asked for money for it? I thought that fences paid burglars for the goods and then resold them. At least that's what they do on TV," Susan qualified her statement.

"Guess not. The officer who talked to me said that they don't have any proof that his story isn't true." Martha shrugged, and took a large ornate jar of English bath oil from the shelf in front of her. "I wonder if this is any good?" She twisted off the cap and put it to her nose for a sniff.

"But why steal the stuff if you aren't going to make any money from it?" Susan protested, seeing that she was losing Martha's attention.

"What?" Martha stopped sniffing and looked at her friend.

"They didn't get any money from the fence so why did they steal the things if not for profit?" Susan asked, grabbing at the bottle of calamine lotion, which was in danger of falling to the floor.

"How should I know?" Martha put the bottle she had opened on the display and took an unopened one. "I think I'll buy this for my mother. She loves junk like this and her birthday's coming up."

"Mrs. Henshaw. Mrs. Henshaw."

"I think someone's calling you," Martha said, nodding at the girl behind the pharmacist's counter.

"Chad's prescription must be ready. Well, I'll be seeing you," Susan ended the conversation, seeing that Martha had lost interest. "Glad to hear that you've got your jewelry back."

"Who got it back? They have to keep it until the fence's case comes to trial. Could be months before I wear my jewels again."

The girl behind the counter looked interested, but Martha had moved on to the row of shampoos and cream rinses. Susan charged her purchases and, waving to her friend, left the store. The sidewalk, slippery where melting snow from the roof had made a puddle on top of yesterday's ice, was hazardous and she walked carefully to her car.

"Susan!" A deep male voice from behind her startled her and, ceasing to pay attention to what she was doing, she slipped and fell, her packages dropping onto the hard cement beside her.

"Well, I've had women fling themselves at my feet, of course, but never with such wild abandon."

Susan didn't have to look up to identify Richard Elliot.

What was he wearing on his feet? Red wellingtons? she wondered, being in a good position to notice such apparel.

"Let me help you with your package, my dear," he offered, bending down slowly. "What is that pink stuff oozing all over everything?" he asked, picking up the leaking paper bag. "What sort of repulsive mixture are you carrying? 'Baboon's blood' or something similar?"

Susan assumed the allusion was literary and let it pass. "Calamine lotion," she answered, poking around in the dripping bag to see if anything else was destroyed.

Richard helped her to her feet and then, cape swirling, left her alone on the sidewalk. "Back in a moment," he promised over his shoulder.

Susan held the sticky mess away from her clothes until he returned.

"Here." He held out a plastic bag with large purple print that she couldn't read. "Put that mess in here before it takes over the world and let's go get some coffee somewhere. I need desperately to talk to you."

"I'll have to call home first. Chad is sick and . . ."

"Of course, the maternal instinct. By all means, make your call and clear your mind of all distractions." By now, he was guiding her down the block in the direction of the bakery Kathleen and Maureen had eaten in the day before. "I know there's a phone here that you can use," he assured her, opening the door to the sweet-smelling shop.

Susan spied the phone on the wall at the back of the room between two red-striped awnings, and quickly called Kathleen to check on Chad's condition.

"Don't worry, Susan. He's still asleep and I think the Tylenol has taken care of his fever. I'm sitting here in your bedroom going through the pile of magazines that was on the floor next to your side of the bed. At least, I assume it's your side of the bed; or does Jed like to peek through *Vogue* and *Family Circle* before dropping off to sleep?

"Listen," she continued, "you talk to Richard. He might give you some valuable information. If all else fails, ask the pompous idiot why Dawn and he stayed married!"

"But you're sure you'll be all right with Chad?" Susan persisted, still worrying about leaving her son.

"Give me the number you're calling from and I'll let you know if anything changes here. Okay?"

"Great!" Susan read out the number and hung up. Returning to the table, she found that Richard had already ordered for them both, and the food was awaiting them. "That looks good," she said, as he pushed a cup of coffee toward her.

"Adequate," was as far as he would go to agreeing with her.

Susan wondered how she was going to begin the conversation, forgetting, that with Richard Elliot, uncomfortable silences weren't a problem.

"Susan, Susan," he began and for a moment she thought he was going to take her hand, but he was just reaching across the table for a pastry. " 'I am a man whom Fortune hath cruelly scratched.' " And he took a bite of pastry.

"You mean Dawn's death," she said.

"Yes." And he sighed deeply before taking another bite. "The loss of one's wife, of one's dearest companion, of the woman who was always by my side . . ." He paused, and Susan wondered if he was thinking about how little his wife had been at his side, or even in the same state much of the time. "And then to be questioned over and over by the police as to where I was when she died, what our relationship was like, as though they consider me a suspect in her murder! It's a low point in an otherwise remarkable life."

There was a profound silence while Susan tried not to laugh. But his next words solved that problem.

"I think, dear Susan, that the police consider your husband and myself the main suspects."

"Why? Why do you think that?" Susan swallowed her food and told herself to calm down.

"Because they are fools!" And Richard displayed that ability to enunciate and project that had made him famous in theaters too poor to afford adequate public address systems all over the country. The girl behind the counter looked over at their table, startled.

"The Hancock police are incapable of doing anything other than looking at the obvious: They suspect me because I'm the husband. As though I would do something so inferior, so mediocre, so pedestrian, so third-rate mystery story-ish. Why, I've never even played in *The Mousetrap*."

"And Jed? Why do they suspect Jed?" Susan asked anxiously.

"Because she appeared in your garage, of course. I told you the obvious: propinquity."

"Is that what they told you?"

"That is what I deduce." And he lowered his head and looked at her with cocked eyebrows. "We are dealing with fools, Susan. And I think it is time we took matters into our own hands."

"I don't understand."

"We must investigate this crime on our own. But I think, yes, I think we need some help."

Susan watched as Richard Elliot took on a series of unique mannerisms: head bent to one side, jerky movements, a series of startling twitches with his shoulders as he spoke. "Help?" she repeated.

"That charming woman I met at your home the other night. What was her name? Kathleen, I believe? Isn't she a private investigator or something?"

"She was a police detective; she's running a security company now," Susan explained, deciding not to tell him that Kathleen was already involved.

"And she is your friend and will help us solve this crime and find the true murderer," Richard said. "You probably wonder how I know this."

"Uh, yes," Susan lied.

"Elementary, my dear. Elementary . . ."

He continued, but Susan wasn't listening. She was too busy watching him mimic a good actor's characterization of Sherlock Holmes, creating a dreadful bastardization that was almost laughable. Or sad; he was so terrible. Momentarily she wondered if Dawn had stayed married to him out of pity. Well, she decided, she might as well get one person's viewpoint.

"Richard," she interrupted his rambling explanation, "why did you and Dawn get married?"

"Why did we—?" He broke off, surprised by the question. "Susan, that is just the type of question that the police have been asking me. I thought you were different. I'm terribly disappointed."

"But you must meet so many interesting women in the theater and, of course, many of them would be interested in you. I just wondered why you chose to get married and . . ."

"This is ridiculous, Susan." He stood up abruptly. "I am not going to sit here and listen to your suspicious questions. I am very disappointed in you, Susan. Very!" And he flung his cape over his shoulder and stalked from the room.

Susan sat there and stared at the uneaten food on the table. "If you're not going to finish that, I can wrap it up and you can take it with you," offered the counter girl helpfully.

"Thank you, but I really don't want it," Susan answered, taking her own coat off the hook on the wall and starting to put it on. She was gathering up her purse and purchases when the girl spoke again.

"Someone is going to have to pay for all that, even if it didn't get eaten, you know."

"You mean he didn't . . . ?"

"Him? Nope. He just ordered and took it to the table. Said you might want something else. He never pays for anything. Probably can't afford it." She shrugged, and brushed her too-long bangs out of her eyes.

Susan had had a hard day and it wasn't even noon yet. "Mr. Elliot is a very wealthy man. He and his family have lived in Hancock for generations and he can certainly pay for a snack at the bakery. He . . ."

"You can't tell me anything about the Elliots. My mother used to be their cleaning woman and she says the family lost most of their money in the stock market crash back in the twenties and then the rest of it in the sixties in some sort of oil swindle. I don't know where Mr. Elliot gets money to live on, but it wasn't left by his family. Maybe he's a more successful actor than he looks.'' She snickered.

Susan had put her purse down on the table and was taking out her wallet. ''How much do I owe you?'' she asked, her voice friendly.

''Eleven twenty-five.''

Susan passed the money across the counter. ''Are you sure about that?'' she asked.

''About the Elliots and their money?'' She put away the cash in a drawer under the counter. ''That's what my mother always said and she would have known. My mother always knows what's going on,'' she added, somewhat ruefully.

''That's interesting,'' Susan commented, trying to keep her voice casual. ''Did your mother have any idea where Richard Elliot got his money from?''

''Well, my mother,'' the girl paused and leaned across the counter, ''my mother said that it was from his wife. You know, the woman who died.''

The door opened behind them and another customer entered the shop.

V

''She was not only married to the idiot, but she was supporting him? This is getting more and more interesting.''

''Well, that's what the girl at the bakery said. We're just assuming that it's true.'' Susan was in the bathroom off her bedroom, unloading the bag from the pharmacy. ''I cannot believe this calamine lotion,'' she added, turning on the water and beginning to wash its pink stickiness off the various tubes and bottles.

Kathleen answered from her seat in the bedroom. ''Well, some of this stuff we can find out for ourselves.''

''How?''

''Wills are public documents. We can find out how much money the Elliots left behind when they died. When did they die?''

"Sometime in the sixties," Susan answered. "They were killed at the same time—in an automobile accident."

"Anything unusual about it?" Kathleen asked.

"Not that I know of. Some teenagers had a party in someone's home and got very drunk and ran smack into the car that Richard's parents were driving home from a party. I think that Richard's father died immediately and his mother lingered on in a coma for a few weeks before dying. But that's all I know about it. Nothing out of the usual, although it's sad. Richard was just a teenager, not grown up. I hate to think of parents dying when their children still need them."

"If there was anything else, I can find out more about it in police records," Kathleen said. "We also need to know whom Dawn left her money to. If she was supporting her husband while she was alive, did she plan to continue to do so after her death?"

"Won't the police know that?" Susan asked, entering the room.

"Of course. All we have to do is get them to tell us."

"Do you think they will?" Susan asked, sitting down at her dressing table.

"Mommy, I itch. I itch all over." The sleepy but insistent voice of her son came from the middle of the king-size bed.

Susan leapt up and rushed over to him. "Chad? How are you feeling, honey?"

"I told you. I itch."

"Well, don't scratch, honey. It will leave scars." She felt her son's head. "You know what will stop that itching? A bath. Why don't I run you a nice cool bath and you can soak for a while?"

"A bath? In the middle of the day?"

Susan smiled. If he had the energy to argue, he wasn't all that sick. "It will make you feel better. And I'll sit outside the door and read to you, if you would like."

"Car magazines?" he requested.

"Anything you want to hear," she promised.

"You have things to do," Kathleen said, getting up. "And so do I. I think I'll pay Detective Sardini a call and see how much information he'll part with about this financial thing. Can I pick up anything for Chad?''

''No, I found another bottle of calamine lotion while I was in the bathroom, so we're okay for a day or two. Thanks.''

''I'll stop over this afternoon and bring you a surprise, Chad,'' Kathleen said, heading for the door. ''And I'll give you a progress report then,'' she added quietly to Susan.

''I'd love the new issue of *Four Wheeler*,'' he suggested quickly.

''Chad!'' his mother admonished him.

''That's okay, Susan. He's sick. I'll see what I can find,'' she answered him. ''To be honest, I didn't even know that there was a magazine named *Four Wheeler*. 'Bye.''

''Chad, you really shouldn't . . .'' She stopped her lecture when she had looked more closely at her son. His spots were increasing every second. ''Let me run that tub for you,'' she continued. ''I know it will make you feel better.''

VI

''All I'm asking for is financial information,'' Kathleen was saying to Officer Mitchell, while Detective Sardini, whom she thought to be intentionally ignoring her, was intently reading through a large pile of papers on his desk. ''You must know a lot about Dawn Elliot by now: tax information, and personal and medical records besides her financial situation. All I want to know now is what her estate was worth and whom she left her assets to.''

''We're not obliged to tell you anything,'' Mitchell reminded her.

Kathleen couldn't argue and so said nothing.

''You're not a member of the department anymore, Mrs. Gordon. You have no more right to information than anyone else in the town of Hancock. Maybe less, in fact, since it is your friend's husband who is a primary suspect in this case. Since it was your friend's garage where Mrs. Elliot's body was found. Since . . .''

"I know all that," Kathleen interrupted, unable to restrain herself any longer.

"Then you understand why Detective Sardini and I won't just casually pass you information," Mitchell replied, a slight grin appearing on his face.

She was determined to stay cool. "Why don't you say something?" she asked the other man, moving closer to his desk. "Why are you ignoring me? I might have some information that you need . . ."

"If you are withholding information that could be valuable to our investigation, you are obstructing justice and, as such, are liable to criminal prosecution. I think," Mitchell leaned across his desk for emphasis, "that you had better tell us what you know right now."

"I am not going to stand here and . . ." Kathleen began again.

"You might make up your mind." Detective Sardini stopped reading and looked up at her, his face betraying nothing of what he was thinking. "You came in here five minutes ago asking questions. Now you are telling us that you possibly know things about Dawn Elliot or her death that we don't know. Are you here to trade information?" He waved his hand to quiet Mitchell, who had been about to jump into the conversation. "My colleague will insist that we do not trade information, but, as a former member of the police department, you know that isn't true.

"Now," he continued. "You are interested in trading what for what?"

"I . . ." Kathleen began, thinking as fast as she could.

"I assume your interest in the Elliots' financial affairs has something to do with all this—you did come in here asking for a look at Mrs. Elliot's will, didn't you?"

Mitchell was smiling nastily and even Sardini was beginning to look as if he was enjoying her confusion.

"You and I both know that after the will is probated, it will become public record . . ." Kathleen began.

"And you are willing to wait until then. Excellent. Then, unless you know something about Mrs. Elliot's death that we don't, I think we will leave you and continue our investigation.'' Detective Sardini slid the papers he was looking at into a manila folder and got up from his seat. ''We will look very carefully into the Elliot family finances, since you seem to think that there is something there worth asking questions about.'' He smiled.

Kathleen left the room without a word, slamming the door behind her.

VII

At five o'clock, she drove into her driveway, the first flakes of snow appearing before the headlights of her car. She left the magazines she had bought for Chad on the seat beside her; she would go to his house later. Right now, she wanted to wash her face, put the morning dishes in the dishwasher, and put a chicken in the oven. If this storm turned out to be anything like the weather people were predicting, Jerry might skip the banquet and come home hungry. She wanted to have a hot meal ready for him. She got out of her car and hurried up the lighted walkway to her house, carefully avoiding places where ice was likely to form during the day.

Feeling cleaner and her kitchen ready for the next meal, she was chopping parsley and onions to put into the cavity of the bird when her phone rang. She reached out for it with one hand and began stuffing with the other. But the serious sound of the voice attracted her attention and she stopped what she was doing to listen after the first few words.

''Kathleen, you'd better get over to Susan's house right away,'' said her husband without any preliminary chat. ''Jed's been arrested for murder.''

FORTY PLUS FIVE

I

"So it was all a mistake," Kathleen said to her husband. He was sitting, head in his hands, at the kitchen table. She was removing an enameled pan from the oven. It contained the remains of last night's chicken dinner: a dark brown lump of skin-covered bones, the result of putting a six-and-a-half-pound roaster in a 325-degree oven and leaving it there for twelve hours.

Jerry looked up. "What's that?"

"Chicken jerky," she answered, dumping it into the trash compactor and tossing the blackened pan into the sink before joining him at the table. "I wish I understood why the police asked Jed to come to the police station last night."

"I assumed he was going to be arrested. That's why I called you. I thought Susan shouldn't be alone when she heard the news."

"She was so distracted by Chad's chicken pox she didn't even wonder why I was there," Kathleen replied, picking out a slightly stale piece of coffee cake from a platter on the table and biting into it. "Yuck. I think this is related to that chicken.

"Actually," she continued, "I was glad for the company.

I hate the thought of you driving home from the city on those slick roads. Do you have to go in today?''

"Yes. And I have to leave right now." He stood up and pulled his tie tighter around his neck. "Don't worry about me. The Cherokee's great on these roads. And I won't be alone. Jed's going in with me. He called for a ride while you were in the shower."

"That's fantastic. Will you . . ."

"I'll call when I get to the office and tell you about what happened last night. At least, I'll tell you everything he tells me. I'm not going to quiz the poor guy all the way to the city, Kathleen. He probably had enough of that last night." He kissed his wife and started to leave the room. "You are going back over to Susan's this morning, aren't you?"

"Of course," she answered. "I don't know what excuse I'll use for being there, but I'm going."

"Then you be careful driving, too. You may be driving a four-wheel-drive car, but not everyone else on the road is, remember."

"I know. Maybe I'll run into someone else with four-wheel drive though, someone who owns a black Jeep," she answered, staring past her husband and out the window into the still-falling snow.

Jerry, already mentally battling the storm, smiled vaguely before leaving. Kathleen was equally distracted, remembering last night. She had dashed over to Susan's immediately after her husband's call, expecting to find the household in tears. Instead she'd discovered that Susan had gathered her children in front of the fireplace, and all three were eating toasted cheese sandwiches and drinking hot chocolate. Kathleen, confused by the difference between her expectations and what she found, decided the best thing to do was accept their offer to join in. Chad, still feverish, had fallen asleep wrapped in a blanket on the couch before half his food was finished. Chrissy, excited by the prospect of another day off from school because of the snow, had joined some of her friends outside in the dark streets for an after-dinner snowball fight. Their shrill cries could be heard through the wind each time Susan opened the door to check how deep the snow was getting.

Kathleen, who didn't really like chocolate, had cupped the warm mug in her hands and sipped absently; now that the children weren't listening, Susan would talk about her husband's arrest. Or so she thought. Instead Susan had calmly related that Jed had called and told her that his lunch with the lawyer had been productive, but too short and he was skipping the banquet to talk with him again. And that he would be coming home late on the train and he'd grab a taxi at the station. Susan's main worry, it appeared, was whether he would be able to find a taxi if the snow continued. Kathleen, undecided about what to do, had called Jerry, hoping to get more information about Jed and just why he thought Jed had been arrested. But the phone rang in an office deserted by people who wanted to be home before the weather made the trip impossible. Deciding not to say anything, she and Susan had spent the evening drowsing in front of the fire, mentioning neither Dawn nor the investigation.

Jed had arrived home around nine, saying nothing about the police, at least in front of Kathleen, and she had left her friends talking over their son's chicken pox and driven through the blizzard to her own home, only to find that Jerry had also skipped the banquet, and had spent the last few hours maneuvering through the weather and around the resulting accidents, arriving in their driveway moments before her. They had admired the mounting drifts in the light of the street lamps and gone inside to bed, only to awaken this morning with more questions and, Kathleen thought, fewer answers.

The only thing to do, she decided, was call Susan and see what had happened. She was dialing the phone before she had even thought about what she was going to say. The phone rang once before it was answered.

"Hi . . . Chrissy. It's Kathleen Gordon. Is your mother free to talk?" She glanced at the clock over the stove while speaking. She hadn't realized how early it was.

Chrissy's answer confirmed her guess. "I'm not sure she's

up yet, Mrs. Gordon. I think—no, wait, don't hang up. I hear her now," the child interrupted herself.

"Hi, Kathleen." Susan's voice came on the line.

"Susan, I'm sorry for calling so early," Kathleen began.

"No problem. I was up early with Chad. And I wanted to ask you for a favor anyway."

"Anything. How is Chad?"

"Not bad. It looks like a mild case so far. That's what's worrying me. He woke up today without a fever and any second now he's going to start getting bored. I might be able to convince him to spend part of the morning with a book, but I hate to think of the afternoon and evening. So I was wondering if you would go to the video store for me and rent some tapes."

"Sure," Kathleen agreed quickly, seeing herself provided with an excuse to see Susan. "What movies does he want?"

"Well, that's the problem. What he would like to see is something along the lines of *Porky's* or anything else about sex and teenage life."

"I gather you're not enthusiastic about that."

"I know he's past *Snow White and the Seven Dwarfs*, but I don't think he's ready for pubescent sex fantasies. And, frankly, there isn't much in between. You'd better head for the PG section, and we'll hope that he's too bored to complain about your selection. Get three or four, if you can. They probably won't have much choice on a day when the kids are off from school. I should have thought of this last night."

"Don't worry. I'll leave right now. They're bound to have something this early in the morning—if they're open. I'll be at your house in half an hour. 'Bye." She hung up quickly before Susan could put off her early arrival.

But she was too early. While the notice on the door informed her that the video store opened at nine A.M. on weekdays, a quick look in the window provided evidence to the contrary. The store was deserted, still locked up for the night. Kathleen slipped through the drifts to the comparative warmth of her car, parked where she could see anyone's arrival. She pulled the collar of her coat up around her neck and composed herself to think about last night's police interest in Jed. But her time alone was short.

"Kathleen! What is this? A stakeout or something?" The voice was accompanied by loud knocking on the now fogged-up window of the passenger's side of the front seat. Kathleen reached over, opened up the door, and discovered the identity of the person on the other side.

"Brigit, what are you doing out so early on such a horrible morning?"

"Same thing you're doing—waiting for the stores to open up." Brigit Frye freed one hand from her heavy heather cloak and waved at the quiet street. "You and me and everyone else in those cars," she added. Kathleen followed her glance and recognized for the first time that the main street of Hancock was parked almost solid with cars and most of the cars had people sitting in them.

They couldn't all be waiting to rent video tapes, Kathleen thought. Brigit answered the question before she asked.

"I'm waiting for the drugstore to open. What about you?"

"Video Visions," Kathleen answered, pointing at the store. "Chad Henshaw has chicken pox and Susan's worried about keeping him amused, so I volunteered to pick up some tapes for him."

"That's better than what I'm doing," Brigit said. "I'm picking up one of those home pregnancy tests. Mind if I come in and get warm? I had to park my car about three blocks away."

"No, of course not." Kathleen hurried to open the door. Maybe there were advantages to being a civilian: Information had never fallen into her lap in this way when she was a police officer. "Is it for you?" she asked, when the other woman had gotten settled into the seat.

"I wouldn't stand out there in the cold for anyone else," Brigit assured her.

"Maybe you're just late, not pregnant," Kathleen suggested, hoping to keep the conversation going.

"That's what I've been telling myself for the last two

weeks. But I'm beginning not to believe it. Thus the test."
She shrugged, seeming unwilling to continue the discussion.

Kathleen wasn't giving up so easily. "Well, maybe you
just miscounted," she suggested.

"I doubt it," came the sour response. "Oh, guess who
called last night? Gloria Bower!"

"Really?" Kathleen said. "Did she mention her temper
tantrum or whatever that was at the Inn the other day?"

"Sure did. She called to apologize, in fact. She said that
she'd had so little sleep taking care of Missy and some sort
of stomach problem that the child is having that she just blew
up for no reason." She shrugged. "Sounds a little fishy to
me, but who am I to talk? I thought I was going insane when
my own kids were babies, and she has to worry about being
approved by the state welfare people on top of all that. Oh,
there's someone removing the closed sign from the door. I'll
be seeing you, Kathleen. And, by the way, don't broadcast
this around town. If I am pregnant, I'm certainly not going
to stay pregnant and I don't want the entire town knowing
about it! That's why I'm waiting here for the store to open
instead of going over to Dan's office." She swept out of the
car and hurried down the slippery sidewalk to the pharmacy.

Kathleen noticed movement in the video tape store and
got out of the car herself, just in time to be splashed by a
snowplow turning the corner. She leapt back off the street as
another truck, following the plow, sprayed grit and salt over
the cleared roadway. "Damn." She looked down at her recently acquired Italian boots, now covered with the caustic
mess, shrugged, and hurried across the street and into the
open store.

II

"Damn. Look at this; the color ran on to my stocking.
You would think that paying over three hundred dollars for a
pair of boots would guarantee that the dye is permanent. Oh,
here are the tapes," Kathleen continued, handing over the
bag she had put down on the floor of Susan's hall. "I hope

there is something there that he'll like. I got *Ferris Bueller's Day Off* and *Short Circuit*. It really isn't easy to pick things out for someone his age, is it?''

''No. It was easier when his favorite movie was *Dumbo*. Much easier. Anyway . . .'' She paused and put Kathleen's boots on some newspaper. ''He's asleep now so we don't have to worry about him. And Chrissy's already off to a friend's house for the day. So we have some time to talk.''

''Great. What did Jed tell the police this time? Has he told you about his affair with Dawn? Or do you get the impression that the police know from anything any one of them has said to you? And what about the lawyer Jed was going to talk to in the city?''

Susan looked up from her task. ''All good questions,'' she said with a sigh.

''You must know the answers to some of them,'' Kathleen urged.

''No.''

''You didn't even ask him about his interview with the lawyer? Or what the police wanted him for? Come on, Susan. You and Jed are so close. You must be at least talking to him these days.''

''Well, Chad napped earlier in the evening and had a hard time getting to sleep. At about midnight the poor kid was so miserable and itchy and I was so tired that Jed took over and told me to go take a shower while he read to Chad. I did and then I fell asleep before he made it to bed. This morning, we didn't have much time to talk. Jed told me not to worry, that the police were asking questions about the sand and small pieces of driftwood that they found in the trunk of the Mercedes. They had gone all the way down to the dealer's to check it out. Can you believe that? Well, once he told them that we had transported driftwood back from the shore to use as firewood, they lost interest. I don't see why they would care about it myself. I guess it was just surprising to find it in the car at this time of the year.''

''That's all?''

''And they asked something strange,'' Susan continued.

"They wanted to know who our doctors are and who has our medical records for the last few years."

"That's interesting," Kathleen said, remembering the autopsy report's analysis about debris on the body, but she didn't enlighten Susan. "And about the lawyer?"

"He didn't mention it. But that doesn't mean anything. He was busy with Chad and calling Jerry for a ride. He just didn't have time to talk. He'll probably call today and . . . That's probably him now," she said as the phone rang.

"Hello? Yes, she's right beside me," Susan said after a pause. With a quizzical look, she handed the receiver to Kathleen.

"Who is it?" Kathleen leaned over to whisper.

"Detective Sardini," Susan said quickly. A loud clunk over her head indicated that Chad might be up. She pointed to indicate her destination and hurried up the stairs.

Kathleen stayed in her seat. "Hello."

"I have some information you might be interested in, Mrs. Gordon," the voice of the detective came on the line. "I could give it to you over the phone but, if you have the time, I'd rather see you in person."

"Of course." No way Kathleen was going to give up this opportunity. "You're at your office in the municipal building?"

"Yes. I'll be waiting for you."

A click indicated the end of the conversation and Kathleen bounded, stocking-footed, up the stairs to find Susan. "I'm meeting Sardini down at his office," she announced, rushing into the room where Susan was sitting with her son. "I'll call you when I find out what's going on. He says he has something to tell me. But I don't think it's anything to worry about," she added quickly. "He seemed very upbeat on the phone." And she dashed out of the room and back downstairs.

Sure he sounds upbeat, Susan thought to herself. He probably always sounds upbeat right before the kill. She ground her molars and concentrated on the thermometer sticking out of her son's mouth.

III

"So," continued Sardini, leaning across his desk to Kathleen. "We know the man's name is Jesse Clark and we have to find him ASAP. His presence has been too convenient: first the night of the party, and then Susan Henshaw saw him near her house yesterday morning. I don't know that we can hold him for anything, but we can certainly try to get some information."

"You have an APB out for him, of course?" Kathleen asked.

"We've been broadcasting his description since yesterday when he was seen near the Henshaw home. We'll find him if he stayed in town or around here. If he headed into the city or got on a plane for the coast, he's probably lost to us."

"You checked on the terms of the will?" Kathleen asked.

"Yes, and it's interesting," Mitchell smiled, taunting her by refusing to give the information without her asking for it again.

"She didn't leave her money to her esteemed husband. She left it to a relative, a Jesse Clark," Sardini explained with a scowl to his associate.

"What?" Kathleen sat up in her chair, astounded.

"It's quite a footnote to all this. And it may have something to do with the murder," Sardini began. "I haven't seen the will itself. It was stored in New York City at her lawyer's office, but I spoke with that gentleman at length on the phone and I believe we have the whole story now.

"Dawn Elliot was born Dawn Clark and the Clarks were a very wealthy family. Most of their money came from shipping. They were heavily involved in shipbuilding along the coast of Maine. And they had the foresight to get out of the business before it became less lucrative in the late forties and early fifties—after which, of course, it dwindled down to nothing. Most of the family had died out by then anyway. There were two brothers representing the Clark family. Joshua Clark, who had one child, Jesse, and Emery Clark, who had two daughters, Dawn and a younger sister who died of meningitis when an infant. So a considerable fortune, valued in millions of dollars, came to Jesse Clark and Dawn when their fathers died.''

"How? When did they die?" Kathleen asked.

"About twenty years ago in a sailing accident.''

"Together?"

"Yes. They were sailing in waters near the family's summer cottage on Deer Isle up in Maine when a storm came up. Their bodies washed up in a small cove the next day. Since they were together, it was assumed that they had almost made it to land before their boat capsized. Anyway, their deaths made both Dawn and Jesse very wealthy young people.''

"Outright? I mean, was the money left in trust funds or did they get their inheritances immediately?" Kathleen asked.

"Yes and no. Joshua Clark was the more conservative brother, it appears; Jesse's money was in a trust fund and he lived on the income of the fund's investments until he was thirty. Which was four years ago. Dawn got her money outright to do with what she wanted. She was twenty-one at the time and one of the first things she did was marry Richard Elliot.''

"And proceed to support him in the style to which he had become accustomed before his parents lost their money,'' Kathleen guessed.

"As far as we know, yes,'' Sardini agreed.

"Did she write a will then? Did she ever leave her money to her husband?'' Kathleen asked.

"Not that we know of. I asked the lawyer and he said that he has always handled her legal affairs, and that he explained to her at the time of her inheritance that she should have a will. She made one leaving everything to Jesse Clark. Evidently, she never changed it.''

"Maybe she didn't think of it?'' Kathleen offered an explanation.

"Not according to this man. He says he reminded her regularly that she should update her will to indicate changes in her life and, in fact, she did add some small legacies over the years—mainly to people she worked with and primarily concerning objects from her professional life, not money. But the bulk of her worth she left to Jesse throughout the years that she was married to Richard Elliot. In fact, Richard Elliot is left only one thing by the will: an early edition of *Bartlett's Familiar Quotations*.'' The detective grinned for the first time since he began this story. ''Seems she knew her husband well.''

''Did he know? Did the lawyer you spoke with have any idea whether Richard Elliot was aware of the terms of his wife's will?''

''He was pretty sure not. He told me that Richard Elliot called his office the morning after he heard of his wife's death and appeared anxious to know just how long it would be before he would have access to Dawn's money. He even spoke of how little money he had available. In fact, the man had no qualms about admitting that he was living off his wife's money. And the lawyer had no qualms about telling him that the free meal had died along with his wife.''

''No wonder his grief appears sincere,'' Kathleen said.

''No one who's ever been exposed to his professional acting could imagine that he is accomplished enough to simulate any emotion,'' Sardini said. ''I dated a woman who was an Off-Broadway theater nut. The most boring evening in my life was spent watching Richard Elliot's portrayal of Dr. Stockman in a revival of *An Enemy of the People*. Of course,'' he added, ''that wasn't true for everyone in the audience; a lot of people seemed to think that the play was a comedy and Richard Elliot was hamming it up intentionally. You can't imagine such laughter in the middle of an Ibsen play.''

Kathleen mulled over this bit of personal information before returning to her original interest. ''So Richard Elliot didn't have any reason to kill his wife.''

''Well, if he killed her for her money, he made a big mistake,'' agreed Sardini. ''But, remember, we have no reason to believe that he had any idea that her money wouldn't be left to him. As far as we know, he didn't suspect the terms of her will.''

"Did the lawyer think that Jesse knew about his legacy?''

"No, but his opinion is that it wouldn't matter. He also handles the affairs of Jesse Clark, and evidently that young man doesn't need any more money. He turned his father's generous legacy into a fortune. He's a broker in broadcasting properties and has been very successful in the last decade. But just because he didn't have a financial reason for murder doesn't mean there wasn't a different motive, as I'm sure you know.''

"Did the lawyer suggest any other motives?''

"No, but interestingly enough, he was in the dark as to why Dawn Elliot married or stayed married to her husband. And he's known her since she was a little girl. He also said that she and her cousin were good friends: He was a business-man, but he was fascinated by her work and often visited her in the field. They regularly kept in touch. I get the impression that Jesse Clark can hardly stand Richard Elliot and that the lawyer feels the same way.

"That's really all I learned from the lawyer,'' Sardini ended. "I thought you might be interested.''

"Yes,'' Kathleen agreed. "I appreciate you telling me.'' She wondered if she could ask about his reasons for calling Jed the night before and decided against it. She didn't want to consider what the sand in the trunk might mean.

"Maybe we can work together a little more,'' said Sardini, getting up from his seat. "I'll be getting in touch with you.''

"Thank you,'' Kathleen responded, confused. Obviously the meeting was over. What had he gained from it? And, once more, he was abruptly dismissing her. She smiled, with as much confidence as possible, and, nodding her head at the unusually silent Mitchell, left the room.

"Well, we certainly gave her something to think about—'' Mitchell began before the door was completely closed behind her.

"Shut up!'' he was interrupted by his superior.

Kathleen made her way to the main reception area of the

building. A small information desk was placed conveniently near the front door. An elderly woman sat behind it.

"Is there a public phone around here?" Kathleen asked.

"Right behind you near the rest rooms," was the answer. Kathleen hurried to follow the directions.

"Hello, Susan. Do you have a few minutes? You won't believe what I just learned from Sardini." And she proceeded to relate the entire story. "I'm going to go over to the aerobics class and think this thing through and then, if I don't come up with something better, I'm going to try to find Richard Elliot. I think it's time to get to the bottom of Dawn's relationship with him. I'll call you if I succeed, okay?"

The voice on the other end of the line agreed with this plan; Kathleen hung up and, slinging her purse over her shoulder, left the municipal center. Susan put down the receiver and turned to her guest.

"They know that you're Dawn's cousin," she said to him.

IV

The man she had spoken to turned from the window he had been staring out of to smile at her. "It was only a matter of time," he said, brushing his slightly long, very straight dark brown hair off his forehead. "I don't want to get you in trouble for hiding me. I don't know much about this type of law, but it certainly isn't legal to conceal someone that the police are looking for."

"I'm not concealing you. You're standing right in front of the window, in full view of any policeman who cares to look in. Besides, that is the least of my troubles. My husband is the major suspect in your cousin's death, you know."

"Because she was dumped in your new car or because of something I don't know?"

Susan stared at the young man. Tall and lanky, with high cheekbones and piercing blue eyes, he was too angular to be good-looking in a traditional way, but he would always get more than his share of attention. She could see the resemblance to his cousin's striking beauty. And his way of talking, half serious, half casual, relaxed her guard. "My husband had an affair with your cousin," she answered honestly.

"So did a lot of other men in this town."

"You knew?"

"Dawn used to kid about it; she called them her handsome Hancock club and said that they gave her an interest in life when she wasn't working."

"That sounds rather crass," Susan said, freezing a little.

"She was crass about her life here," the man agreed easily. "Wasn't she?" He sat down on the couch on the other side of the room.

"I don't know," Susan responded. "I'm just beginning to realize how little I knew Dawn. How little any of us in Hancock knew her, in fact."

"That wasn't your fault. She hated being here—not that she didn't admit to the virtues of the suburbs, she just felt more at home in other environments."

"So why did she come here?" Susan asked, a bit indignantly. If she didn't like it here, why come and have affairs with the husbands in town? She was just about to ask out loud when Jesse Clark answered the question.

"She had an agreement with Richard Elliot to spend a certain part of each year with him in Hancock. I gather it was important to him to be here and uphold his standing in the community or some such nonsense. Evidently he felt that he needed a wife at his side to do so."

"It helped his standing in the community that she was sleeping with people other than him?"

"I know. It doesn't make sense. The only thought I have on the subject is that Richard Elliot is such a fool that he didn't know. Or maybe such an egotist that he didn't care." He shook his head.

"You don't like him." It was a statement rather than a question.

"Does anyone?"

"Then why . . . ?"

"Did Dawn marry him?" he finished for her. "Good question. I've asked myself once or twice, although Dawn was a very private person and didn't talk about her life to others—even relatives. But Richard Elliot has always been a puzzle. He was a fool when she married him. She was young, just twenty-one, but she was smart and she must have seen what he was. And then, if she did mistake his personality earlier, why stay married to him for all these years? Why not divorce him?'' He looked straight into her eyes. "I think the answer to that question died along with my cousin.''

"Unless Richard knows,'' Susan reminded him.

"Maybe. My own opinion is that he's such an egotist that he probably thought she adored him for years despite all evidence to the contrary. God, I don't know. Her life with him—her life here—it's all a mystery to me. The Dawn I knew was passionate about her work, and fulfilled by it. What her life was like here in Connecticut is a mystery to me.''

"Why have you been hanging around my house?''

"You saw me?''

"Yes. Your car is pretty distinct, you know, with that smash in the side.''

"Actually, the car belongs to Dawn. I just bought a new sports car and I didn't want to drive it on these roads, and she had ordered this Jeep that she was going to drive out to her digs in Mexico next month and asked me to pick it up for her a week ago. With this bad weather I thought it was a good time to try it out. Dawn wasn't sure about how it would handle. She didn't learn to drive until a year ago.''

Susan thought that was a strange insight into the life of a woman she would have described as very independent, but didn't say anything.

"Mommy, the tape machine is broken. I can't get the tapes to run anymore.'' This wail came from a pajama-clad spotty child standing in the doorway.

"Oh, Chad . . .'' Susan began, just stopping herself from telling him that she had forgotten him with the arrival of Jesse Clark. "I'll check on the machine right now. It's probably just overheated or something.'' Like most mothers, Susan had developed more than a passing acquaintance with many machines, from video tape players to vaporizers to computer games. And there were some who said that most of a person's learning took place before he was twenty.

"If you want me to look at it," Jesse offered.

"No, it's an old machine. It probably did overheat. I have a fan attached to it. It will only take a second." She started to get up.

"Is that your car out front?" Chad demanded, still standing in the doorway.

"Sure is. You interested in cars?"

"In a Ferrari 328 GTB? You bet I am!" Chad moved toward the man as he spoke.

His mother grabbed him gently by the shoulder. "Don't forget you're sick, honey."

"It's all right, Mrs. Henshaw. I've had chicken pox. And people who love cars like to talk together, right, Chad?" He smiled as he spoke.

But Chad wasn't heading for Jesse Clark, but for the window. He stood in the middle, staring out at the car in the driveway. "Wow. It looks brand-new."

"Three weeks old. But it's hardly been driven. The weather has been so bad that I was borrowing a Jeep from . . . from a friend," he ended with a quick glance at Susan. "When you get well, I'll give you a ride in it," he offered.

"Oh, you don't have to do that," Susan began.

"I'd love to," he insisted. "I think I owe you one after the mess I made. Besides, us car lovers have to stick together, right, Chad?"

"A ride in a Ferrari 328 GTB. Wow," was Chad's only comment. He hadn't moved from the window.

"You have to get well first," his mother reminded him.

"I think I'll go look it up in my books," Chad responded, forgetting his problem and leaving the room. "Thank you," he paused and turned around to call out to Jesse Clark before bounding up the stairs to his bedroom.

"He seems to be feeling much better," Susan said, relieved that the worst of the disease appeared over and dreading the boredom that would set in as recuperation began. She sighed.

"I think I'd better be going," Jesse said, standing up and reaching for his coat. "I gather from what I heard of your conversation that the police are looking for me. I think it's time to show up at their offices. Maybe once I explain everything, I'll be able to start driving the Jeep again. This snow . . ." He stopped and looked out the window. "This snow isn't the environment the designers envisioned when they thought up the 328 GTB."

V

"Look, it's no problem for me. I haven't got anything happening this week. Gotta fly to D.C. next Monday and meet with the Feds about a shitty little problem out in Pittsburgh, but I can spend the day right here at the Club if necessary." Guy Frye took a sip of his coffee and rocked back in his chair, a position that displayed his bulging stomach fully.

"I'm okay unless someone decides to have a baby a little early. But they can call me." Dan Hallard patted his beeper, unconsciously imitating fictional cowboys speaking of their trusty six-shooter. He was also drinking coffee.

The third member of their party was talking on the phone that the bartender had plugged into the jack under the table where they sat. Few of his words could be overheard, but apparently there were problems on the other end of the line. After running his hands through his hair a few times and crumbling a croissant all over his plate and a large portion of the tablecloth, he grew impatient with the person he was speaking to. "Listen, I know things are backing up, but with this lousy weather and the new baby and all, I've had problems just getting into the city. And concentrating at my house is impossible. Gloria is in such a tizzy about the whole approval process for Missy's adoption that she does nothing but wash the baby and vacuum the floor. Just tell him that I'm snowed in and I'll write both reports today and have them on his desk first thing tomorrow morning. I don't know how! Just tell him!'' And Harvey Bower angrily slammed down the phone. "Why is it that every good secretary I find gets pregnant?'' he asked rhetorically and reached for the silver pot of coffee that had been placed on the table. "Is this stuff still hot?''

As if on cue, the white-jacketed waiter moved from behind the bar and placed a fresh steaming pot before the men. Two of them, having a late brunch in the bar of the Hancock Field Club, where they were all members, didn't notice the efficiency. But Dan Hallard smiled. He'd waited on tables to get spending money in college and medical school, and he knew exceptional service when he saw it. The other two men, raised in towns like Hancock, took such service as their due. He reached across the table and refilled the cups before speaking. "Now that we have our work schedules figured out, I think we'd better do some serious thinking. Why don't we start by pooling our information?''

"What's there to pool?'' Harvey Bower pushed his hair back again. "I thought we talked about all this on the phone last night. We three had affairs with Dawn Elliot over the years. We also know that Jed Henshaw did. She was murdered and turned up in his garage. Not in one of our garages but in his. The question is do we go to the police and tell them that Jed slept with her?''

"Or did he already tell them himself?'' said Guy Frye. "Look, I've got the day to kill, so I don't care, but I don't understand why we're here.'' He carefully picked the largest piece of crumb cake from the platter in the middle of the table. "Those cops from Hartford seem to know what they're doing. They'll check out Jed's relationship with Dawn and they'll find out that he slept with her . . .''

"And what if they don't?'' interrupted Harvey, sloshing the coffee from his cup as he leaned closer to the table. "Suppose they don't find out that Jed slept with her? Suppose he didn't tell them about it the way we did? Suppose they figure that he had nothing to do with Dawn Elliot and someone slipped her body into his garage to incriminate him and get themselves off? Then whom will the police come to? One of us, damn it! And what if a policeman shows up during a spot inspection from the state? How would that look? It might not make any difference to you, but this investigation could wreck my life. I want this whole thing over as soon as possible and if Jed killed Dawn so that Susan wouldn't know he slept with her, then he should be arrested for it!''

''First things first,'' came the calm voice of Dan Hallard. ''We may be jumping to conclusions. Sex may have nothing to do with the motive for Dawn's murder. For all any of us know, they're looking into her relationship with her husband . . .''

''And sex had nothing to do with that relationship,'' Guy added, snickering and wiping powdered sugar from the front of his shirt.

''Possibly not, but that has nothing to do with the fact that the three of us had uncomfortably close relationships with a murdered woman, and we have to decide if we are going to tell the police that there is a fourth. Now. If we wait, that will look suspicious too.'' Dan Hallard reached toward his coffee as his beeper sounded. ''Dawn . . . I mean, damn. I'll get it at the phone over there.''

''How about this . . . ?'' began Harvey, waving at the phone sitting on the table.

''No. More confidential over there. No offense, but you have to be careful in a town this size. Can't have rumors starting about who's having trouble with their ovaries and who isn't.'' He got up and left the table.

Guy rearranged his position slightly so that his back was to the doctor before he spoke. '' 'Dawn . . . I mean damn'?'' he quoted, with a broad smile on his face. ''Do you think that means something?''

''Maybe that we all have Dawn Elliot's death on our minds,'' was Harvey's rejoinder. ''I doubt that he murdered her, if that's what you're suggesting.''

''Someone did.''

''I won't argue that.''

''So what about Colin Small?'' Guy asked. ''Brigit says

that he slept with Dawn too. Evidently Maureen thinks that he's going to use it as an excuse to leave her and the girls or something. How come he isn't here?"

"I called him last night," Dan Hallard replied, returning to the table. "He had some important work to do today. But the police know about Dawn and him, and he'll go along with anything we decide about telling them about Jed. The Henshaw/Elliot affair was a surprise to him, though. I don't know what that means, but I vote that we call Sardini and tell him that Jed Henshaw was Dawn's lover, too. After all, we've confessed, so we're suspects. Why should Jed get off the hook?"

"I doubt if he is. After all, her body was found in his car," Harvey reminded him. "But, as it happens, I agree with you. I think we should tell what we know because otherwise we're keeping information from the police, and that in itself could get us into trouble."

"So what are we waiting for?" Guy said impatiently.

"Nothing," came the reply as a dull thumping noise began from under their feet.

Harvey looked up first. "What is that banging noise? It doesn't sound like it's coming from the squash courts—too rhythmic. And this is coming from the basement, isn't it?"

The men listened to the muffled pounding. "Aerobics classes," Dan Hallard decided after a few moments. "The bartender was telling me about them. They just began yesterday and he says they're driving him crazy."

"That's right. Gloria said something about joining. I think there's even a sitting service provided for the younger kids and she thought it might be good for Missy to get out some. I wonder if they're down there right now," Harvey said.

"How are they doing?" Dan asked. "Missy looks like a healthy, happy child. You were lucky to get her. There aren't a lot of children available for adoption these days."

"Don't we know it. Listen, why don't we hurry up here and maybe I can grab a few minutes with my new enlarged family before getting back to work," Harvey said, suddenly serious.

"Good idea," agreed Guy. "We think one of us should tell the police what's what about Jed and Dawn. Do you agree?"

"Fine. Who's going to be the one to do it?" Dan Hallard answered. "I can't see any reason for all three of us going together, do you?"

"I'll do it," volunteered Guy Frye, standing up. "In fact, I'll go do it right now."

"Fine," agreed the doctor. "You agree, Harvey?"

"Sure. Are you going to mention this meeting to them? Not that I think you should keep it a secret," he added quickly.

"I'll say that we all know about the affair and think that they should too, okay?"

"Excellent. They will contact us if they think it necessary," Dan Hallard said, "and I think that's just fine." He paused and signed the check that had discreetly been left on the edge of the table.

"Then I'll be off. See you both around." And Guy Frye pulled on the leather bomber's jacket that had been hanging on the back of his chair, nodded his good-byes, and started for the door.

"That bastard is going to enjoy it," Harvey Bower said, feeling slightly sick.

"Probably," was Dan Hallard's assessment, wondering if Colin Small really was so busy he had to miss this meeting. He returned to the present. "Why don't we see if your new daughter is around here somewhere?"

But it turned out that Gloria and Missy weren't attending the aerobics class this morning and only Kathleen, taking a break in her leg lifts, was there to see Dan Hallard and Harvey together on this weekday morning.

VI

"Well, I don't understand why you are giving information to Kathleen Gordon. It seems to me that we should keep what we know to ourselves,'' Mitchell was saying, a self-righteous tone to his voice.

''But it is my choice. I'm in charge of this case,'' Sardini replied, not looking up from the papers in front of him. He was more than a little tired of having every decision he made second-guessed by this man. ''Yes? What is it?'' he angrily asked the woman who had come knocking at his door.

''Two gentlemen to see you, sir,'' she reported. ''That is, there are two gentlemen here to see you, but they didn't come together and they don't want to see you together. One's name is . . .'' she paused to check the slip of paper she carried, ''one's name is Jesse Clark and the other is Guy Frye. Do you want to see either of them?''

''I want to see them both. Especially Jesse Clark, but I need to spend more time with him. Tell you what. Ask Mr. Frye to come in first but make sure Jesse Clark waits. In fact, if he has any inclination to leave, call one of your men to hold him on some pretense. They can call me if they need any suggestions. Got that?''

''Yes, sir!''

''And there's an APB out on Jesse Clark right now. You may as well call it off since he's here.''

''Yes, sir.''

''Bring in Guy Frye,'' he urged her as she seemed about to take root in the doorway.

''Yes, sir!''

She must have hurried because the man appeared in her place almost immediately. ''Hello again, Detective,'' he said, and, getting right to the point, ''I have some information about the death of Dawn Elliot that I think you might be interested in.''

''Please come in, Mr. Frye. We're interested in all information about Mrs. Elliot, and we appreciate you coming in to tell us what you know.''

Guy Frye came in and sat down, and told his story in the nastiest way he knew how.

''That is very interesting, Mr. Frye,'' Sardini said when the man was finished. ''It gives us a lot to think over and we certainly appreciate that you came in and told us about it. No matter how painful it is to talk about a good friend, this is just the information we need. Thank you very much,'' Sardini said, ushering the man out the door.

There almost wasn't time enough for Guy Frye to get angry about how quickly he was dismissed. Almost. As the door closed behind him, he would have been interested if he could have heard Mitchell's comment.

''Well, that wasn't anything we didn't know. Not only did Mr. Frye's wife already tell us about that, but we heard the same thing from that obstetrician, didn't we? A man named Hallard or something, wasn't it?''

''Yes,'' Sardini agreed for once. ''Dr. Dan Hallard.'' He rearranged a small tape recorder that was sitting to one side of his desk before speaking again. ''I think it's time that we saw Jesse Clark.''

VII

''I have very little time, Mrs. Gordon. I am flying to the coast tonight and I must pack.''

''Just a few minutes then. I promise I'll be brief.''

Kathleen stood outside the entrance to the large white brick Colonial where the Elliots lived when they were in town and tried to convince Richard Elliot to let her in. He was standing in the doorway so that she couldn't even see inside. Unlike his usual pseudo-English sartorial display, he was wearing carefully bleached jeans, an even lighter blue silky chambray shirt, Gucci loafers, and no socks. He looked like what people thought Southern Californians look like. Except for his ankles: They looked cold.

Maybe it was the icy breeze that convinced him, but he suddenly stepped aside and suggested she come in. Before he could change his mind, she did.

''Thank you. I really won't take much time,'' she began.

He waved away all such concerns with his right hand while closing the door with his other. ''I'll manage. I have learned to travel light while following my shining star. Come in, dear lady, come in. You will be my last guest at this house; the last person to visit the home of my parents.'' And, with a suitably expansive gesture, he led her into the large living room off the spacious center hall.

''What a lovely room,'' she commented, feeling something was expected of her.

''It is exactly the way it was in my parents' day. Of course some of the furniture wore out and had to be replaced, but Dawn saw to it that the replacements found were as close to the originals as possible. In many cases, she found exact duplicates.'' He continued, but Kathleen wasn't really listening. The room into which she had been ushered was decorated as one would expect the Colonial home of an upper middle class family in the fifties to be decorated. A little too much pine, a little too many ruffled prints and cotton calicos, certainly too many wrought iron knickknacks, but not without its charm and a lot of comfort. Dawn Elliot had lived here?

''It's nice that your wife liked your parents' taste,'' she said, feeling that some sort of comment was again expected.

''She hated it,'' came the terse reply.

Kathleen, startled, looked carefully into the face of the man sitting on the couch across from her. He was looking around the room and fiddling with a replica butter churn. Kathleen thought that his last statement might have been the only impromptu thing she had ever heard him say.

''You think that she wanted to change it?'' she asked.

''She made no secret to me of how little she liked it. She said we lived in a museum dedicated to mediocrity.''

''Then why . . . ?''

''Because she had to, that's why!'' Richard Elliot toppled over the churn in his anger. It fell toward Kathleen and she reached to pick it up. ''Just leave it,'' he ordered. ''It's not my problem now.'' He focused all his attention on Kathleen. ''She left me nothing in her will you know. Absolutely nothing. Everything goes to that cousin of hers, as if he needed more money. The man is a millionaire! A goddamn millionaire and now he has everything of hers too! It makes me sick! And after all I did for her, too!''

"All you did?" Kathleen repeated the phrase slowly.

"Yes, all I did," he repeated sarcastically. "She would have gone to jail, if it hadn't been for me!"

"To jail? For what?"

"For murder, that's what. There, that surprises you, doesn't it?" He sat back in his chair, and crossed his arms. "You haven't been in this town very long, but I know that everyone thinks that Dawn was too good for me. I know that no one knows why we married, why we stayed married, why she was supporting me with her money, why she came to live in this house that she hated and pretended that our marriage was real for a few months each year. No one knows the truth because I told no one the truth. But now that she's dead, I have no obligation to support her lies anymore, do I?"

"No," came the honest reply.

"So . . ." He took a deep breath. "So I will tell you the truth. You were a meter maid or something, you'll know what to do."

Kathleen nodded, ignoring the insult. "Of course."

"My wife, Dawn Elliot, the woman whom everyone thought was so superior, so educated, so brilliant, so everything perfect . . . My wife killed people. Two children."

"How?"

"She ran over them. She was driving home from a Halloween party in 1969, and she ran over two little children out trick-or-treating, and killed them. What do you think about that?"

"How do you know?" Kathleen asked, not doubting the truth of what he was saying. He was such an incompetent actor that she knew he couldn't be lying, but she needed to hear more of the story.

"I was with her. In fact, she was driving my car!" And he sat back and looked smug. "Oh, how I've waited to tell this to someone," he continued. "You see, we had just begun dating. Oh, I had known Dawn for a long time. We were in college together, but she hadn't had time to go out with me. She was always busy studying. But we ran into each other at a party, a costume party in fact. I never found out who her date was but he had driven her to the party in her car—a Jaguar XKE—and had left the lights on and the battery was dead when they got ready to leave. Well, Dawn and he had an argument or something. I never heard the whole story. Anyway, she wanted to get home in a hurry so I offered to give her a lift. Dawn agreed, as long as she could drive, and we left her date to find someone to jump-start her car and took off. The party was here in Hancock and she was living in the city doing some research work at NYU. It wasn't late, only a little past nine, and there were still children out trick-or-treating. Dawn had been drinking—we all had—and she was driving a little recklessly. You know how hilly and curvy the streets are around here, and, in the fall, the gardeners pile the leaves that they sweep off the lawns into the street, near the curb. That night, Dawn was driving a little too fast and running the tires of my old Corvair into those piles and making the leaves blow up into the air when . . .'' He paused and Kathleen thought that, for the first time, he was moved. ''. . . when there was this awful thud. We both knew that she had hit something. The car had even risen a little into the air as we rolled over it . . . them. When we got out of the car, we found two children. One was dressed as a clown in red-and-white polka dots with ruffles of red and white stripes. The other a black witch with a tall pointed hat. Both costumes were bloody. And the children were dead.

''I didn't know what to do. I think I was frozen. But Dawn didn't stop to grieve. I remember exactly what she said: that no one had seen us, that there was nothing we could do to help these children now, that it would ruin her life if anyone discovered that she had been driving the car that hit them, that we should get out of there immediately and shut up about it. And then she reached down and picked up a Tootsie Roll that was lying on the ground and took off the wrapper and popped it in her mouth. She got back into my car, still chewing on the candy, but this time in the passenger's seat. She said we should get the hell out of there.

"And we did. I drove away from there as fast as I could. And she was right. No one knew my car had killed those kids. No one knew Dawn was driving; neither of us was ever connected with the deaths."

"You drove her to her apartment?"

"Yes, she was upset and she asked me to spend the night and I did, of course."

"Of course," she agreed, feeling sick.

"In fact, and I don't like to be indiscreet, but we spent the next week in her apartment. We only left to go to the deli around the corner for food and the liquor store for wine. We didn't read the papers; we didn't turn on the TV; we just enjoyed our solitude. We were married on Thanksgiving Day in the Episcopal church where my parents were married. At first I thought nothing had changed for Dawn, except for the fact that she wouldn't drive a car. I thought that was understandable after what she had been through. But the moment we were married she became a self-centered woman, determined to carry on with her career despite the demands of my life."

"You lived in this house?"

"Not at first. My parents died about a year later and I was left this property. I insisted that we keep it up and live in it for a while each year. Dawn didn't like Hancock but she had to do what I wanted."

"She did?" Kathleen asked, beginning to understand the convoluted and destructive relationship that had been the Elliots' marriage.

"Of course. I could always go to the authorities and tell who killed those two little children, couldn't I?"

"But I understand you had moved from Hancock for the past three years," Kathleen said.

"Yes. Dawn's life—her sex life—was making me crazy. I couldn't stand it anymore. You know why she slept with all these men around here, don't you?"

"No."

"She did it to get back at me for making her live here. She hated me," Richard Elliot said. "She not only slept with half the men in this town, she talked about it, even bragged about it. 'For thou thyself hast been a libertine, As sensual as the brutish sting itself; And all the embossed sores and headed evils That thou with licence of free foot has caught, Wouldst thou disgorge into the general world' was how Shakespeare put it in *As You Like It*. That woman was out to get me!''

And Kathleen wondered if it was her imagination that she saw tears in his eyes.

VIII

''And then he told me that he was going to Los Angeles— or 'the coast' as he, of course, called it. That he had to meet with some television network executives tomorrow morning and that he wouldn't be around for Dawn's memorial service tomorrow.''

''And then you left?'' Susan asked, pulling the phone cord up and around the towel rack on which it had become caught. She put down the six tubes of bright red lipstick (one color, six different names) that she had in one hand, and concentrated on Kathleen's call.

''Yes. I'm in that phone booth near the library. I'm on the way over to the Hallards' house. Martha called late yesterday afternoon while I was putting dinner in the oven and asked me to do a consult on their home security system. Seems that last burglary scared them.''

''Or maybe Dan is off to another convention and Marty is expecting a munificent gift of jewelry,'' was Susan's bitchy reply.

''Maybe. Anyway, I didn't want her to hear this, but I did want to let you know right away. Listen, I have to go. I'll stop over as soon as I talk to Martha, if you don't mind.''

''Of course not. I'll be looking forward to the company. Chad's supposed to be napping and I'm keeping busy cleaning out drawers and cupboards. Right now I'm going through the medicine cabinets in the bathroom. You would not believe what's here,'' she said, removing a small tube of baby teething ointment from the rear of a top shelf over her sink and throwing it into the large brown paper bag she had brought upstairs for that purpose.

"When you get done there, you can start on mine," Kathleen said. "See you later." And she hung up.

Susan whisked the plastic tubes of lipstick off the counter and into the garbage and turned her attention to a half-empty packet of birth control pills. How long had it been since she used that particular form of birth control? she wondered. She shrugged, and it followed the rest of the mess into the bag.

"Mom, when do you think I'll be well enough to go for a ride in that Ferrari?"

"Chad, you're supposed to be resting, not thinking about cars," Susan called back to him.

"Mom, I always think about cars. What else is there to think about?"

Oh, how about your father being arrested for murder? she thought. Damn, this was all getting to her. "Why don't you read the *Car and Driver* magazines that Kathleen brought you?"

"Will you read them to me?" came the plaintive cry from the adjoining room.

Susan sighed. Well, why not? After all, he was sick and maybe he would learn something—certainly she would. She put the paper bag in a corner near the enameled pink wastebasket and went into her bedroom. Chad was sitting in the middle of the king-size bed she shared with her husband and, surrounding him, twisted in and around the cotton sheets and the down comforters, were a dozen or more magazines, their covers embellished with gleaming low-slung cars or imposing trucks on wheels so high that her son could have walked under them without brushing his feverish forehead on their chassis. "What do you want me to read?"

"This . . . It's about the 959."

"The wh . . ."

"It's the new Porsche, Mom. Don't you know anything?"

"Chad, I don't expect to be spoken to that way, even if

you are sick.'' She put her hand out and caressed his hair as she spoke.

''Okay,'' he agreed. ''Here's the article.''

Susan looked down at the picture of a remarkable car and, resisting an urge to check just how many pages the article ran, began to read.

FORTY PLUS SIX

I

"So Richard Elliot isn't going to be at the memorial service. I truly don't believe that man," Jed said, tightening the knot of his rep silk tie around his neck.

"But you'll be home . . . ." Susan began, digging through her sock drawer for stockings.

"In plenty of time for the service. Do you want me to meet you here or at the church?" he interrupted, picking up a heavy Harris tweed jacket.

Susan pulled a pair of periwinkle blue opaque panty hose from her drawer before answering. "Meet me there. I think I'll ask Kathleen if I can go with her. There are some things I'd like to talk to her about."

"Jerry says that her business is picking up since the burglaries last week."

"Yes. Do you know, Martha Hallard called her in for a consult on their security system? She did it yesterday. She stopped over here afterward but we didn't get much of a chance to talk. Chad was being something of a pest."

"Well, maybe now that he's getting well you can get away some. He did seem better last night."

"I hope so. You know, Chrissy was pretty sick with chicken pox but I had never thought it was a serious disease until I was talking with the nurse at Chad's school and she said one of the girls in his class had a mild case, then it got in her lungs and she got pneumonia and ended up in the hospital.''

"Have you taken Chad to the pediatrician?''

"No, I just talked to him on the phone. He told me what to look for, though. It's just that Chad's older now and I'm not used to his being sick, I guess. And all this with Dawn, of course . . .''

Her husband looked across the room at her and Susan froze, one leg in her stockings and one out. Was he going to say something about Dawn? Was he going to tell her about the affair? But he just smiled and the moment vanished; whatever had been about to happen stored, for the present, in the past. "I think I hear Chad now. I'd better hurry and get dressed.''

"I'll check on him and make some coffee before I leave,'' Jed offered. "Oh and, honey . . .'' he paused. "I wonder if you would mind picking up the Mercedes this morning? They called the office yesterday afternoon and said it was finished.''

"Sure,'' she answered, as her husband left the room. Then she picked up her shoe and threw it at the wall. "Damn all cars!'' she exclaimed.

II

"I still don't understand why we're going to a memorial service for a woman we've never even met. The only time we even saw her she was laid out on the slab at the police morgue in Hartford, damn it,'' Mitchell was saying as angrily as he dared to his boss.

Sardini looked up from the bacon and scrambled eggs that he was eating at the local diner. The eggs weren't properly mixed and bits of white floated throughout the yellow. The bacon had been fried last week and reheated in the microwave an hour ago. All this and Mitchell, too. He ignored him and continued eating. His partner for fifteen years had retired last month; this pairing with Mitchell was just a tryout and, as far as he was concerned, it was going to end with this case. If the case ever ended. Sardini dutifully ate what was on his plate and considered what it would be like to have a partner like Kathleen Gordon: beautiful, bright, and, from all reports, a creative problem solver. He shook his head. Why think about it? It would only make Mitchell more unbearable.

"We're going because everyone involved in this case will probably be there. And, even if some don't appear, that may be significant. We're going to see if we can recognize the murderer in a room full—or in this case a church full—of suspects."

III

"I do not understand why we have to go to her memorial service!" was the echo in the Small house across town as Maureen poured coffee into a mug for her husband.

"Because it wouldn't look right for us to not be there. Everyone will be there, damn it. We have to act like everyone else," her husband replied angrily, pushing bread into the toaster oven and slamming the door. "Now look, we have to do everything that everyone else is doing. It's important that we don't single ourselves out in any way."

"But you told me last night that we didn't have to worry anymore," Maureen protested.

"I told you that Guy told the police about Jed and Dawn's affair . . ."

"So he's the logical suspect! If we don't have to worry anymore, why do we have to go to this funeral?"

"I keep telling you: We have to do what everyone else does. We can't draw attention to ourselves. Now do you understand?" Colin reached for the butter and dropped it on the floor. "Shit! Now look what you made me do!"

"I didn't make you do anything. I don't think you can blame the girls and me this time," his wife replied, her voice raising angrily.

"What other solution was there? Tell me that! You . . ."

"What a pleasant way to begin the day." Unlike her parents' voices, the girl that stood in the doorway sounded calm and in control: her hair rigorously styled to appear casual;

her sweater hand-spun and hand-knit; her high boots under the short skirt made from soft Italian leather. She was a model of what most exclusive stores said a teenager was supposed to look like.

"Jenny!" Her mother's face dissolved into a bright smile. "I didn't know you were downstairs already. Your father and I were just having a disagreement about . . . uh," she paused. "About the car . . ."

"Don't tell me that one of them is broken again. I thought that the reason we leased cars instead of buying them was so that someone else had to worry about maintenance. I promised Jeremy he could drive the Jaguar when he takes me to the movies tomorrow night." The girl walked over to the counter and took the toast that her father had waiting for him and popped a piece of it, still unbuttered, in her mouth.

"I don't see why your dates have to drive our—" her father began, his voice still angry.

"Colin. I promised Jenny that she could have the car Friday night," Maureen said quickly, with an anxious glance at her daughter. "Now what time do we have to be at the church for the funeral?"

"Noon. I'll leave work early and come home and pick you up. That is, if there's a car available for me to drive into the city and back," he added, subdued but still angry.

"Of course," his daughter answered quietly. "Trevor Anderson is picking us all up and taking us to school. He just got a BMW for his seventeenth birthday." She started out the door. "Some parents' don't make their children borrow cars. They buy them for them." And she speeded up her pace a little as though she thought she might have gone just a little too far.

"Shit!" her father roared and slammed out the back door.

Maureen just shrugged and bent over to pick up the spilled butter.

IV

"Not that I really feel like getting into black for the woman who had an affair with my husband, but Harvey says we have to be there and he's right. Besides, he wasn't married to me when he slept with Dawn.''

There was a smugness in her voice that could be heard over the phone and Brigit felt the need to explain that her position wasn't that of the injured wife either. ''Well, you know that Guy and I have an open marriage so I don't worry about such things. Besides I have this wonderful new steel-gray Donna Karan wrap dress that will be perfect for the occasion. I was calling because I wondered if you wanted to drive over together. Guy's afraid that he'll be late so he's going to come by himself.''

''Great. I was going to be going alone. Harvey really can't get away from the office in the middle of the day. He's been taking so much time off from work because of all the legal work involved in adopting Missy that he says he's almost a month behind. And I'd like the company. Why don't I pick you up? I'll have to get the car out to pick up the sitter for Missy. You wouldn't believe how long it took me to find a sitter last night.''

''I remember those days,'' Brigit answered. ''What time should I expect you? I think the service starts at noon.''

They continued to plan their transportation and their ward-robes. Guy Frye walked through the kitchen where his wife was sitting at her built-in desk and looked at her with a question mark in his eyes. She responded by putting her hand over the mouthpiece and whispering, ''It's all set. I'm going with her,'' in a voice that Gloria couldn't hear.

''See you later then,'' and, without a kiss or a caress, he left his home.

V

''I didn't know she was coming,'' Kathleen was saying to Susan, who was sitting beside her in her idling car in the Henshaw driveway. ''She called just as I was leaving the house and asked for a ride. I didn't see how I could say no, since she might see that I was stopping over here to pick you up. We'll have to wait a bit to talk privately, though.''

"Well, I'm just glad we're together. I hate funerals—memorial services—whatever."

"Really?" Kathleen commented, watching out the windows of the car.

"Yes. More all the time, in fact."

"Because we're getting older and more aware of our own mortality?" Kathleen suggested.

"I don't think so. Although I suppose that's true. But, you know, every funeral I go to reminds me of the ones I've already been to. It's almost like I start to miss everyone I know who's died all over again with each new death." She paused. "I remember the first person I knew who was my age and died. It was Samantha Bower. I'll never forget it. Of course, she had cancer and we had been expecting it, but that didn't make it any easier. She died on a Saturday night and I remember going to the grocery store on Monday morning and in all the aisles there were groups of women talking about her. It sounds stupid, but I can still see Martha Hallard standing in front of the dairy case, her grocery cart overflowing, and she was sobbing loudly." She checked in her purse to see if she had a handkerchief along. "So where's Martha? Are we going over to her house?"

"No, she said she'd keep a watch out the window and come over here when I arrived. She's so organized that she should be . . . Oh, there she is now," Kathleen answered, considering the image Susan had just presented as a very unemotional, very put-together Martha Hallard cut across the snowy lawn to them.

"I'm sorry. I couldn't find the scarf I always wear with this coat," she said, opening the car door and revealing a dark, shimmering mink that hung open at the neck to reveal a large silk rectangle woven in muted tones of brown and emerald. "I thought I had lost it and was looking everywhere and all the time it was stuffed on the floor of my closet. I guess the dog must have pulled it off the hanger. But I can't imagine why Toto would do something like that. And, you know," she added, "it smells a little. I hope Toto didn't have an accident on it. But, anyway, we won't be late. It's only a few minutes to the Episcopal church.''

"That scarf's gorgeous. I noticed it the night of Susan's party,'' Kathleen said, putting the car into reverse and guiding it out of the driveway.

"Dan brought it to me from India one fall and then bought this coat to match the following Christmas,'' Martha said, pulling the fur from beneath her where it had folded itself. "It's my favorite.''

Your favorite bribe or your favorite present or merely your favorite present from your husband, Kathleen thought, wondering if all three were identical. There was silence as they drove down the road.

"It might be easier to park in the back lot. Then we don't have to worry about skidding across that slippery spot out front,'' Susan said as they turned the corner behind the dark brown shingled church with glossy red-painted doors and trim. She took a few deep breaths as Kathleen followed her suggestion and parked the car; her companions were composing themselves too.

"I'm not looking forward to this,'' Martha commented quietly, as the three of them got out of the car and started toward the building.

"The service is going to be in the smaller chapel,'' Susan commented. "Jesse didn't think that there would be many people here and he thought an empty church would be depressing.''

"How do you . . . ?'' Kathleen began.

"Ladies . . . Good to see you on this sad occasion.'' Dr. Doubleday Sterling stood in front of them.

Martha Hallard, noticing the handful of dropping daffodils he held, started to smile rather superiorly. Susan, noticing the same flowers at the same minute, felt she was going to cry at his gesture. She reached out and kissed his cheek.

"Thank you, my dear. It's good to see a familiar face,'' Day said, brushing a tear away from his eye.

Kathleen introduced him to Martha and the four of them stood together a little awkwardly, no one knowing exactly what to say. Then Martha absented herself with a garbled mumble about the ladies' room and, in her absence, the threesome relaxed a little.

"I wish that more of Dawn's colleagues were present. I understand that there's a group coming from NYU but I don't see any of them," Day said, looking around.

"That would be nice. You know, Dawn didn't spend much time in Hancock; not many people knew her here," Susan said, trying to apologize for the sparseness of the crowd in the lobby of the church.

"Maybe we should go inside," Kathleen suggested. "Maybe there are more people there."

"I think I see some people I know," Day answered, looking out the still-open door into the lot. "If you will excuse me . . . ?"

"Of course," Susan said. "Please go meet your friends," she added, as organ music began to be heard.

"Why don't we go in and sit down," was Kathleen's next suggestion and, Susan agreeing, they headed to the door.

"Oh no," Kathleen exclaimed.

"Well," Susan said, following her gaze. "What did you expect? The Elliots really didn't spend much time in Hancock and not all that many people knew Dawn, and . . ."

"Yes, but I thought that someone besides ourselves would come."

"Ladies, if you're looking for the Elliot service, its location was changed to the main sanctuary at the last minute," a dignified man in a black suit stood up from where he had been sitting in the back row of the chapel. "I can show you the way . . ."

"Thank you, we know it," Susan assured him, and she and Kathleen hurried off. "We're going to be late, although I don't suppose it matters much." There was no one in the narthex outside the church and they hurried in. "Oh . . . !" Susan was so surprised that she slapped her hand over her mouth to shut in the words she would have liked to have said. The room was jammed!

VI

"Well, that was very, very interesting. I don't think I've ever been to a Quaker memorial service before," Kathleen said, as they stood up in the back pew where they had squeezed in an hour before.

"Especially not one in an Episcopal church," Susan agreed. "But you know it was a service like Dawn and I think she would have liked it—if you know what I mean."

"I do." Kathleen smiled. "But I think we're lucky that so many of her colleagues from the city showed up. Did you notice that no one from Hancock spoke?"

"Except for Miss Saldes, the elderly lady in the pink dress. She's the research librarian downtown," Susan said.

"Oh, I didn't know who she was. I thought she was talking about a university library when she spoke about Dawn doing research from early in the morning until late at night."

"It does seem a little difficult to envision Dawn doing research on extinct Indians in the Hancock Library. Maybe she was looking up something else."

"Maybe. Did you notice that Sardini and Mitchell were there? I wonder if they have any information," Kathleen said, looking around the room.

"Susan! Jed didn't come to the service? Colin just left. He had so much work to do, but he certainly didn't want to miss paying his last respects to Dawn." Maureen Small came over to them, a blob of wet tissues in one hand.

"Jed's here somewhere," Susan replied, hoping it was true. She had looked around during the service but couldn't spot him. "He had to be in the city earlier so we came separately."

"All these men, just rushing in and rushing out. Colin. Jed," Kathleen said, smiling at Maureen. "I want to find Jesse Clark and offer my condolences. Have you seen him?"

"Jesse Clark?" Maureen asked.

"Dawn's cousin," Kathleen explained. "The man who was riding around town in her black Jeep—the one that I ran into and smashed one side of," she added.

"The man who was in the black Jeep the night of Susan's party?" Maureen looked anxiously around the room while asking the question.

"Yes . . . where are you going?" Kathleen asked as Maureen turned around quickly.

"I just thought of something I forgot to tell Colin. Maybe I can catch him before he leaves." And she pushed her way through the crowd toward the door.

"I wonder what that was all about," Susan said quietly to Kathleen.

"Looks to me like she didn't want to run into Jesse Clark," Kathleen said.

"She didn't even know who he is," Susan protested.

"Maybe I told her all that she needed to know."

"What?"

"Maybe she has good reason to fear the man in the black Jeep no matter who he is," Kathleen said.

"Are you talking about me?" Jesse Clark appeared at Kathleen's side.

"Jesse! What are you doing here? I thought you'd be greeting mourners at the door," Susan exclaimed.

"I thought about it but decided it would be inappropriate. No one in Hancock knows me except for you two and I had very little contact with her professional friends and colleagues. Dawn wrote fairly specific instructions for this service in her will and she didn't mention a chief mourner so I thought I would just dispense with that."

"When I didn't see you, I was a little afraid that the police had held you. The last time I saw you, you were off to their offices downtown," Susan reminded him.

"No. They questioned me for a few hours, and then said a very polite thank you and let me go. I didn't even get the impression that I was a suspect. They asked why I appeared at the front door the night of your party, of course. But I told them the same thing I told you: that Dawn had asked me to meet her in front of your house. And, when she wasn't there, I decided to knock to see if she had gone inside. It was silly of me not to explain to the man who came to the door."

"The police knew that Dawn was planning on being at the party?" Susan asked, wondering if she would have preferred Dawn's alive presence to her dead one.

"Yes. One of the other guests had invited her along and had already mentioned that to the police, I understand.

"They were also very interested in finding out what I had seen outside of your house and the house next door while the party was going on—not where I was at the time she was killed or even when she was moved into the garage. That is, as far as I can tell. It may be presumptuous of me to think that I knew where their questions were leading."

"But what does that mean?" Susan asked. "I mean, I'm glad you're not a suspect; I never thought you were, remember. But why are they interested in what was going on outside the house?"

"An excellent question," Kathleen said. "And I think I may know the answer." And she turned and left the group quickly.

"But she's not going to tell me," Susan commented. "No one tells me anything." She turned back to her companion. "Were you surprised to see how many people arrived for the service? I thought it was going to be in the chapel."

"I was shocked. But I shouldn't have been. The sensational coverage this has gotten in the news brought out people. Actually, I was a little offended by that at first but, when I thought about it, I decided that Dawn would probably enjoy a laugh over it." He shrugged. "So why should I let it bother me?"

Susan, noticing for the first time his very red eyes, realized she had been remiss. "I shouldn't be talking about the police when you're feeling her death so much. I'm sorry."

"Don't worry about it. I find that the more I think about it, the more I want her killer found. No one should kill someone and then get away with it!"

"Susan, did you notice that Richard isn't here? I thought I might have missed him so I found one of the men from the funeral home and they said that he wasn't present—that he hadn't even stopped in to see the body!'' Gloria Bower was obviously thrilled. "Can you believe it!''

"Richard Elliot is in California—Los Angeles, I believe,'' Jesse Clark told her.

"Really? I don't think I know . . .'' Gloria began, looking up at him.

Susan quickly introduced them and then asked a question of her own. "Why is he there? Kathleen saw him and told me that he was leaving, but I really don't think of him as a Hollywood actor.''

"He did do some commercials out there a year or so ago,'' Gloria said. "I remember him telling me about it last summer. But he claimed to hate Hollywood and films and that type of thing.''

"Probably because no one out there would hire him. You can tell he's overacting from the back of a theater with a large house—think how he would look on the screen,'' Susan suggested.

"That's just what someone has done evidently,'' Jesse said. "He called early this morning—I hate to think what time it was on the coast—he purported to be thinking about Dawn and her memorial service but what he really wanted to report was that he's been offered a role in a movie. He said it was a starring role, but I don't know that we can go by that.''

"But what is he going to play?'' Gloria asked.

"An aging Shakespearean actor, from what I could tell between quotes. I assume the movie is a comedy.''

"You mean someone is going to make a fool out of him,'' Susan said.

"No more than he's been making out of himself for the past decade.''

VII

"There's going to be an arrest.''

"What?'' Susan spun around and stared at Kathleen. "Who?''

"I don't know. That damn Sardini wouldn't tell me. I wouldn't know about the arrest except that Mitchell opened his mouth once too often—as usual. Get into the car and I'll explain.'' The two women were back in the lot behind the church, after having met more of Dawn's colleagues and running into Dan Hallard, who was driving his wife home. Jed hadn't appeared.

Susan connected his absence to what Kathleen was saying. "Did they make an arrest? Did they arrest Jed? Is that why . . ."

"Of course not. You'd know if Jed were under arrest," Kathleen assured her. "It's not something the police keep from the family. Don't worry." She got into the driver's seat and waited for Susan to get in the other side before continuing. "What I don't understand is why Sardini and Mitchell were at the service if they're going to arrest someone this afternoon, unless . . ."

"Unless they're going to arrest someone at the service. Kathleen, don't start the car. We've got to go back inside and—"

"No, they already drove off. I watched them out the window of the narthex. The arrest isn't going to be made here."

"Then where?" Susan asked, as Kathleen turned the key and started the engine.

"Good question. Where are you going?"

"Home. I need to check on Chad. Poor kid isn't getting as much attention as he deserves for someone as sick as he is."

But, when they arrived at her home, they found out that she was wrong. Chad and his father were sitting in the study, sipping hot chocolate in front of the fire, in the middle of a game of Trivial Pursuit.

"Hi!" Chad looked up from the rectangle of cardboard that he had been reading to his father. "I'm winning!"

"Hi, hon. Hello, Kathleen. Is the service over?" Jed stood up and kissed his wife.

"What are you doing here?" she asked, returning his kiss.

"I made good time coming out of the city and thought that I'd stop here and check on Chad before going to the service and he talked me into a game. Listen, I'd like some coffee.

Maybe Kathleen can take my place for a few minutes while we go in the kitchen and get something to munch on.''

"Sure," Kathleen sat down immediately. "You're not going to ask me a question about some little-known king in fifteenth-century England, are you?''

Chad grinned. "How much do you know about geology?''

"You're in luck. Nothing," she answered as his parents left the room.

"Why did you stay here? Was something wrong when you checked?'' Susan asked, immediately after the kitchen door closed behind them.

"No. The poor kid just looked so spotty and lonely that I decided that it wasn't necessary to go to the service. Was I missed?''

Susan told him about the crowd and assured him of the contrary before mentioning the impending arrest. Jed was busy looking into a cupboard so she couldn't see his face, but she didn't have to when he spoke.

"You thought that they had arrested me, didn't you?'' he asked quietly and, she thought, sadly.

"I thought that maybe . . .''

"Susan, Jed. What kind of car do Maureen and Colin drive?'' Kathleen came into the room asking.

'What kind of what?'' Susan couldn't change her thoughts so quickly.

"What kind of car? Chad was just telling me that they had a new Jaguar sedan,'' she insisted.

"That's right,'' Jed answered. "But I don't think they own it. I think Colin just rents it. At least I know he was doing that until a few years ago.''

"Is this important right now?'' Susan demanded.

"Yes. I think I may know who's going to be arrested,'' Kathleen answered.

FORTY PLUS SEVEN

I

"I KNEW YOU WOULD SAY THAT SO I CALLED HEATHER last night and the party's on. I even heard her check with her mother. So we just have to go out and buy her a present. I know just what she wants." Chrissy, still in her nightclothes (this time a pair of pink sweat pants, green and yellow tweed baggy socks, and a gray sweatshirt professing to be the property of the New York Mets) got up from her seat at the kitchen table and went to the window. "I really don't think the snow's all that deep," she added.

"Chrissy! How can you say that? There must be twelve inches out there and the plows haven't come around yet. Your father's had a long week and I am not going to wake him up to take care of your brother while we try to find an open store to buy a present for Heather . . ."

"Not just any store, Mom. I want to go to A Feather in Her Cap. They have the cutest ski mittens and Heather really wants them . . ."

"You're not listening to me. I said that I wasn't going to talk about this until the roads were clear and your father was up and I meant that . . . What was that?" she interrupted herself at a loud crash that sounded as if it were coming from under her feet.

"Something in the basement? Did the furnace blow up again?" Chrissy asked, remembering last month's crisis, and following her mother to the basement stairs.

Susan, not believing that a furnace a month old would explode, was relieved that there was no smoke curling up from below. No loud noises followed the first one but, surprised to find the lights on, she started down the stairs. At the bottom, she looked around the large wood-paneled rec room. With a living room, a study, and family room on the first floor as well as the dining room and kitchen, their family of four had found little use for this space. The furniture was from the apartment in the city and very worn. A small HO gauge train was half set up over a rustic wood wet bar that the previous owner had installed and that had never been used while the Henshaws lived there. Three doors led from this room. The one to Susan's laundry room was open and three built-in bins overflowing with clothes reminded her that she had better run the washing machine today. She should probably pull the sheets off Chad's bed and get some clean ones for him while she was about it.

"Did I smell coffee?"

"What are you doing down here?" Susan was startled as her husband's head popped out of the door to her left.

"Cleaning. I'm thinking of knocking down the wall between this room and the next one and giving myself a bigger workshop. Chad's getting old enough to be building things and I want to get him a workbench of his own and maybe some simple hand tools and things. We really don't use the stuff in there," (he pointed toward the last closed door) "so I thought this might be a good idea. What do you think?"

"Great idea! I'll get you some coffee and be right back!" Susan almost ran up the stairs to the kitchen. Although she suspected that Chad's enthusiasm for this plan would equal that he felt for the train his father had bought him, she was happy. This was just what Jed needed: a new project. She delayed getting the coffee only long enough to run to the second floor and peek into her son's room. Glad that he was still asleep, she hurried back to the kitchen and microwaved some frozen coffee cake to take with the coffee. Everything on a tray, she returned to Jed. He was busily pulling a top-of-the-line Tunturi stationary bicycle through one of the doors and into the space in front of her.

"Let me help," Susan offered, putting the food down next to the train and hurrying over. She picked up the back end and together they placed it in one corner of the room.

"I wonder if we should have a garage sale and try to clear out some of this stuff," Jed said, waving back into the room he had just left. An exercise track was still in place. A weight-lifting bench was resting on its side against one wall. "We get enough exercise down at the Club and no one uses this stuff here."

Susan thought guiltily of her ever-present plans to "start tomorrow" and decided to put off anything definite. After all, she might wake up one morning and really do it. Or maybe Chrissy . . . "Why don't we just shove it all into the corner of this room for now?" she suggested. "After all, we don't come down here much, and no one holds garage sales in March. Next month we'll have a better chance of getting rid of it."

"Good idea. Will you help me move the Nordic Trac? Or, if you're busy, I could ask Chrissy . . ."

"It won't take any time at all. We can do it in a few seconds. But, Jed, the plows haven't been through yet. If you need anything at the hardware store . . ."

"Not now. I'm just going to be tearing down this morning. And everything should be cleared by the afternoon."

Susan glanced into the room he called his shop and wondered if the hardware store could possibly be as well equipped. For years, Jed had amused himself on weekends buying up every kind of tool and gadget available to the suburban handyman. So why was she always calling repairmen and carpenters when this treasure trove of materials lay beneath her feet? Maybe she should skip exercising and take a course in carpentry.

They had just finished rearranging the last of the weights when Chad appeared at the top of the stairs. "Hey, a bench press. They have some at the high school. That's just what I need. I was thinking about trying out for the wrestling team next year.'' He hurried down and stroked the dusty plastic covering the top.

''You were?'' Susan asked, not sure how she felt about this revelation.

''Did I ever tell you I was on the wrestling team in high school?'' His father's enthusiasm was apparent.

''You are not to do anything with those weights until I have checked your temperature,'' Susan insisted, despite her husband's attitude. He needed a distraction from his worries and she was thrilled that he was involved with a new project, but Chad's health came first.

The boy started to protest, but his parents stuck together. ''It will only take a minute, Chad. And you should get on a robe or something. It's pretty cold down here. You go with your mother now. I'll be here when you're through. Is someone going to get that phone?'' he added.

''Chrissy's upstairs,'' Susan said.

''She's taking a shower, Mom,'' Chad informed her. ''At least she was when I got up,'' he said to her departing back.

''Hello?'' Susan gasped, having tripped on the last step into the kitchen, fallen down and skinned her elbow on the quarry tile floor. ''Oh, Kathleen,'' she identified the caller. ''Could you hold on a second?'' She reached across the room and pulled a dish towel from a drawer. ''That's better,'' she continued, placing it over her bleeding arm. ''How are you today?''

''Fine. Susan, Jerry says that the party is on for tonight. I gather that these people from California are only free tonight and, since everything is arranged for a car to drive them out from the city, we're going to go on as planned, despite the snow.''

''As planned?'' Susan asked, wondering what she was talking about, thinking only of the sleepover that Chrissy had been talking about.

''What I called for was to ask if you wanted to bring Chad along. He can stay upstairs in our guest room and watch TV or sleep. I thought you might not want to leave him when he's sick. Chrissy can come, too, of course.''

''Kathleen, what are you talking about?'' Susan gave up trying to fake it.

''My dinner party tonight. The one that . . .''

''Of course! I had forgotten,'' Susan cried. She and Kathleen had been planning this for over a month. Two couples from a company in Los Angeles were in town for a week and the Gordons were having them to dinner along with some people from Hancock: the Hallards, the Fryes, and the Bowers, come to think of it. The point of the party was to be half business and half social; now it would be half business and half talk about the murder.

''Jerry says we have to keep the talk away from Dawn's death,'' Kathleen stated, reading Susan's mind over the phone wire. ''But I really want to talk to you about the arrest. Could you possibly come over for an hour or so this afternoon?''

''I think so. Let me check with Jed and call you back, okay? And, was I supposed to bring something tonight? I seem to remember . . .''

''Nothing,'' Kathleen lied and added ''pick up rolls at bakery'' to the list she was scribbling.

''I'll . . . Chad, don't drink that juice! How will I ever get an accurate reading on the thermometer if you gulp down cold juice?'' Susan interrupted herself to stop her son, standing in front of the open refrigerator with the Tropicana carton raised to his mouth. ''And you know not to drink from the carton! Especially when you're sick! I . . .''

''Call me back,'' Kathleen said from her end of the line. ''I'll be here all day, cooking and cleaning and everything.''

Jed appeared at the top of the stairs as Susan hung up the phone. ''That was Kathleen calling about the party tonight. I had forgotten all about it.''

''It's pretty important, Sue. The people coming in from the coast are big clients of the firm and Jerry has to do well by them. I encouraged him to give this party, so I feel pretty responsible . . .''

''Kathleen and I were just figuring out what to wear,''

Susan lied, forgetting that she was about to try to convince her husband to beg off. They would go. They would be merry. After all, Kathleen had just told her that Colin and Maureen had been arrested.

II

"I tend to agree with you, Martha. But Harvey's been giving me grief ever since last night. He thinks that this is all part of some sort of quasi-official investigation into Dawn's death," went the voice on the phone.

Martha Hallard, sitting on the gray satin bedspread in her bedroom, kicked her right foot nervously while she listened. She finally had to interrupt. "I don't see what there is to worry about. In the first place, the arrest last night proves that the police think Colin and Maureen killed Dawn. Although it doesn't sound right to me. Besides, this party was planned over a month ago—long before Dawn was murdered—so how could it have anything to do with her death? Anyway, it's really being given for business reasons. Jerry has two big clients coming in from the West Coast and he's giving this party for them and their wives. We're just frosting on the suburban cake."

"I told Harvey all of that," Gloria Bower said, getting up from her chair at the kitchen table and moving over to the counter, her husband being busy with a new snowblower just outside of the window. "But he says that won't stop Kathleen. He says that the party is going to be a sham and, since we have this snowstorm to use as an excuse, we should beg off."

"Well, you have to do what you think best," Martha agreed, her kicking becoming so violent that she flicked her shoe off her foot and across the room. "Is that Missy crying?" she asked hopefully, anxious to end the conversation.

"That's the snowblower," was the indignant reply. "Or, maybe . . ." Gloria became aware of a more high-pitched hum in the background. "You have good ears. That is Missy.

Time for her midmorning feeding!'' An anxious new mother, she hung up without saying good-bye.

Martha put down her white and gold enameled receiver with a slight laugh.

"Who was on the phone?" Her son's sleepy face appeared in the doorway.

"No one for you. Mrs. Bower was calling about the party we're going to tonight. You certainly are late getting up," his mother continued as he came in and sat down on the bed beside her.

"Mo-o-om!" He pulled away as his mother reached out to smooth down his hair. "Can I call someone to play with today? Or do you think Chad will be able to come out?"

"Chad will definitely not be able to play outside in the snow. Chicken pox isn't a twenty-four-hour disease. You can call someone else later. It's still a little early in the morning. And, when you call, make sure it's someone who lives close by. I don't think the roads are going to be good for a while today."

"Dad at the hospital?"

"Yes, he had a call about eleven last night. He probably delivered the baby and decided to spend the night in the doctor's lounge when he found out how bad the storm had gotten. I was just going to call him. But why don't we go downstairs? I'll use the kitchen phone and make you some pancakes at the same time."

But the phone ringing as they entered the kitchen preempted her plans. The child rushed over to pick it up. "Hello? . . . Oh, yeah . . . Hi, Dad . . . She's right here." And he handed the receiver to his mother. "Can you make breakfast while you talk?" he asked, plaintively. "I'm awfully hungry."

"You can turn on the TV," his mother replied, "and I'll start mixing and stirring."

The boy laughed. The whole town knew that if any "homemade" food came out of this kitchen, it was from a caterer. His mother was no cook.

As if to prove it, she turned to the freezer and pulled out

microwavable pancakes. Her son smiled and went over to the bay window's built-in banquette and table and turned on the small TV conveniently mounted in one wall. A brightly colored robot appeared on the screen, waving his arms out at the audience. His attention was riveted.

"Dan. Bad case or was the snow too deep for you to get home?"

"Neither. The delivery was normal and I didn't get a chance to find out if the snow was deep or not."

"Then why . . . ?"

"I didn't come home last night because I was doing a little research."

"Research?" Martha asked, a little inattentively. She had just ripped a fingernail trying to open the cardboard box encasing the pancakes.

"Let's just say that I'm looking into motives for a murder," her husband teased.

"But the Smalls were arrested," his wife protested.

"That may be so, but there are still some things that need further investigation. Is the party on at the Gordons' for tonight?"

"I assume so, but I was just talking to Gloria, and she says Harvey's trying to convince her to make up an excuse to stay home. He evidently thinks that the arrest isn't going to stop Kathleen's investigation, and he doesn't want to be a part of it." She closed the oven door and set the timer before returning to the refrigerator for maple syrup.

"He may have good reason to avoid it."

"He what?" The microwave timer buzzed as she spoke.

"I said, he may have good reason to avoid an investigation," her husband repeated.

"What do you know?" Martha asked quickly.

"I think I may have found the motive. But I don't want to talk about it on this line. It goes through the hospital switchboard. I'll get the car out of the lot and be home in about fifteen minutes. See you then."

"In this snow?" Martha began, but he had already hung up.

''Mom, you left the pancakes in the microwave after they were done. They're going to be all gunky now. You have to take them out right away.''

''Dump those in the garbage and I'll put some more in,'' she replied. ''Your father's on his way home,'' she added. ''Can you look out the front window and see if there's another drift of snow across the driveway? You know how he hates parking in the street. I don't know why we pay so much money to those plow people if they're not going to get here immediately after the snow stops.''

''Okay. Call me just as soon as my pancakes are ready.'' And off he ran.

When he was out of sight, Martha put the frozen pancakes in the oven, threw the empty carton toward the sink, and began to cry. She hated all this confusion; she desperately needed some relief. Sometimes she felt that a whole lifetime had gone by since she had stood in the Henshaws' garage a week ago and watched Dawn Elliot's silver-covered arm tumble from the open car door.

III

''Storm or no storm, someone has to go to the liquor store and pick out wine for tonight.''

''Can't you do it on the phone? Talk to that nice man with the long gray hair; he knows more about wine than we do. And they'll deliver the order this afternoon.'' Kathleen watched the blades of her Cuisinart spin around and around as she poured water down into the bowl. In seconds, the pâté brisée was done. She put the ball of buttery dough down on her counter and began to roll it out into a flat circle.

''I already called. That 'nice man'—George—is skiing in Vermont this weekend, and they can't deliver this afternoon or any other afternoon this week. Their van was in an accident last night. There's nothing to do but go on down. But I can do the rest of the errands for the party at the same time. Why don't you make out a list?''

''I have one right here.'' Kathleen picked up a long piece

of lined paper with a very floury hand. "And I'd love it if you would do the errands for me. I seem to be a little behind. But could you lay a fire in the fireplace in the living room before you go? I cleaned it out yesterday, so it just needs setting up, but I never seem to put enough kindling in or something. And it would be nice to have a blazing fire going when everyone arrives."

"I'll do it right now." Jerry leaned across his wife's shoulder and snitched a raw mushroom from the pile she was slicing into the unbaked crust before leaving to do as she asked.

Kathleen nervously pushed her hair from her forehead. Your first formal dinner party is your first formal dinner party whether you're twenty-one or thirty-five, it seemed. Why hadn't she agreed with Jerry a month ago and hired a caterer and bartenders and the whole bit? The truth was that she had watched Susan pull off events like this with ease for an entire year, and she wanted to show that she could do it, too. Of course, Susan had been entertaining on this lavish scale for a decade or more. Kathleen, on a police officer's salary, was more likely to pick up Chinese and invite her friends in at the last moment. Had she been trying to prove something when she decided to do this? Was this some sort of statement? An announcement that she belonged in Hancock? She hadn't answered that question when Jerry returned to the room, pulling his ski jacket on.

"I'll head down to the liquor store and then . . ." He glanced down at the list in his hand. "And then I don't know where I'll go," he continued. "You gave me the wrong list."

"The wrong . . . ?"

"This seems to be a list of suspects and their motives for murdering Dawn."

"Oh, damn. A very incomplete list of motives too. That isn't going to do either of us any good. I gave you the wrong paper." She reached across to the pile of lists on the windowsill. She gave him the correct sheet of paper and, as he went off to do his errands, she put the other list resolutely back with the others. She had to concentrate on this meal; wild mushroom pie wouldn't make itself.

Jerry pulled out of his driveway slowly. The group he contracted with each fall had done their job, and his property was plowed. Not true of the streets. Luckily, he was driving the Cherokee; he shifted into four-wheel drive and slowly made his way down the curving street. A half mile from home he saw a familiar figure standing on the side of the road. He carefully pulled his car over. Although hidden by the snow, he knew there was a ditch here somewhere.

"Jerry. Thank god. I called the police on the car phone, but they said it would be hours before a tow truck got here. Seems there's some sort of problem out on the highway. Where are you going? Can I catch a ride?"

"Get inside and get warm, Harvey. I'm on my way downtown to do some errands for the party tonight, but I'll take you wherever you need to go," Jerry said, opening the door.

"Uh . . . great. I was going downtown too; to the liquor store to get a bottle of wine to bring to your house tonight, in fact." Harvey Bower got into the car and slapped his glove-covered hands together to warm them.

"Fine, that was my first stop too," Jerry said. "Although you don't really have to bring a gift."

"Well, why don't I go with you that far and then I can call Gloria and we can figure out a way to get home? I know you must be busy. Wives can keep you running for days before a dinner party. And we're sure looking forward to this one. It will be our first night out without the baby. Gloria insisted on bringing Missy to the Henshaws' last week, you know. But tonight Gloria's mother is coming to sit—no one can say that's an irresponsible choice—so we'll be free as two newlyweds."

"Fine. Now if I can just keep this snow plow from running me off the road . . ."

IV

"What time did you expect the limo company to pick them up, for heaven's sake?" Kathleen asked, impatient with this interruption of her work. She peered anxiously into the oven. Why had she ever even considered hors d'oeuvres that had to be prepared at the last minute? Some good pâté, interesting cheeses . . . Oh well, it was too late to replan her menu. "When do you think the Henshaws are going to get here?"

"Jed and Susan? Why are you worrying about them? They're driving themselves over. What I'm talking about is our California guests; they're not used to this weather, and I can't understand why the limo I reserved hasn't arrived at their hotel yet. I keep trying to call the company, but no one answers. I don't know what to do, Kath. I'm running out of excuses and they keep calling me up . . ." He leaned back against the kitchen table, endangering the thin-stemmed glassware standing on it.

"Jerry. Be careful," his wife warned him. "And don't worry. You said they didn't sound terribly upset on the phone, and I'm sure the limo will get there soon. It's a very reliable company, you said so yourself. Now will you please go check to see if the fire's burning, and if there's enough ice in the ice bucket in the living room? I need to concentrate on things out here."

"You're probably concentrating too much when you don't hear your first guests arrive." Jed Henshaw stuck his head around the door and into the kitchen.

"Je . . ." Kathleen began, turning away from her oven.

"Don't move, Kathleen. I'm going to take your husband from you, and check out the bar situation in the living room. Susan said she talked to you earlier and she's taking Chad upstairs to your bedroom as planned. She'll be down in a few minutes. Now don't either of you worry about a thing."

"You won't say that when you hear about what that limo service has done," Jerry Gordon insisted, following Jed out the door.

Kathleen sighed and glanced back at her homemade cheese straws. Weren't they ever going to brown?

As much as she wanted to do this herself, Susan's presence came as a relief. "Why aren't these things getting done?" Kathleen asked, not even bothering to say hello.

"Was the oven hot when they went in?" Susan asked. "If not, it just takes a little longer. Be patient, no one's here yet. Now tell me what you think about the arrest while I . . ." she paused to look around the room, ". . . while I stir that stuff bubbling on top of the stove."

"My wine sauce!" Kathleen began. "Oh, fine, you handle it."

"So what do you think about the arrest?" Susan repeated.

"I was very surprised," Kathleen said. "Not that some people in town aren't financially overextended, of course, and Maureen never tried to hide the amount of money they needed to maintain their life-style, but I think they must have been awfully desperate to become common burglars."

"Burglars? What about murderers?"

Kathleen stopped her vigil over the cheese straws and turned to Susan. "They were arrested for the burglaries, not Dawn's murder."

"What?"

"They were arrested as suspects in the burglaries that took place during your party, not for Dawn's murder. In fact, the police don't think the two are connected in any way, except for an accident of timing. I thought you knew."

"No. I had no idea."

"No idea about what?" Martha Hallard said, sticking her head in the door.

"Come on in," Kathleen greeted her guest with a kiss on the cheek and hurried back to her stove. "I'm glad to see you."

"Just as long as you're not depending on me to actually cook anything," Martha said, adjusting large cuff bracelets of heavy silver on either arm as if to demonstrate how little equipped she was for any domestic task.

"We have everything well in hand," Kathleen lied. "Why

don't you just pour us each a glass of wine?'' She nodded to where supplies waited on the table.

"That I'm good at,'' Martha agreed. Before she had a chance to begin, however, both of the other couples arrived, Brigit and Gloria coming directly to the kitchen, leaving their husbands and their host to deal with discarded coats, scarves, and boots in the hallway.

"Hey, don't open that,'' Brigit said, as Martha pulled the lead foil off a bottle. "I brought some Australian wine that the man down at the shop said we should try.'' She held up two beribboned bottles. "Look, red and white; that's enough choice for everybody.''

"More than enough,'' Kathleen agreed. "Why don't you and Martha open them and then we can offer the men some.''

"The men were drinking Scotch practically before they got through the door. I don't think we have to worry about them,'' Gloria said, coming over and picking up a glass from the table. "This is beautiful crystal, Kathleen. Was it Jerry's?''

Susan thought it was a tactless question until she realized that both Gloria and Kathleen had married widowers. Maybe they accepted living with another woman's things more than anyone else would.

"No, they were a wedding present from my colleagues back in Hartford. Beautiful, aren't they? They're antiques.''

"Gorgeous,'' Martha agreed, pouring white wine into one of them. "Is that smoke?'' she asked Kathleen while handing Brigit the first glass. "You be the taster, Brigit.''

"In case it's poisoned?'' Brigit kidded, before taking a sip.

Susan turned and glanced at her sharply.

"Oh, no! They're burning!'' Kathleen wailed, sharply jerking open the oven door.

Susan rushed to her side, potholders in hand. "No, no, just a little scorched. Take that pan off the burner, turn off the gas and I'll take care of them,'' she suggested, reaching into the oven. She pulled the smoking cookie sheets from within and placed them side by side on top of the stove.

"Now don't worry about anything," she said, looking carefully at the food. The backs are a little burnt—your oven must heat unevenly—but we'll cut off the brown bits and dip them in more parmesan and no one will ever know."

"Except us . . ." Brigit began, passing a glass of red wine to Martha.

"And wives don't count," Gloria added complacently.

"Oh, we count. How else would everyone get taken care of and fed?" Martha said. "You know," she turned to Brigit, "this is really good."

"I'm waiting for Susan to try it. She's the one who knows wine," Brigit replied.

"Well, I can drink and snip off the ends here easily," Susan said, and a glass was handed to her.

Kathleen, watching her friends and neighbors chatting happily because of her hospitality, felt warm and happy. This was the best of life in suburbia or anywhere, she thought.

V

"Evidently the car picked them up a few minutes ago. I couldn't reach them in their rooms and the main desk suggested I speak to the concierge. He was very helpful. He not only told me about their departure, but he managed to inform me that they were in a good mood, despite the delay. They had been waiting in the small bar off the lobby for an hour or so, and were very relaxed," Jerry reported, hanging up the phone and looking around at his guests.

"Well, that calls for a small celebration," Dan Hallard said, picking up the bottle of wine in front of him and refilling everyone's glass.

"When do you think they'll arrive?" Susan asked, pushing the tray of cheese straws closer to Dan; maybe they would absorb some of the alcohol he was drinking so quickly.

"In this weather, we'll be lucky if they get here within the hour," Jerry answered.

"An hour?!" Kathleen exclaimed, and even Martha knew that she was thinking of her dinner.

"Well, I think we've all been through enough in the last week or so to find something to talk about, don't you, Harvey?" Dan Hallard asked, slouching into the couch he was sitting on.

Harvey Bower looked up from his glass of Scotch, but seemed unable to find an answer.

"What do you mean, Dan?" Gloria asked, standing in the doorway on her way back from the phone in the kitchen, where she had been checking up on her new daughter.

At her appearance, Dan Hallard seemed to change his mind about what he was about to say. "Nothing at all. Just that a lot has happened in the last week." He took another large sip of his drink.

Kathleen, losing interest in her job as hostess, peered from the Bowers to Dan and back again.

"You know," Gloria Bower began in a voice a little too loud. "Harvey and I should have known that the Smalls were the burglars. We saw Colin drive out of your driveway alone just as we were arriving for the party, and we were pretty late getting there because of Missy and all the confusion about the sitter." She smiled at her husband and he picked up the story.

"Yes, he must have been going out to commit the burglaries right then," Harvey said, patting a spot on the sofa beside him to indicate that his wife should sit there.

"Then that's how they knew that no one was going to be home at your house," Susan cried. "I had been wondering about that all along. It made sense that everyone else who was burgled had an empty house, but not yours. Since Missy should have been there with a sitter." She felt triumphant about this discovery.

"That's right," Jerry agreed. "You know, Sue, it was Chad's talk about cars that made Kathleen start thinking about that very thing. And, when she told Sardini what Chad had said, he checked out the comings and goings around your house with Jesse Clark, and discovered that Colin Small had indeed left your house during the party—or at least his new Jaguar had left with a man in it. Sardini checked out their financial situation and, when he confronted the Smalls with the information, they confessed. At least, that's the way Kathleen tells it. She also said that they got the idea from their own burglaries. Seems that they had been broken into so many times that they decided to try it for themselves.''

"What about Chad and the clue?" Susan asked.

"Yes. Are you saying that he knew who was coming and going just because he notices every car that passes him?" her husband asked, his voice proud. "Well, what about that? I guess all that interest in cars is paying off after all.'' He beamed at everyone in the room and poured himself another Scotch.

"And just what are you two talking about?" Harvey Bower asked. Kathleen had been sitting on the arm of the couch, talking to Dan Hallard throughout her husband's revelation.

"Nothing important," Kathleen assured him. "Why don't we all have a toast to Chad? I'll even go upstairs and bring him down. He should know exactly how proud of him we are. Susan, will you make sure everyone's glass is filled?" And she left the room, the tray of hors d'oeuvres she had been bringing to her guests still in her hand.

Guy Frye laughed. "I love to watch the hostess at the beginning of the party."

"That's because you men don't know how much work putting on something like this is," Susan told him, filling up his glass before moving over to his wife. "Right, Brigit?"

"I'll say," she agreed, drinking down the last of her white wine and holding out the glass for a refill. "We do almost all our entertaining in restaurants these days. It's so much easier."

"And cheaper than a divorce," Guy added.

"I know what you mean," Gloria Bower agreed. "Harvey and I had our first fight and our first dinner party on the same day. Didn't we . . . ?"

"And we're going to have another right now unless we get out of here," was her husband's surprising response. He had been staring at the doorway Kathleen had just departed through and he appeared to have suddenly made up his mind.

He stood up and took his wife's arm. "Sorry to drink and run, but we're leaving now."

And he pulled her out of the room and, without getting their coats, out the front door.

"What's going on?" Susan asked, standing in the middle of the room, a bottle of wine in either hand. "What happened?"

"What's going to happen is that they are going to be arrested for the murder of Dawn Elliot," Kathleen said, reentering the room with Chad right behind her. The platter of hors d'oeuvres had evidently vanished like the Bowers. Instead, she held a rectangle of silk in her hand.

"My scarf!" Martha Hallard cried.

"Arrested?" Jed and Jerry said simultaneously.

"Just as long as Sardini and the rest of the police catch up with their car," Kathleen said, ignoring Martha.

"They will. Their Porsche is fast, but not really very good with snow on the road," Chad piped up. "Are you drinking both of those?" he asked his mother.

Susan looked from the wine to her son to Kathleen, and then at the spot on the couch that the Bowers had occupied until a few moments ago. "Maybe," she answered vaguely.

"I'll get that," Brigit Frye offered, hearing the doorbell.

"It's probably Sardini," Kathleen said. "He told me that he would stop by as soon as the Bowers were captured. And they had a car on the block watching us, so it couldn't have taken any time at all . . ."

"Jerry, I think these very tan people are here to see you." Brigit reentered the room, followed by four rather dazed strangers.

"Do you all know that there are four police cars and about a dozen armed men on your front lawn?" one of them asked. "Maybe this isn't a good night for us to get together?"

FORTY PLUS EIGHT

"THANK GOODNESS THEY WERE GOOD SPORTS ABOUT IT all," Jerry said. "For one moment there, I saw the whole account going down the drain."

"I still don't understand everything," Jed Henshaw said. "Susan invited you both over to get an explanation, so I hope you're going to give one to me. Susan and I sat up last night trying to figure it all out, but we still don't understand how you knew that the Bowers were the murderers, Kathleen." He was sitting in front of the fire in his study with the Gordons the morning after the party. "Not that I have the faintest idea where Susan is now," he added.

"That's okay. I was on the phone with her before you or Jerry were out of bed this morning. She knows the whole story. She said to tell you that she had an errand to do," Kathleen answered.

"If your wife isn't going to explain, will you?" Jed asked Jerry.

"I'll tell you right now," Kathleen said. "You should be pretty proud. Once again, it was Chad who gave me the clue that led to the truth." She smiled at the child, who was sitting in a recessed window, a car magazine in his lap, staring out into the glare of bright morning sunlight on yesterday's snow.

"You see, Chad asked the right question: 'Why did the Bowers bring their big car to the party instead of the Porsche?' And the answer was simple. Because they couldn't fit Dawn's body into the trunk of their Porsche.''

"I don't think that's quite a complete explanation," Jed said. "I don't suppose you could start with why?''

"It was Dan Hallard who supplied the motive," Kathleen said. "He found it in the hospital records and very unprofessionally told me about it: Harvey Bower was sterile because he had gonorrhea—a disease that he shared with Dawn years and years ago. The police had been looking into the records, too. Remember they asked who had your family's medical records? And even Richard Elliot told me that the last time I saw him—in one of his endless Shakespearean quotes—that Dawn had had a venereal disease.''

"I still don't understand," Jed said.

"Harvey Bower killed Dawn because she knew that he had had VD, that he had been unfaithful to his first wife and was unable to have children of his own as a result. Harvey and Gloria were anxious to make sure that the information stayed hidden—especially now,'' Kathleen said. ''Because they had so much to lose, you see. They were afraid that if this information got to the state child welfare people, they wouldn't be allowed to keep Missy. There are a lot of people looking to adopt babies these days, and Harvey and Gloria couldn't risk looking anything but perfect. There were, of course, more than a few people who were trying to hide their past lives with Dawn, but no one except the Bowers had so much to lose: their chance for a child of their own.''

Jed looked into the fire, thinking that Gloria and Harvey had lost everything now. ''But where did they kill her? Why bring the body to my house?''

"They killed her in their own home. Harvey told the police that they invited Dawn over and then shot her. The carpet fibers on her body will undoubtedly be found to match those in the Bower house. I think bringing her to your house was an impromptu idea. They killed her, put her in the car trunk and then, remembering Susan's party, decided to leave her there. I had told Gloria about the Volvo, I'm afraid, and they hit on leaving the body in the car as a way to not only deflect guilt from themselves, but spread it around a little.

"Unfortunately, while opening the garage door, they laid the body out on the driftwood that you brought back from the shore, and it picked up sand and particles of wood that matched the ones found in the trunk of your Mercedes, Jed. That made the police look at you as a primary suspect. They didn't think that you would be stupid enough to leave Susan a dead body for a birthday present, but they couldn't figure out the evidence that they had collected. They were stumped, and so was I.

"And then Martha was complaining about the smell of her silk scarf, and Susan had complained about the smell of your bedroom from Missy's stomach problems, and it occurred to me that maybe Missy had been left alone on your bed—and leaving a baby in the middle of a pile of coats and scarfs is probably as safe as can be—while the Bowers were away together."

"Moving the body!" Jed exclaimed.

"Exactly," Jerry agreed. "In fact, I saw Gloria on her way to the garage. She said she was going to throw one of Missy's diapers into the garbage cans out there to keep the smell out of the house. But, actually, she was using that as an excuse to meet Harvey, and help him move Dawn's body."

"And so it all fits together," Jed said quietly. "They wanted something so much that they were willing to kill for it, and then, of course, they had to lose it." He was silent for a moment and then seemed to remember that this conversation might not be appropriate for his son. He turned to Chad, who was still sitting in the window, but no longer quiet.

"I don't believe it," the child was saying. "I don't believe it." And he jumped up and ran toward the front door, which had just opened to reveal his mother. "Where did it come from? Are you going to keep it? Can I . . . ?"

"Enough, Chad. Please don't get excited. You're still sick," she answered, putting her hand on his forehead.

"But is it ours?" he insisted loudly.

"It's ours. I just wrote a very large check to pay for it. It's all ours." She smiled at him as, unable to contain himself, he ran back to the window. She turned to Kathleen. "You explained everything? The whole story?"

"Sure did."

The phone rang and Jed got up to answer it. He was only talking for a few minutes when he hung up and glanced out the window to see what his son was looking at. "That was Mitchell. He says we can pick up the Volvo at any time . . . what is that?" He walked over to the window and squinted out into the bright light.

Susan turned to her friends before answering. "I can't bear the thought of driving that Volvo now." She looked straight at her husband, a wide smile on her face, and answered his question.

"It's a Maserati Spyder convertible. I thought I deserved another fortieth birthday present."

ABOUT THE AUTHOR

Valerie Wolzien is also the author of MURDER AT THE PTA
LUNCHEON. She makes her home in Tenafly, New Jersey.